The

Disapparation

of

James

The
Disapparation
of
James

Anne Ursu

AN IMPRINT OF HYPERION
NEW YORK

Library of Congress Cataloging-in-Publication Data

Ursu, Anne.
    The disapparation of James / Anne Ursu.—1st ed.
      p. cm.
    ISBN 0-7868-6779-5
      1. Missing children—Fiction. 2. Magic tricks—Fiction.
3. Circus—Fiction. I. Title
PS3621.R78 D47 2003
813'.6—dc21
                    2002027324

Hyperion books are available for special promotions and premiums.
For details contact Hyperion Special Markets, 77 West 66th Street,
11th floor, New York, New York 10023, or call 212-456-0133.

FIRST EDITION

10 9 8 7 6 5 4 3 2 1

for my big brother,

who always showed me how

the trick was done

The Disapparation of James

James Woodrow's parents have

never seen him so excited. The boy sits between Hannah and Justin in their orchestra-section seats, bobbing up and down on his springy plush chair and singing some James-like song to himself. His father caresses his thin orange hair and assures him, "The show will start soon, buddy, settle down, okay?" while exchanging puzzled glances with his wife. James's sister, Greta, is rhythmically kicking the chair in front of her, squawking emphatically. Their mother, strategically placed in between the children, whispers, "Shhhh, Greta, sweetie, don't do that."

Hannah and Justin Woodrow are not alone; parents all over the auditorium of the Lindbergh Performing Arts Center are shushing and soothing, cajoling and threatening—a steady murmur underneath the screeches, babbles, and cries of the ten-and-under set. It is two minutes after the Razzlers Circus Stage Show should have begun, and the children are restless.

"Mom, they're *late*," Greta shrieks, pointing at her pink plastic watch. She kicks all the harder and, inspired, James begins to bounce more furiously in rhythm.

There is nothing at all unusual about Greta kicking things and shrieking, but Hannah and Justin do not know what has come over their son. He is usually the quietest boy. Enthusiasm manifests itself as a single syllable, a small smile. James can go hours without making a noise; sometimes his parents half-wonder if he has forgotten how to talk. He spends his days in his own corner of the playroom, solemnly working with his building blocks. At dinner, he sits in his chair assiduously arranging shapes with his slices of hot dog, then he returns to his construction projects until it is time for bath. He is a baby-sitter's dream; "James is so good," they say, "that sometimes you forget he is even there."

But not today. Today, James has been the picture of disobedience. He has been messing, spilling, breaking. He spent the afternoon running laps around the playroom, throwing stuffed animals, gnawing on crayons. For Justin, who has become used to more sedentary afternoons, today was a flashback to when Greta was this age; back then, by the end of the day, Justin would be ready for bed well before his daughter.

When Hannah came home early from work this afternoon, she found Justin on his back in the center of the playroom floor.

"You look as if you could use medical attention," she said. "What happened?"

He sighed theatrically. "Something has possessed your son. Look!"

Justin pointed vaguely in the direction of James's favorite corner, today a mess of broken crayons and scattered blocks, where James was jumping up and down, higher and higher each time, whooping, "Up up up up up!"

Hannah exchanged a glance with her husband, then approached her son carefully. "Hi Jamesie! What are you so excited about, big guy? Is it the circus?"

And, in response, James bent his knees close to the floor, readying himself for the biggest little-boy-jump in the history of the world, and exploded, yelling, "*Circus!*"

Hannah smiled at her son, then turned back to her still-prone husband. "If this is James," she said, "I can't imagine what Greta will be like."

Today is Greta Woodrow's seventh birthday. Seven is, as Greta would be happy to explain to you, a very momentous age indeed. Six is just like Five, and her little brother is just Five, and he's a baby. But Seven is much closer to Ten and that means you are a full-fledged Big Kid.

A momentous occasion requires a momentous celebration: Greta will come home from school to a lavishly decorated house, she will feast on macaroni and cheese and chocolate birthday cake with strawberry ice cream, then the family will head downtown and she will be treated to the best seats in the house for the Razzlers Circus Stage Show. (The tickets are compliments of Stewart Martin, theater writer for the local newspaper and college friend of Justin's. "I got extra," he said. "Take the Munchkins.")

At dinner on her Birthday Eve, Greta cross-examined her father on the exact nature of the entertainment planned for the next evening. Greta has always been skilled at the art of interrogation; she stealthily discomfits the deposed by becoming steadily shriller with each passing question.

"Daddy?" she began, "are there gonna be lions?"

"No. This isn't that kind of circus."

"Daddy, are there gonna be elephants?"

"No."

"Daddy, are there gonna be puppies?"

"Oh, yes, actually, one. And trained birds!"

"Daddy, are there gonna be silly songs?"

"Probably."

"Daddy, are there gonna be jokes?"

"Yes! Lots and lots of jokes!"

"Daddy, are there gonna be clowns?"

"I'm afraid so."

"Are there gonna be tricks?"

"Tricks? Like acrobats?"

Greta's pitch was nearly inhumanly high by then, and Justin had just prepared his answer when James chimed in to ask:

"MAGIC tricks??!"

Justin turned to look at James. "Well I . . . I don't know . . ." he said, shrugging at Hannah.

Now, the show is four minutes late, and Justin and Hannah, for possibly the first time, have to divide their parental attention between their two children. James has stopped bouncing; now he kicks the chair in front of him with a wild giggle, as if to compliment his sister on her most excellent idea for a diversion, and Justin must use his best paternal tone, "James. James, don't do that, I mean it."

In truth, Justin has not exactly been looking forward to the circus. Justin does not like clowns. He says he had a bad experience at his eighth birthday party—he has never elaborated; when pressed, all he will say is, "He just kept coming and coming."

As for Hannah, she would prefer to be in the bath right now with a magazine and a cup of mint tea, but she has no objection to the circus, per se, and seeing James so excited certainly makes her happy. Once the show starts and the children quiet down, she can look forward to one hundred and twenty minutes of sitting—even without a magazine or tea, this is always a good thing. So Hannah Woodrow would be in a reasonably good mood right now, if her evening had not been so handily spoiled in the lobby just moments ago.

A few weeks ago, a chance meeting with Dr. Lewis would have meant nothing—Hannah knows him professionally, of course—but now, things are different, and Hannah could not believe it when he tapped her on the shoulder with a bellowing, "Hello, there, Hannah Woodrow!" And then the doctor looked at James—who was hiding behind Justin's leg—as if he were considering him, inspecting him, diagnosing him right in the lobby. Hannah moved toward her son instinctively—this is not right. Here, here on Greta's birthday, here

6

with the whole family out together, she did not want to be reminded of her son's appointment with the eminent pediatrician next week.

Now, six minutes after the show should have started, Hannah finds herself feeling prickly again, and she wonders where Dr. Lewis is sitting. They have not explained to James that he will be going to a new doctor; he's always hated his physicals and there's no need, yet, to tell him what is about to happen to him. But if he were to find out from Dr. Lewis instead of them, Hannah would never forgive herself—

And now, there!—seven minutes after the show should have started, the lights begin to go down in the auditorium. Three hundred parents let out a sigh of relief, and Hannah whispers to her brood, "Okay, guys, the show is starting, settle down now." At that, Justin lets out a small, "ha"-like noise, and she mutters across James's bouncing head, "You're not helping."

But the instant the lights begin to dance, the music sounds, and the performers explode onto the stage, both children become still. Ten bodies come tumbling onstage, four fly in on trapezes, another storms in on stilts playing the violin, three jump rope, two ride a tandem bike, and a shaggy little puppy jumps up and down in the center of it all. The stage is a flurry of bodies and motion and color and light, and even Greta cannot speak.

The music bounces, bodies flit, and a rubbery man in a tailcoat, clown nose, top hat, and funny pants enters the fracas and tries desperately to command attention. He waves comically and screams and jumps up and down and the children in the audience begin to point and laugh. He takes off his hat and slowly scratches his thick dark brown hair. Finally, the thin man disappears offstage, and then emerges again, slowly pushing a whistle the size of a baby elephant. He stops, looks around, winks at the audience, and blows—a shriek pierces the auditorium, and all the performers stop, start, and hightail it off the stage.

The thin man, now alone amid the chaos the tumblers have left, smiles at the audience, "That's better." Everyone laughs. The man clears his throat. "Hi, I'm Mike the Clown. I'll be your emcee for the evening." He bows dramatically, juggles a few balls, drops them everywhere, then introduces the next act—a woman and her dancing puppy for which Greta lets out a shriek that seems to crack several lighting instruments. Hannah settles back in her chair and James continues to monitor the action onstage intently.

There are acrobats and trapeze artists and bicyclists and jugglers, balance artists and trained birds and, in between each act, Mike the Clown jokes with the audience. At one point he gets a wallet from someone in the front row and turns it into a bouquet of flowers. Justin pats his son on the head and whispers, "See, buddy? There's a magic trick for you."

At intermission, Greta stands up and shouts, "This is the best show EVER!" James is still wide-eyed and quiet—that's the James they know—and Justin squeezes his hand and asks gently, "Are you enjoying the show, big guy?" James looks at his father, he is all eyes, and he nods slowly, seriously.

And the lights come up again, the second half starts, act follows act, and the children begin to get squirrelly. They never know how to end things on time for kids, Hannah thinks. Springs squeak and feet kick all over the auditorium. Parents check their programs; one act left, something with the clown—and then the finale. Shh, just a little more, guys, don't you want to see what happens next? The curtain closes and Mike the Clown walks onstage in front of it.

"And now ladies and gentlepeople," he proclaims, "the moment you've been waiting for all evening . . . Can I have a drumroll? . . . MY ACT!!!"

A spotlight flicks on and appreciative laughter rumbles through the auditorium. This clown is a good entertainer, Justin thinks. He knows how to command a room—even this room.

With ceremony and panache, the clown proceeds to balance a plate, then a broom, then a pool cue, then a folding chair on his chin. And then a bike. The audience cheers. Justin rubs his own chin sympathetically.

"Ohhh, but that's not all!" the clown proclaims, "Mike the Clown has more tricks up his sleeve. Now, I will need a volunteer from the audience."

Children's arms fly up all over the auditorium. Greta's hand shoots up right away; she stands on her seat and shrieks. This is to be expected; Hannah and Justin look at her and smile as parents do. And then something flits in the corner of their eyes. An arm. A hand. They do not believe it: James has raised his hand.

Hannah and Justin exchange a look—what has gotten into their boy tonight? Greta is too busy popping up and down to notice. The clown comes down into the audience—he trips down the stairs and three hundred children squeal. He wades down the aisle—their aisle— he comes closer and closer until, finally, he is next to the Woodrows. His clown nose is very close to Justin's head. Next to Justin, James has his arm up, calmly, stiffly—he seems like an alien among all these screaming "pick me"-ers. The clown leans forward and smiles at James. "How about you, little boy? Do you want to come onstage?"

And James beams and looks up at the clown with his beautiful wide little boy eyes. The clown grabs his hand and pulls him into the aisle.

At this moment, it occurs to Hannah that James could make a fool of himself. This is a clown, not a child psychologist. If James freezes up, panics before the crowd, the clown won't know what to do. He is expecting an outgoing child. He will make jokes at James's expense. The crowd will laugh at James, James will be humiliated, and he will never, ever, ever recover. He will lead his life as a misfit, a recluse, unable to function in public. And then, when he's thirty, after ten years of psychotherapy he will finally be able to confront his mother, "Why did you let me volunteer for the circus, Mom? You're supposed to protect me, Mom. That ruined my life, Mom."

Justin reaches across James's empty chair and strokes her hand a little. "Hannah, it's okay." (Justin always thinks everything is going to be okay; it can be terribly annoying sometimes.)

The clown has James by the hand, and they are heading away from the Woodrows. James follows like a puppy and the clown asks him, just loudly enough for Hannah and Justin to hear, "What's your name, young man?"

There is a pause. The parents watch their son carefully across the rows of heads. Greta, meanwhile, is jumping up and down, shouting her brother's name for the whole auditorium to hear. Justin unconsciously moves into James's seat, channeling all his thoughts toward his son, and Hannah clasps his hand. One breath. Two breaths. Three—and then their son's little voice says, proudly, firmly:

"James."

They exhale.

James and the clown walk down the aisle, chatting and holding hands the whole way, and James is smiling, and the audience is applauding—applauding their son. Greta cannot contain herself, she shrieks, "THAT'S MY BROTHER!" Families turn around to look at them, smiling and pointing. And Justin begins to feel a beneficence toward, not just this clown, but all clowns. "Look at my son!" he wants to shout. "That's my son!"

And there! James is on the stage holding the clown's hand. Greta is still now, enraptured, she doesn't take her eyes off the stage as she tugs on her mom's sleeve, "Mom, do you see him? Do you see James? What are they going to do to him? What do you think he's going to do?"

"Shhh, honey, I don't know . . . Shhhh, watch now."

The clown and James stand side by side, two lone figures on a vast stage. The clown says to the audience, "I'd like you to meet my friend James. James is going to do just what I do, right James?" The clown nods to James.

And then—James nods right back to the clown. The clown smiles. James smiles. The clown waves at the audience. And then, James waves at the audience! The clown grins widely. And then, James grins widely! Everyone laughs and cheers! The clown tips his head toward James, "Look at the kid!" James tips his head to the clown. The clown jumps. James jumps! The clown turns around, grabs the waiting chair, and ceremoniously plops it down in front of him. James turns around, grabs an invisible chair, and mimes plunking it down. The clown giggles. James giggles. The clown mimes sitting down in the chair. James copies him exactly. No, no, the clown seems to say, YOU sit in the chair, and James mimics, YOU sit in the chair. The clown points at him, and at the chair. The boy does the same! The clown slides the chair over to James. James slides it right back!

The audience is nearly in hysterics, laughing and applauding and cheering for their son! For James! Hannah and Justin are mesmerized. Will you look at that? Will you look at our boy? Before his parents' eyes, James grows, James glows, he is energized, electrified. James is brilliant. He's playing the audience! James will be a showman, he will be a star, he will be whatever he wants to be—he will be all right, our son, he will be just fine.

Finally, the clown negotiates James into the chair and gives the audience a triumphant bow. James kicks his legs up in the air and squeals. "He wants more," Justin whispers to Hannah, eyes shining, "He wants to play more."

Greta begins to pull on her mother's arm, "What's he doing, Mom? Huh? What's he doing?!"

The clown then begins to lift James and the chair up into the air. Greta gasps loudly. James lets out a giggling squeal to the heavens. Hannah is too busy watching the expression on her son's face to worry that he might fall and break his neck or otherwise injure his spinal cord. The clown lifts James above his head, and then right above his upward-turned face.

"Wow," says Justin.

"Wow," says Hannah.

"He's gonna put James on his faaaaaaaaace!" explodes Greta.

And that's exactly what the clown does. He sticks his chin up in the air and places the rear chair leg on it. And then, the drumroll starts, he takes his hands away and sticks his arms out to the sides, and there is James, on top of the world. And James—their James—is not scared at all, but delighted, and his glow intensifies; Justin and Hannah can never remember seeing him happier than right now and each tries to grab on to the moment and put it away somewhere where it will be safe forever.

The drumroll continues, the clown staggers back and forth a bit, but James never wobbles, and then, the clown sticks his arms up straight in the air, the drumroll flourishes, and then—

And then, James is gone.

Just gone.

Poof!

The audience is stunned for a moment, silent, and then they get on their feet and begin to yell and cheer. The clown lurches forward, looks up at the chair and blinks.

Hannah and Justin are speechless.

"Wow."

"Wow."

Greta seems to explode next to them, *"He made James disappear!"* she shrieks. After a moment's pause, the clown takes his bows. And again. The applause lasts and lasts. Hannah and Justin mouth the words they will say to their son when he comes back:

James. James, you did well. James, we are so proud of you.

Finally, the applause fades. The lights go down and the curtain opens on the finale—a swinging, swooping, sparkling affair—with no sign of James. And Hannah shifts in her seat and looks around the auditorium and whispers to her husband, "When do you suppose they're going to bring him back?"

Earlier That Day

It is morning in the Woodrow

household, and nothing seems out of the ordinary. Justin is making breakfast—pancakes, because it's Greta's birthday—amid the quotidian bustle of a quotidian morning. There are no funny colors in the sky, no strange smells, no perversions of gravity, no metaphysical rumblings. There's nothing at all to portend the break in the laws of the universe that will happen tonight. The only thing that's wrong, now, is that Justin can't find the good spatula. It lives in the utensil drawer, it's always there—Justin knows it's always there because he's the one who puts the dishes away. His kitchen is very orderly; he's quite proud of it actually. But the spatula is gone. There is no explanation. The drawer is in perfect order, there are no signs of Greta-esque rummaging. The dishwasher is empty, it's not in any of the other drawers. It's not possible that Hannah moved it, Hannah is the inspiration for all his order. And she doesn't usually do anything in the kitchen that requires spatulas.

Justin looks through the drawer a third time to no avail. There's batter bubbling on the griddle and Justin sighs and settles for the second-string spatula. "Come on," he encourages, "it's your chance to shine." He gives it a little pat, and together, they flip the pancakes, one by one, and the cakes do flip quite well—frankly Justin excels at making pancakes—nothing sticks to the griddle, and they come out perfectly round, even though Greta would probably prefer funny-shaped ones, but the loss of the good spatula has made Justin feel a need for symmetry. Justin mutters a "Yes!" with each perfect flip, and right on schedule, the birthday girl herself comes barreling down the stairs yelling, "I SMELL PANCAAAAAAKES!"

Justin smiles. "Good morning, Pumpkin!"

"Hi, Daddy!" Greta is dressed in checkered bright pink pants and a light pink peasant top, her orangy hair hangs down in two elaborate braids, and her face seems to have fallen victim to a glitter outbreak.

"You're very sparkly this morning," Justin says as he brings her a plate.

"Mom did it. Because it's my *birthday*."

"Oh, is it?"

"Dad!"

Greta, Justin notices, seems to have finally grown out of her annual tradition of running around the house screaming, "IT'S MY BIRTH-DAY! IT'S MY BIRTHDAY! BIRTHDAY BIRTHDAY BIRTH-DAY!" Justin indulges himself in a "Sunrise, Sunset" moment, then lets it pass. "Have you seen your brother?" he asks.

"He's getting dressed. Slowpoke!"

"Greta, he likes to take his time."

This is an understatement. Each day, endless minutes pass between the time when James gets out of bed and when he emerges downstairs for breakfast. Hannah and Justin cannot figure out what he does with all that time. And it does not seem to serve him well; he isn't quite clear on some of the fundamentals of dressing, no matter how many times they've shown him how to dress himself. Now, when he comes plopping down the stairs, he is wearing one sock, sweatpants, and his pajama top. Something inside Justin twinges.

"Morning, big guy!" Justin says cheerfully, as James plunks down in his chair. "You want pancakes? Here, let me cut them up for you."

Greta stares at her brother meaningfully. "Hi!"

"Hi Getie," James says. He stares at her face. "Sparkles!"

"Don't you know what today is?" she asks pointedly.

James stares at his sister.

"It's my *birthday*!"

James turns up a corner of his mouth. Greta grins.

This is the way Greta and James communicate—they speak in gestures and facial twitches. When they're together, they converse in their own hidden sibling language—always communicating, always connected. Sometimes, when James's English is less than good, when his gestures or facial expressions aren't clear, the parents turn to Greta. "What did he say, honey?" She always knows.

"Thank you!" Greta smiles. "Are you gonna come to my party tomorrow? You better. There's gonna be cake."

Tomorrow, ten girls from Greta's second-grade class will invade the Woodrow house for two hours. They have been planning for months. The house itself seems to be quivering with anticipation.

"This is gonna be the best birthday ever," she explains. "I'm gonna be seven, you know. Are you coming tonight? We're gonna go to the—"

"CIRCUS?" James explodes. "TONIGHT?"

"Ow!" Greta pokes her brother. "Loud!"

Justin fixes a bemused smile on his son. "Yeah, big guy, tonight's the circus show, remember? Are you excited?"

"Ohhhhh!" James's eyes grow very wide. He drops his fork. He blinks, then he springs out of his chair and runs up the stairs.

Greta turns and watches him go. "Hey, where're you *going*? Aren't you gonna eat your *pancakes*?"

No answer comes from the fleeing form of James, and Greta is left to turn around and inquire of her father, "What's with him?"

"I don't know."

Greta shrugs and proceeds to go over the party plans with her father, who listens solemnly and nods at the appropriate times. As Greta is running through the guest list for the second time, Hannah emerges from the stairwell. She smiles at her family.

"How's my birthday girl?" She kisses Greta on the forehead.

"Good! Thank you for my sparkles!"

"Well, you look gorgeous." Hannah smiles and turns to her husband. "No screaming this year?"

"Not yet. Do you want pancakes?"

"Ohhh . . . I'm late. But it smells delicious."

"No breakfast? You're the doctor."

She grins. "I'll grab something at work, don't worry. Where's James?"

"He ran away."

"Oh. What time are the festivities?"

"Six. The show starts at eight . . . Should I call and invite Catherine to the party tomorrow?"

Hannah frowns. "I don't know. I don't want her to feel obligated—"

"Well," Justin shrugs, "she's your sister. I think she'd be delighted to come, though. And she'll get Greta a present anyway. You know that."

"I'll call her," Hannah says offhandedly. "I'll try to get home early to help you, too." She turns to Greta. "Be good to your father, honey. Happy Birthday."

"Thanks, Mom!"

Hannah touches her husband's hand. "I'd like to find James for his good-bye before I go. Any suggestions on where I might look?"

"He went thataway." Justin points up the stairs.

"Thanks, honey. I'll see you this afternoon."

"Hey, Han?"

She stops. "What?"

"Have you seen the spatula?"

She blinks. "It's in your hand."

"No, I mean . . . never mind. Have a good day."

Welcome to daily life at the Woodrows, where the husband sees off the wife every morning on her way to a hard day at the office. This is Justin's life now, and he wouldn't trade it for anything. Justin Thomas Woodrow is a stay-at-home mom, a hausfrau, an officially registered board-certified homemaker. He makes breakfast, kisses his wife good-bye, sees Greta off to school, takes James to preschool two afternoons a week, cleans the house, does the laundry, manages the bills, does the shopping, welcomes Greta home, sees Greta off to piano or gymnastics or ballet or T-ball or soccer or karate, welcomes his wife home, cooks dinner, and, mostly, takes care of his son. Hannah's father used to hem and haw when asked what his son-in-law did for a living, but to him it was at least better than when Justin wanted to be an actor.

Justin can understand. He was obnoxious when he wanted to be an actor. During college he subsisted on cigarettes, coffee, and beer and spent all his time talking to his friend Stewart (who is now theater critic for the paper and gave them tickets to the circus show tonight) about saving the world (or at least the Midwest) through experimental theater, at least when they weren't talking about girls. After college, Stewart went to grad school at the U to experiment some more and Justin fell in love with Hannah. Suddenly, Justin stopped being the center of his own universe. He started going to bed on time. He stopped drinking beer and smoking. He started to eat well-balanced meals. He bought an iron. With Hannah, all his ambitions changed— Justin found himself suffering from an intense desire to seem responsible to this woman, this miracle, and got a job teaching at the local private high school. And there is nothing like being with high school boys on a day-to-day basis to make a man want to be a grown-up.

Justin taught courses in speech, acting and directing, and the literature of the theater. He directed two plays a year—a drama in the fall and a musical every spring. In his last year, the school got a medal at state in the one-act competition.

Well before Hannah became pregnant with Greta, the couple decided that it made more sense for Justin to take parental leave from the school for the baby's first year than for Hannah to take so much time away from the practice. It was Hannah's idea—she broached it so cautiously—but Justin was thrilled. He scheduled his leave with alacrity, telling everyone who would listen, "I'm going to be a dad!" Nothing made him grin more than the words, "parental leave."

Being home with the baby was the brightest joy of his life. He had already planned to take a second year off to be with Greta even before James began to manifest. Then he took a third year. Even then, the school made clear to him that the job would be there for him when he wanted it; attendance at the school plays had decreased dramatically since his departure.

But he has not gone back. One year off became seven, and there is nothing in the world Justin would rather do than stay at home with these children of theirs. Their words and shapes flicker behind his dreams. This is what life is for—his son smiles, his daughter sparkles, he has spatulas to spare.

This will not be forever. In the play of Justin's life, this is just the second act. When the kids are older he will do something else, perhaps go back to teaching or go back to school himself. He has considered freelancing as a speech coach for executives or teaching acting techniques at corporate retreats, that sort of thing. Stewart has offered to let him write occasional reviews for the newspaper. (Whatever he does, he wants to be home for his children when they finish school each day.) It doesn't matter, yet—it will all work out. Anyway, he has noticed that life has a funny way of making plans for you; it rarely plays by your rules. Justin has been taken by surprise too many times not to have learned his lesson. The future will bring what it wants; for now, Justin will spend his days taking care of his son.

It is well after lunchtime, but Hannah hasn't eaten the leftover lasagna that Justin packed for her this morning. She wanted to squeeze all her patients in early today; she has promised Justin she will try to be home in the afternoon to help with the birthday preparations. She was able to swallow a bagel that one of her colleagues slipped her between her ten and ten-twenty this morning, but as she sits in her office talking to her one-thirty, she silently hopes her stomach isn't growling too audibly.

At the beginning of every appointment, Hannah takes some time to chat with her patients. Her practice is devoted to the care of the whole individual; too many of her colleagues work in places that pressure them to get patients in and out as if they were working on an assembly line. In the Kenwood Medical Group, the doctors begin each appointment not in the examining room, but in their cozy, book-lined offices. As a result, the practice is teeming with patients. "It's so nice," Hannah's patients tell her, "so nice to have doctors who actually seem interested in you." As far as Hannah is concerned, this personal attention is only proper. How can you diagnose or treat a person you do not know? Clues to illness lie everywhere; in examination, yes, but also in experience, voice, posture, eye contact.

Hannah does not usually let these chats turn to her; she's in charge of keeping these people well, that's all they need to know. Most of the people who come into her office are only too happy to oblige—so, now she's taken aback when Ginny Klausen, a longtime patient, after talking a bit about her weekend to come, asks:

"And you, Dr. Woodrow?"

"What?"

"Any plans for the weekend?"

"Oh . . . Well. Yes . . . I'm . . . It's my daughter's birthday . . . We're having a party, all her school friends are coming." Hannah shifts in her seat.

"How old is she?"

"Um, seven."

"You know," Ginny shakes her head, "I didn't even know you had a daughter. Is she your only child?"

"No . . . I have a son too." Hannah's eyes travel unconsciously to the framed photo on her desk.

"Those are your children?" Ginny smiles. "Can I see?"

Hannah clears her throat. "Sure. Yes. This is Greta."

"And that one?"

"That's James. He's five."

Ginny blinks. "He's five? Small for five . . ."

"Well," Hannah hits a stack of papers against the desk, "should we get started? What brings you here today?"

After several minutes of questions, they go to the examining room. Hannah has a system. She begins, usually, with a brief physical. Eyes, ears, throat. Lungs. Heart. Abdomen. Muscles and reflexes. Leave nothing out. Assume nothing. Start from the beginning. The body will tell you its secrets if you only listen well enough. Everything can be diagnosed, if you only have patience.

Hannah is a good doctor. She does not look at this as something to be proud of—it is a necessity. Of all the professions out there, hers demands skill—she is a doctor, therefore she must be a good one. She has a responsibility to the people who come to her for care, and Hannah has always accepted her responsibilities.

She wanted to be a doctor since she was a child—when her classmates were playing pilot and fireman, she was in the corner with the plastic stethoscope. She set up a free clinic for her dolls and monitored her sister Catherine's temperature daily. Hannah had a plan, an ambition, and she worked hard to achieve it. For quite a while, she believed that that was just the way people worked, they were born with a destiny. She was very confused in high school when she realized most people didn't have any idea what they were put on this earth for.

When Hannah first knew Justin, he told her acting was his lifelong ambition, but Hannah knew better very early on; all his life all he really wanted to do was to be a dad. Once, when Justin and Hannah were dating, she went with him to a relative's house for a birthday party. Justin spent the afternoon on the floor completely engrossed with the toddlers. His cousin Beth watched, shaking her head, and told Hannah, "I'm going to feel sorry for the woman Justin marries. After they have children he's never going to pay attention to her again."

If character were destiny, Hannah would have married a nice lawyer or doctor. They would have a marriage just like her parents did, all shiny and loveless. They would be a formidable couple, they would move out of the city to a ritzy suburb where they would know all the right people, they would have a grand collection of fine lambswool sweaters, their house would be heavy with silence, they would be trim and tan.

But Hannah does not tan, she freckles.

Hannah had many suitors in med school. She was particularly popular among those medical students who wore a tie to every class. They took her out for expensive, boring dinners, they talked largely about themselves, and afterward Hannah would go home and study.

One day, during midterms her first year, Del's Deli closed due to a plumbing malfunction. Hannah had to find somewhere else to get her lunch. So she went two blocks farther from the medical quad and ended up at the Sandwich Box. Justin, who had been working there since graduation, was late for his lunch break, but his replacement was in the bathroom, and so he waited on the most beautiful woman he had ever seen. She tossed her red hair and ordered a turkey sandwich with provolone, avocado, just a bit of mayo, lettuce, tomatoes, hold the onions. When she left the shop, he pulled off his hat and apron and followed her. She went into the medical library and he went in behind her. He sat down next to her and asked to borrow one of her anatomy books. That's all. He never actually said he was a medical student, so he didn't tell a lie, per se. True, when he asked her for a date, he may have implied it was a study date, but eyewitness accounts still differ on that matter. He didn't confess until midway through dinner. A man has to be very careful in a situation like that—there is a fine line between pursuing and stalking, and his actions could have been construed as either charming or creepy, but Hannah was evidently in the mood to think the former, and he has loved her for it ever since.

In the following years, they would lie in bed talking about the wonder of being young and in love. "You could have worked at any sandwich shop. You could have had a different shift."

"It had to have happened. If not then, some other time."

"I always went to Del's. But they were closed that day. And I needed lunch. I had that exam. If Del's hadn't been closed—"

"We would have met anyway. It had to happen. It couldn't *not* have happened."

Fate or chance? Hannah wonders. Is there one person out there for each of us that we are destined to meet? Or are we just bouncing around aimlessly in this empty universe?

"It was meant to be," said Justin.

"But what if it wasn't," said Hannah. "What if it was all just . . . random?"

"It can't be random. I won't believe that. The world can't be just *like* that. It can't be true that it was just luck that I met you."

"You believe there's a plan?"

"I don't know. But I can't believe there isn't."

"I had a plan," she said. "You weren't part of it."

"That's why I love you, Hannah Bennett. You're willing to be taken by surprise."

And surprised by him she is, every day. He wakes up in the morning with love for the day ahead—she's never met anyone like that before. And while there was a time she imagined herself with a man who would do great things, now, for her, there's no greater thing than what he does each day. Hannah's colleagues at the practice can't believe how lucky she is. They complain about nannies and day care and how little their own husbands do. The Woodrows' system works out beautifully for Hannah—she doesn't have to feel some atavistic maternal guilt, and Justin couldn't be happier. It is nice for the kids, to have Dad at home like that. And he is just much better at parenting than she would be anyway. And, instead, she can become better at what she has always wanted to do.

Hannah is always learning how to be a doctor, every day. Complacency is the worst enemy of the physician. The body is a teacher, the body is full of lessons—you are only its humble student. If you understand this, you will never be surprised. If you think you have learned everything from the body, you will make errors, and you will fail.

Ginny Klausen has gastritis, Hannah is fairly sure. It may be an ulcer, but it is prudent and efficient to rule gastritis out first. Dr. Woodrow will give her something to calm the acid in her stomach. If that doesn't work, they will look deeper.

After Ginny leaves, Hannah calls the appointment desk—there have been no last-minute appointments, no emergencies. The city is well today, and Hannah can go home early. She will get home before Greta. She'll get to her house, kiss Justin and James, help set up for the party—and have some lunch. They will have a family dinner and for once she will not be too exhausted by the exigencies of the day to enjoy it. And then tonight—oh that's right—tonight after dinner the family is going to the circus.

The Show Is Over Now

"Excuse me, sir, where's my son?"

"Huh?" The pimply usher blinks.

The show is over now. The lights have come up in Lindbergh Auditorium, the bows have been taken. Chattering families flood the aisles next to the Woodrows—heading to the lobby to buy balloons, T-shirts, clown noses, batons, wigs, CDs, hats, posters, commemorative programs—the glow of the rousing grand finale still on their faces. James disappeared, the audience roared, the clown bowed, the orchestra sounded, the cast took the stage. Acrobats jumped and tumbled and twirled, colored lights danced, flaming torches flew, unicyclists cycled in unison. The auditorium cheered, the acrobats mounted their last stand, and meanwhile, next to Justin, little Greta started wiggling in her seat.

James's disappearance was the second-to-last act, though Justin thinks it would have made a pretty darned good finale on its own. Justin knows a little about conjuring, about the manipulation of illusion, but he has never seen an act quite like that. (Hannah must be dying to know what the trick is—Hannah is the one who always looks for the wires.)

During the finale, Justin searched among the lights and the cyclists and the confetti and the torches for his son, but James was nowhere onstage. It would have been a nice touch, he thought. A nice bit of showbiz—have the boy reappear onstage like that, because usually when someone or something disappears during a trick, they reappear again—that's part of the whole trick, really, it's the payoff. It would have been nice for James, too, to get the applause. Justin didn't see the clown onstage for the finale either; he hoped he was off holding James's hand. James doesn't like to be alone too much, and Justin and Hannah started exchanging looks—the invisible line between parents and son had become stretched too taut. Hannah raised her eyebrows, Justin shrugged, they glanced at each other. No, this is fine; he'll be back after the show, they just didn't want to disturb the audience by returning him to his seat. He's fine, of course he's fine. We'll just wait.

Now, with the show over and no sign of his son, Justin has grabbed the nearest boy in a red vest. The lights are up, the audience presses out beyond them, families move inexorably toward the restrooms. All the energy in the auditorium rushes out toward the front doors, and the usher sways slightly in the current.

"Where's my son?" Justin repeats with a patient smile. "He just volunteered? He was in the chair? Great trick, but, uh, can you bring him back? We like him." He smiles. Greta squeals and tugs on his coat. "Dadd-ee!"

"Just a second, sweetie," he hushes. The usher is still standing, staring at them. "My son?" Justin feels his smile rework to express a touch of the aggravated pity he used to reserve for his particularly recalcitrant sophomore boys.

"Uhhhh... yeah..." The usher straightens his vest. "Um, I'm on auditorium duty right now so I can't go to the lobby, because that's Team A's job? But all the performers are out in the lobby, you know, signing things and stuff? I bet your boy's out there. I'd go out with you, but, you know, I'm Team B."

"Sure," Justin says accommodatingly, just loud enough to mask Hannah's snort. Greta hops up and down next to them squeaking out a steady chorus of, "Dadd-ee, Dadd-ee, Dadd-ee!"

"Yeah. Uhhh... The boy's with Mike, I'm sure."

"Mike?"

"Yeah. Mike the Clown."

"Mike the Clown."

"In the lobby." The usher beams.

"Okay," Justin sighs. "You've been a big help." The usher rubs his nose and slouches toward the Team B command central.

Justin turns to face his family. "I'll go get him," he says. "I'll meet you guys—" he smiles at Greta and realizes she is squeezing her legs together and wincing "—in front of the ladies' room."

"THANK you!" Greta exhales and pulls her mother into the aisle. Hannah sighs and says to Justin, "Don't forget James's jacket."

In the lobby, Justin works his way through the masses of people push-ing toward the Lindbergh front entrance. Little knots of children are gathered here and there around heavily made-up performers who are signing programs. A few talk and laugh with the kids, others seem to wear their smiles like surgical implants. Justin stops and scans the faces. A succession of children bump into him.

Then, there, next to the refreshment counter, in the middle of the biggest knot of all, he sees a bobbing top hat. Mike. Programs wave in the air attached to small grasping hands. Justin expects to see his son—the star, the victor, the champion—maybe on the clown's back, or next to him, signing autographs himself. But James is nowhere to be seen in the throng, and Justin breathes away a nagging of something that has begun to inhabit his stomach.

"Excuse me!" Justin stands behind the crowd and shouts. "Excuse me, Mike?" He waves his program up in the air, to no avail. He begins to work his way through the crowd, reaching over it to tap Mike on the shoulder, but he can't get close enough.

He shouts again. The clown looks over at him blankly. Makeup is running down his face in sweat droplets, and there's a large scar on his forehead that suddenly strikes Justin as rather menacing. The chil-

dren around him are jumping and squealing and chattering and singing. Justin bellows, "Excuse me!" and the clown waves him off.

"Sir, you'll have to wait your turn."

"No!" Justin shouts. The thing in his stomach will not be breathed
away. Justin has worked his way right up to Mike; now he can touch
him. "I don't want an autograph, I want my son. Where's my son?" The
children around him are quiet now, watching this red-faced man shout.

"Who?" The clown regards him more closely. Is he shaking?—
the clown might be shaking underneath that calm, but it might be
Justin as well.

"My son. James. Your volunteer? Where is he?"

"Oh. Well. Um." The clown's lips disappear inside his head.

"Yes?"

"Well..." His eyes fall down to the ground for a second, then
back up. "Um, I made him disappear."

"Yes, I saw that, but where is he now?" The clown is starting to
back away. Justin finds himself softly moving children aside to get
closer to him.

He shakes his head and says softly, "I don't know."

"What do you mean, you don't know?"

"I'm sorry. I'm very sorry. I don't know."

"Jesus Christ!" Justin grabs his shirt. The crowd around them
seems to have grown bigger. "Is this a joke? Are you playing some
kind of game?"

"No, I—"

"Well, where the hell is the trapdoor? Where the hell are the
invisible wires? Where's the secret chamber?" This is what Justin
wants to say, but really he says something like, "Where in the hell did
you put him?"

Next to Justin, a little girl starts to cry. The clown looks around
for escape. "I didn't. I didn't. I'm sorry."

Justin breathes. He breathes again. The world stops for a moment, two moments. He opens his mouth. He speaks very slowly and carefully, "I'm just going to ask you this one more time. Your little disappearing trick? How does it work? Where did you put my boy? Where is my son?"

Most of the Lindbergh audience seems to have gathered around them. Justin has backed the clown nearly against the wall. Mike begins to whimper.

"I'm sorry, I just don't know." The clown coughs. "He must've scampered away. Little tyke." He laughs weakly. "Probably just backstage somewhere." The clown is shifting his weight back and forth, and will not meet Justin's eyes.

"Listen, you shit." Justin spits the words out. "I don't know what the hell you have done with my son, but if you do not bring him to me right now, I will kill you, is that clear? I will actually kill you."

He feels a tap on his shoulder. An usher stands behind him, gathering strength. "Sir, what seems to be the problem?"

"Get the manager."

"Sir, I . . ."

"I want to see the God Damn Manager. Now." Justin grips Mike's arm and fixes his gaze. The crowd stares at them in turn. There is no noise, no motion, no air.

This is not happening. This is not happening. This is not happening. This is—

This is what the nightmares are like. The ones that started even before Greta was born, even before Hannah was first pregnant. A crowd—a park, a grocery store, a shopping mall. The child is at hand. The child is holding your hand. You open your hand for a moment—just a moment—and the hand slips away. Where's the child? Where's my child? The crowds around you keep moving on, carrying their packages, talking, laughing, living, and in the waves of bodies in motion the child has slipped through the seams. You are alone. Your hand is cold. You wake up, shuddering, to find your wife is next to you, sleeping peacefully—it was a dream. Just a dream. It's all right. This is going to be all right. This is—

This is not happening.

Justin feels it now, the chill in his hand, the weight of the emptiness. What he wants, right now, the only thing he wants in the world is his son's hand in his. If he closes his eyes, if he wishes it there, will it come back? Justin will hold on and hold on to that warm, sticky little boy hand—

"Sir." A man in a security uniform has come up behind Justin. His voice sounds like marching. It's not quite threatening, yet, but it carries the promise of force. "I must ask you to let go of this man."

Justin does not let go. He breathes in. He breathes out. He opens his mouth. Listen. "Listen." His voice cracks. "This bastard has done something with my son." Justin pauses and blinks. He turns to the security guard. His eyes are full. He holds out James's jacket, a small blue puffy offering. "Please. Please. Make him find my son."

Hannah and Greta come out of the ladies' room, hand in hand, and stand by the door waiting for Justin. And then they hear sounds like shouting, and then mother and daughter look around the corner and see a big crowd of people and a security guard leading away a man in a top hat and clown's nose. It's the same clown, James's clown. And then, before this thought really processes in Hannah's mind, Greta says, "Daddy!" and there is Justin, in the center of the crowd of people. Hannah opens her mouth and then shuts it. Hannah stands quite still. Hannah knows:

The clown has done something with my son.

Hannah grips Greta's hand and stares at Justin across the lobby. Maybe that's not my husband. Maybe that's someone else's husband. Maybe my husband is buying cotton candy and a clown nose for James and is about to come around the corner behind us and say, what are you looking at? That's someone else's husband and someone else's lost child. That poor man. His poor wife. How awful, awful.

If he does not look at me, if he does not seek me out, that is not my husband. If he does not meet my eyes then he belongs to someone else.

The man who looks like Hannah's husband watches the security guard and the clown go off into the theater. The man who looks like Hannah's husband stands for a while as the crowd buzzes around him. The man who looks like Hannah's husband begins to search the crowd, the lobby, his eyes roam over every face, peer into every shadow. The man who looks like Hannah's husband searches over the buzzing heads toward the hallway where the bathrooms are and then the man who looks like Hannah's husband looks at Hannah, he meets her eyes, and Hannah knows he belongs to her.

"What was James wearing when

he disappeared?"

Hannah is in a room behind the box office. She can see figures moving around in the lobby. She never knew there were rooms behind the box office before; she had never thought about it. There must be rooms in so many places, rooms no one even thinks about. A policeman is asking her some questions, and she is answering them promptly.

"Jeans. Blue jeans. White tennis shoes. And, um—a sweater."

"What color?"

What color? Was it the green or the navy? Hannah loves him in both. With his light skin and green eyes and red hair either color looks so good on him. It's getting so cold now, it's getting to be fall and it's sweater season. Justin bought him new sweaters when he went back-to-school shopping with Greta. You have to get kids new sweaters every year, they grow so quickly, it's ridiculous. "Be sure to get a navy blue and a green one," Hannah said. James doesn't like sweaters, they make his arms itch; he'd run around in a T-shirt and shorts all year if he could, James was not born for these winters. Greta doesn't like sweaters either. Greta is on her way home with Catherine now. Greta might know which sweater James was wearing, she remembers things like that, but Hannah doesn't know if Catherine has a cell phone. This is the problem with not being very close to your younger sister, you don't know if she has a cell phone. Everyone should have a cell phone, in case someone needs to reach them to ask what color sweater her son was wearing.

"Mrs. Woodrow?"

"I don't remember," she says. "It was either the green or the blue. My husband will know. Where's my husband? You should ask him." She nods matter-of-factly. "Yes, he'll definitely know."

Justin is running. The police tell him to stay but he runs all the same. He pushes past the impatient families trapped in the lobby waiting for the police to let them out. He runs into the auditorium and on the stage. He yells and yells. He looks up. He climbs the catwalk. He yells some more. He goes back onto the stage. He opens the trapdoors. He jumps into the orchestra pit. He lands on his ankle funny. He swears. He opens the doors and stumbles through the hallways. He opens dressing room doors, he looks in cabinets and under desks. He runs backstage and looks under every pile, in every corner. His throat cracks. There's a police officer following him. Justin turns to him. "I have to go outside." The police officer shakes his head. "It's my son," Justin says, "you come with me, we'll look." The police officer goes too, but he can barely keep up with Justin, who hobbles all around the building, again and again, and again. He yells until he has no breath left. The police officer says, "Come on, let's go back inside. We're using every available resource. We're good at this. Come on, they want to ask you some questions."

Hello. I'll be in charge of the investigation. I'm wearing a gray blazer to show you I am a professional and I have moved up enough in the hierarchy of the police force to wear a blazer. They are not sending some monkey to help you find your son.

The new man is saying something like this. His mouth is moving, anyway, and Hannah must supply the words.

I am the top banana. I am going to use this soothing tone of voice

*with you. It matches the soothing color of my blazer. Don't you monkey
with the monkey.*

Hannah nods.

*Have you remembered the color of his sweater yet? You really should
remember. A good mother would remember. We will never find your son
unless you remember. Green or blue?*

Hannah nods again.

Mrs. Woodrow?

"Hmmh?"

"Mrs. Woodrow?" The man in the gray blazer is looking down
at her. "Do you have a picture of your son with you? In your purse?"

"Oh, yes," she says. "I always carry one with me." She may have
gotten the sweater question wrong, but now she has the right answer.
Hannah always carries pictures of her children, she does that.

"I'll need to borrow that for a while, if I could."

"Certainly," she says. "Certainly you can."

The police keep multiplying. At first there were just the two. And
then they said some things on their radios and then more came.
And then more still. They are at the doors, keeping people from leaving the auditorium. They are in every available room, interviewing
troupe members, audience members, crew. They are talking into radios, reading names off of driver's licenses. They are at computers,
scanning and faxing. They are talking into phones. They are all
through the building, looking up, down, inside, out, behind, between,
over, under, and around. There are police officers setting up road-
blocks. There are police officers in the parking lot, shining their lights
inside and under cars, searching each car as it leaves. There are police
cars coming to the building with police dogs. There are FBI agents
on the way. There is a helicopter on the way. There is procedure,
there is action, there is machinery at work, there is everything but
James.

• • •

"All right," the man in the gray blazer says to an official-looking woman. "That's the description. James Woodrow, five years old. White male. Red hair, green eyes, thirty-five pounds, thirty-eight inches. Green or navy sweater, blue jeans, white tennis shoes."

(*Three-foot-two, jeans of blue, oh what those blue jeans can do, has anybody seen my boy?*)

"Okay, Detective Blair. What next?" says the woman.

"Start gathering volunteers for a search party."

"Got it."

The woman leaves the room behind the box office. The man in the gray blazer says, "That's Detective Henry. She's my partner."

Hannah nods. That's nice.

"Mrs. Woodrow—"

"Call me Hannah," she says politely.

"Do you have something of James's on you? An article of clothing?"

"Oh, no! No, but my husband has his jacket. The jacket is blue."

"Good. We'll need it for the dogs. They'll be here any minute." He checks his watch. "Damn. I'm sorry, we're going to just miss the ten o'clock news."

Hannah doesn't want to seem rude, but why would they want to watch the news?

"We're calling a press conference but it's going to take a half hour to get together. They'll break into local programming, but most people won't see the story until tomorrow. It'll be all over the news tomorrow anyway, if we haven't found your son by then. It's better than nothing."

Oh. "A press conference? Do we have to?" Hannah is so confused. He keeps talking in time. Ten o'clock. A half hour. Doesn't he know that time isn't working right anymore? Time is sitting still, an obstinate elephant in the doorway. Shouldn't somebody tell him?

"Mrs. Woodrow, the story will get out. It's best we are the ones who control it. Besides the media is our greatest ally in these cases. Do you want to speak for the cameras?"

Hannah opens her mouth and closes it again. She shakes her head. She doesn't want to speak at all anymore, not until they've brought her son back to her.

Parents with young children are allowed to leave. Police officers escort them to their cars. A lot of people stay to help with the search party. They all want to find James. The lady detective has gathered them all in the lobby.

"You must wear these badges. You must let me make a copy of your photo ID. You need to stay with your team at all times. Your team leader will give you specific instructions on where to search. You must check back in with me before you go home. If you do not check back in with me, you will be considered a suspect. Is that clear?"

Two officers are carrying the clown off in handcuffs. He has a black eye—the security guard punched him.

People point and whisper. Hannah watches from behind the glass partition of the box office. She could sell tickets if she wanted to, step right up, come see my worst nightmare and yours.

Hannah knows what they're all thinking. They all think she is somebody different, marked for tragedy, a different species somehow; you all think I am Someone Else, but no, I'm just like you.

She hasn't seen her husband since he went off with the police officer. Did someone take him too?

Cameras and lights fill the lobby. Detective Blair and Detective Henry stand side-by-side.

"Around nine-fifteen tonight, five-year-old James Woodrow disappeared from Lindbergh Performing Arts Center. We have a suspect in custody, but the boy is still missing. You're all getting copies of his photograph. He's three feet, two inches and thirty-five pounds. He's wearing a blue sweater, jeans, and white tennis shoes. He has red hair and green eyes. We are using every available resource to find him. We have set up a hot line for him. Anyone with any information on James Woodrow should call 1-800-555-3262. Are there any questions?"

The man in the gray blazer says, "Now, Mrs. Woodrow, do you have any questions?"

"Yes. Where's my husband?"

"He's talking to another officer. You'll see him soon. Now," he says softly, leaning forward, "I want you to tell me in your own words what happened."

Justin and Hannah sit at a long

table in some kind of boardroom. Justin holds Hannah's hand. His eyes are red, and he's trembling. Hannah is all white. Detectives mill around, whispering to each other. For a while, Justin and Hannah were in two separate rooms because the detectives just had to ask them a few questions:

"Is this your first marriage?"

"Are you James's natural parent?"

"Is your husband/wife James's natural parent?"

"Would you say yours is a happy marriage?"

"Have there been any disturbances in your neighborhood lately?"

"What other adults have regular contact with James?"

"Has your son ever shown any signs of abuse?"

"Have you ever suspected anyone of abusing your son?"

"Have you ever suspected your husband/wife?"

"Is there anyone who would want to hurt your son?"

"Is there anyone who would want to hurt you?"

"What do you think happened to your son?"

Hannah did not cry. Hannah answered the questions. Hannah answered the questions as carefully and completely as she could. Justin and I are his natural parents. We are very happy. We have always been happy. My parents are dead. My sister lives in town; she loves James. No one would hurt him. No one would touch him.

Justin cried silently. He talked through his tears like they weren't there. He pretended there was air in the room but really there wasn't. He was talking so quickly, his heart kept pounding, he wanted to jump up out of his chair and scream. He doesn't remember the questions, but he knows he just kept saying *Yes. Yes. No, No, No. No.*

The world is so funny sometimes. You think it is real but then it proves to be just an illusion.

Now they sit together, Hannah and Justin, inside this room with the long table. Police officers are scattered in corners like misplaced statues. Justin can't hold Hannah's hand hard enough. It's the only thing keeping him where he is. He doesn't know what's wrong with these people; they keep expecting him to sit still. Don't they realize he has to find his son? Don't they realize he needs to be running and yelling, that he obviously has not run and yelled enough because if he did he would have his son back? The police officer who went outside with him took him to a little room behind the coat closet. A woman officer was waiting for him, "I'm sorry, we won't be here long." At that moment, Justin didn't know where anyone in his family was, his wife, his daughter, or his dear little son. "No," he said. "I can't sit here. Please. We have to do something."

"Talking to me is doing something," the woman said. "You can help us look for your son. Why don't you tell me in your own words what happened?"

Justin feels himself now ready to burst. His heart keeps beating so fast. How long can it keep this up? He should ask Hannah, Hannah's a doctor and knows these things. He could ask her about it if they'd just let him get up and get his son back. Then they could all sit down and have a nice conversation about heart rates.

Someone rolls a television and VCR into the room with the long table. "Detective Blair will be right in," someone else says. Hannah has not blinked for hours—her eyes are dry like dead things.

The detective in the gray blazer follows the VCR in. "Mr. Woodrow, Dr. Woodrow," he nods at them. "We're still doing interviews downstairs. It was Simmons's first show with the group, they say. He's local, and he was a last-minute sub. None of them had met him before."

A woman walks in. Detective Henry. Hannah has met her before. Detective Henry has a videotape in her hand. "Good call," she says to Detective Blair in the gray blazer. "They were taping the show, the tour was."

The woman detective flashes the same brief sympathetic smile to them that each detective walking into the room gives. Hannah briefly wonders if they learn it at the academy. Today is smile day, class. You must communicate empathy and authority. You must show that you care but you aren't emotionally involved. Nothing will get in the way of your competence. You have a job to do. You are hard like steel and you are not afraid to show it.

A doctor's smile is different. They don't teach it to you in med school but you learn it just the same. A doctor must know just how to smile—a doctor must care with authority, yes; a doctor must radiate competence and empathy, yes; a doctor must not be afraid, yes; but unlike the detectives, a doctor is not supposed to look on her patients as suspects.

All the suspicious detectives gather around the long table. Detective Blair puts the videotape into the VCR and says, "Let's see what we can see."

Static, black, and then, before their eyes, the circus starts again. The troupe rushes on stage, tumblers tumble, jugglers juggle, clowns clown.

"It was near the end," Hannah says. "Right before the finale."

Detective Blair attends to the remote control and the images on screen fly by. Acrobats move at superhuman speed, unicyclists zoom by, balls whiz through the air, and in between each act is Mike the Clown, bumbling and chattering.

Justin can't believe they're all sitting there—he's moving as fast as the images on the tape. Maybe his heart will explode, maybe that's what happens—

"Not that one. No, not yet. Not yet. Later. It's later." Hannah must say this. Justin won't talk. Hannah can talk, she can talk all she wants, she'll do whatever she has to do, just find James, find James, find James—

The tape is not going fast enough, nothing is going fast enough, but these are the police, the police are here, it's Hannah's job to help them so they can find James, find James, find James—

And then, after the big man rides his little bicycle through a flaming hoop, the curtain falls, and Mike comes on again.

"There," says Hannah quickly. "That one."

Mike the Clown is saying, "I've been trying to get some balance in my life." Laughter. He balances a plate, a pool cue, a broom, then a chair. And then a tandem bike. Applause. Then he says, "I need an audience volunteer."

The camera doesn't capture the children jumping up and down in their seats, nor does it get Mike tripping through the aisles, nor does it get little James raising his hand toward the ceiling. It does not get Hannah and Justin as they exchange a surprised look, nor does it get Mike the Clown come over and pick James out of all the kids in the audience. It does not get James as he takes Mike's hand and walks back to the stage. But then, the odd couple reappears—James looking so small next to that tall tall man. James is grinning, beaming—you can't quite tell on the camera, but he is, Hannah knows he is. Audience members whisper to each other, "That boy is so cute," but it just sounds like static. All the camera shows is their James playing along with the clown, mimicking his every movement, pretending to squat in an invisible chair. The clown shakes his head and points at James. James shines. The clown puts James in the chair. James holds on to the sides. The clown lifts James-in-the-chair up and puts James-in-the-chair on his chin. The clown's arms go out to his sides and he staggers about a bit—applause starts—and then, all of a sudden, he bends and sways, there is a gasp, and then . . .

And then James disappears.

In the room with the long table, Justin and Hannah Woodrow stop—heart, breath, mind. This is not at all what they thought. This is not even the same world anymore, this is a whole new universe. It's right there, on the video. James has not been kidnapped. James is not lost. James has just gone.

Poof.

Hannah starts to tremble. Justin's skin begins to burn. The detectives still have the appearance of people who believe in the laws of the universe—they do not see it, they do not know, and they will not be able to help. From that point on the Woodrows exist in a completely different sphere than everyone else; they are on their own. The detectives say, "We better look at that again," but Justin and Hannah do not need to look at it again. Even as the detectives rewind and watch the tape again and again and say, "We need to figure out how that was done," Justin and Hannah need nothing else. They do not need to go over it in slow motion or stop motion because they know exactly what they just saw. Now Hannah and Justin Woodrow know that they live in a world where little boys can disappear into thin air.

James Was an Accident

James was an accident. They'd

never admit this to anyone, of course. If you asked, Hannah and Justin would tell you that they had every intention of having the children so close together; they had planned it that way from the beginning.

But they had intended to wait. They wanted to have their children three years apart; three years apart is a good range for siblings they heard, and three years would give Hannah and Justin time to recover from the first baby. They had a good, solid plan—and Hannah getting pregnant again when Greta was less than a year old was not part of it.

The thing about birth control is, it's supposed to work.

Greta was no accident. Greta was the product of years of planning—Justin scheduled his leave of absence at the school a year in advance, Hannah studied her pay scale and negotiated with her practice, together they pored over fertility charts, read all the literature, absorbed everything there was to know about prenatal care—until years of birth control gave way to basal thermometers, carefully marked calendars, and concomitant couplings.

Had it been up to Hannah, she would have waited longer to have Greta. A few more years maybe, until she felt more prepared. Before, she had expected that by the time it became Time, something would change inside her, she would feel ready—but she wasn't ready. From the year Justin proposed on, Hannah would find herself sitting somewhere, just sitting, minding her own business, and a shudder of panic would run through her: *I am not fit*. Children—such helpless, malleable, needy things. And this baby-making, this *person*-making . . . this transformation from woman to mother. *I do not want to change my identity. I am selfish, you see how selfish I am? I am not fit.* What would happen to her space, her time, her self? Who will she become?

I am not fit. We mother like we were mothered, right? Despite her best intentions, Hannah Woodrow would be doomed to teach her children to be quiet so as not to disturb mommy.

And her marriage—Justin and she had a delicate balance, based in the delight of mutual discovery. He was so unlike anyone she expected to fall in love with—all the men around her had always been steeped in ambition—he viewed life as something to enjoy, not to win. This, to her, was a being that needed exploring. She wanted to spend more time with him before they lost each other to the family; she didn't know how much time, but more, more, more. She'd never seen a healthy marriage before—her own parents didn't speak for all of her childhood and were divorced when she was fifteen. Hannah wanted to spend as much time learning about hers as possible.

And there was the conversation that she had with Justin one thousand times in her imagination. It went something like this:

I don't think I can have a child, Justin.

Why not, sweetheart?

Because I don't know how I could go on, loving something that much. How do you contain so much love and still exist?

How do you do it? How do you go on? How do you live from day to day when there are speeding cars and balls that roll in the street, evil men with welcoming hands, death that creeps in on babies in the night, disease that eats at bodies silently, there are household chemicals, angry kids with an arsenal at their disposal, school buses with drivers who do not pay attention, open wires, crashing waves— there are so many wrong places and wrong times, and how on earth do you keep your kids from them—

How do you love something that much when you could just lose it, just like that? Justin—

But they had never had that conversation in real life, and it was Time to Start. Hannah's first missed period came right on schedule. Justin was elated when she became pregnant—he glowed, he became her source of light and heat. He tucked her in at night and kissed her belly in the morning and set out her vitamins and stroked her neck and she would think, *I will miss him.*

Hannah spent her pregnancy reading every book on parenting she possibly could. She had a stash under her desk at work and, between patients, instead of reading medical journals she would learn how to potty train and how to teach her child to eat right and love reading and respect humanity. None of the books said the same things. There are so many ways to screw up a child irrevocably. And what Hannah didn't know then, what not one single person told her, is that every single book is just filled with lies. If someone just had told her that, it would have saved her a lot of time.

Justin, meanwhile, spent the nine months reading everything he could about a healthy pregnancy. He made her do a yoga-for-expectant-mothers tape, threw away every piece of food in the house that had ingredients of more than four syllables, and tried to get her to stop working one month before her due date.

Soon, Hannah's womb became the unborn child's personal gymnasium. Greta kicked and tumbled and rumbled around with such alacrity that Justin would shake his head and say, "I think you're going to give birth to a monkey."

Greta emerged from the womb like a shot. Hannah held her and every piece of her body and soul melded to this baby and she could hardly bear the beautiful pain of all that love. *We are in love, you and I—it's a secret—shh, never tell, never tell.*

Greta responded with a series of spirited wails and never stopped vocalizing after that. She would carry on entire conversations in baby syllables with such unalloyed confidence that soon Justin and Hannah half-wondered if she weren't fluent in Chinese.

The baby woke up at five-thirty every morning, and Hannah with her. Greta's wails and gurgles mirrored the state of Hannah's insides as she woke up each morning and realized, "I am a mother. That is my child." Greta was the most precious, tiny little thing; Hannah could barely look at her without wanting to cry. Hannah would sit and hold her, feed her at her breast, melt with joy, all the time praying, *Please let me be a good mother. Please let me be worthy of you.*

How do you go on, loving something this much?

It was hard. Sometimes the baby would cry and she would find herself feeling annoyed, and then she'd wonder where her heart was. Or she didn't know if she was holding the baby too much, or not enough, if she should be feeding her whenever she wanted to be fed, and if she was in danger of messing her daughter up, irrevocably. She had nightmares small and large, from bee stings to illnesses to hate-filled rants. In one, her infant daughter sits across from her and begins to calmly explain why she is a bad mother. *You are too cold. You do not know how to love. You are too afraid.*

She got advice everywhere. The world is full of mothers. You forget; you think that everyone is just a person until you become a mother yourself. And then you learn you have joined a very special club in which all of the members are entitled to tell you exactly what you are doing wrong.

She would sit outside with Greta by the lake, and the other mothers with their strollers would stop and ask:

She's so cute. Is she a good baby?

No, Hannah wanted to say. She is one of those bad babies that you hear so much about.

(What they meant was, Does she sleep well? Does she cry a lot? Because if she does not sleep well, and she cries a lot, then you are clearly a bad mother, and you are going to screw her up, irrevocably.)

The mothers didn't really have to ask, because while their babies were all snuggled up fast asleep, Greta would, without fail, be screaming and wailing so all the world could see.

People stare. Your baby is crying. Can't you see? There's something you're doing wrong. You should feed your baby. There's something wrong with your baby. You should hold your baby. Can't you see?

Do you let your baby cry herself to sleep or do you comfort her until she sleeps? You're supposed to let your child cry for longer and longer periods of time before going in to comfort her. Your baby should learn to fall asleep by herself.

Hannah wants to grab her daughter and run, hide in her house away from this world full of mothers. They have all these opinions, they know all these things, and anyway how do they all know things that she does not know?

It isn't safe to go anywhere. Grocery stores, walks in the park, lunches with friends. Everyone has opinions on the things Hannah is doing wrong. And Greta just keeps on crying.

Greta cries, and all Hannah wants to do is have her stop, because she can't stand for her baby to be in pain, because she cannot go on loving something this much, because her baby needs something and she would give her anything, anything, anything to make her happy and protect her from the world, but Hannah doesn't know how to do that, she can't do that, she has no idea what to do, and what do they do if Hannah cries herself to sleep?

You should comfort her, Justin says.

But the books say we're not supposed to, Hannah says, helplessly.

Do you think if you comfort her you're going to ruin her irrevocably? Justin asks.

What did her mother do? Hannah never dared to ask. Probably she just shut the door and tried to tune out the awful noise.

Is your baby a good baby? How long does she sleep? Really? Mine sleeps five hours already. He is a perfect little dream. I can take him anywhere.

And even Justin, her source of light and heat, began to change. He was so good with Greta. The baby would just cry and cry and cry with Hannah but when Justin held her she gurgled and sang and played with his hair. How did he know? His own father ignored him, then left him when he was eight, how come he gets to be such a great dad?

Hannah counted down to the day when she would go back to work and Justin would stay home. He is better equipped for this because he believes everything generally works out for the best. He believes if you act in good faith, the world will give you good faith back. He will raise Greta perfectly, because that's how he does things. And she can go back to work, and then she will not be able to harm her baby, irrevocably.

Hannah was thirty-two when Greta was born. She began to feel that one child was all she could ever manage. It is too much—this person-making. Three years seemed too short; she would rather wait until Greta was at least twenty-four to try this again. But then, without aid of calendar, thermometer, or chart, little James Woodrow began to make his presence felt. At night, in bed, Hannah leaned over and whispered to her husband:

"Justin? I think I'm pregnant again."

"No!"

"Yes."

"Not really."

"Yes."

"How do you know?"

"Well, you know how I had a checkup today?"

"Dr. Bandu says you're pregnant?"

"Yeah."

"So it's pretty sure then."

"Yeah."

"Wow."

She didn't want to tell anybody about the pregnancy, at first, but Justin refused to keep it a secret—that is, he didn't have it in him to contain the news. He was swelling over with it, and no one who saw him could fail to ask, "Justin, what is it?"

"It's a gift. It was meant to be. You must be so happy." And Hannah, Dr. Hannah, would find herself lying in bed at night feeling her body grow again, these words echoing in her head, and would wonder, *This child—miracle or accident? Fate or mistake?*

What if they were all wrong? What if—what if the baby was never meant to be? What if his birth threw off this delicate balance?

Everything with Greta's birth had gone according to plan, to schedule. Their hypothetical planned sibling was going to be so perfect, in three years' time. But what would this flesh and bone accident be like?

And soon, she began to have new nightmares. This baby, this thing growing in her stomach, would be a two-headed thing, an alien, a fish, a monster, an alien fish monster that she would let loose on the world.

She never told Justin about her nightmares. He would—no, he wouldn't laugh, Justin would never laugh at her—but he would angle his head and bite his lip as if his world had just silently altered, just a bit. She would not put him through that. Justin—for whom parenthood was manifest destiny, who had unconsciously dedicated his life to expiating the sins of his own father, who had just signed on for a second year of paternity leave—would never comprehend that a child could bring anything but joy. What would he think of her? What kind of a woman was she? She could not tell Justin because she would not—could not—give these feelings the body and breath of words.

(*Doesn't anyone understand that I can't possibly have another baby right now? I'm still trying not to break this one.*)

But one night, when sleep would not come, she leaned over and whispered in his ear, *Justin? Do you want to have this baby?*

And Justin paused, and then angled his head and bit his lip.

Hannah . . . ? Yes . . . yes, of course. Don't you?

Of course. Of course.

When James Joseph Woodrow was born, Hannah saw that he had only one head. And he had two legs. He had just the right amount of everything, in fact. He was no fish, no alien, no evil thing. He was a baby. Just like Greta. A sweet little baby.

And for a moment, when Hannah held James for the first time, her fear washed away. *James, my James, my baby boy*, she whispered— *You are special, you are a miracle, you are my love*—and it took persuading on Justin's part for her to let him hold the baby too.

She promised him at that moment she would watch over him. She would make all her fears and doubts up to him. *We are in love, you and I. Let it be our secret. Never tell, never tell.*

They had been worried about Greta's reaction to the new baby. It was not fair to her, in a way, to give her a brother so soon; firstborns should have a good two to three years thinking they are the center of the universe before the awful truth is revealed.

But Greta, little squawking Greta, too young to have things explained to her, somehow knew right away. She would bring her chubby hand up to her mother's swelling belly and rest it there, unmoving—for once silent and watchful.

From the beginning, Greta adored James. She progressed into toddlerhood in constant orbit around her baby brother. Hannah and Justin would watch her carefully, of course. "You must be gentle with the baby, Greta. You must be quiet around the baby." But they needn't have worried. Greta treated James like a glass thing. He absorbed her, and she became glass too, and together they inhabited their own glass people world. Apart from her brother, Greta motored around the house commanding the air, but with him, she was a creature of serenity. She leaned next to his crib and talked to him endlessly—never using the real words that she was accumulating like so many heartbeats, but in her old fluency of burbles and coos.

And James, little baby James, so quiet around everyone else— James would mew right back to her, and the parents could only stand outside the glass surface and watch.

James was so different from Greta—even when he was born, he simply squawked in momentary astonishment, and then fell silent. The nurse said she had never seen a baby enter the world with so little protest.

He was the good baby, the one you could sit in a restaurant with, the one who made all the other mothers look bad.

It took a while for the problems to surface. He developed more slowly than his sister, certainly. He was slow to roll over, slow to crawl, slow to walk, talk, run. He conversed better in the mews of the glass people world than he ever had—has—in English. James is so quiet all the time, so shy, and so much smaller than the other children.

The other parents began to notice. "Well, everyone grows at their own pace," gradually turned into, "Really, he's not walking yet?" Eyebrows went up, meaningful glances were exchanged. "What does his doctor say?"

Hannah couldn't take it anymore; the entire world is full of mothers, all of whom have opinions about your children. The same women who posited that perhaps Greta was hyperactive and could be medicated had all kinds of theories about James. You go to Water Babies and Musical Trolley and SuperTots and the mothers begin to grill you: What are you feeding him? Have you tried organic food? Are you reading to him? Have you tried seeing a developmental specialist? Have you tested him for food allergies? What kind of chemicals do you clean with? Have you tried a new doctor? Have you tried a special preschool? Have you tried a clinic? Have you tried medication?

"James is fine," Hannah would reply stiffly. "Everyone grows at their own pace."

His preschool teacher spends their parent conferences talking in an extremely serious voice; she worries, she worries about his shyness, she worries about how quiet he is, she worries that he is behind his peers. "He's so quiet," she says. "Is there something wrong at home?"

Hannah bristles and Justin has to calm her down, "She just wants to help, Hannah."

"Can't they all just leave him alone?"

"Han, it's her job . . ."

And of course it is. Hannah knows that, she knows everyone just wants to help. She's a doctor, she's not supposed to scowl at the pediatrician when he shows them that James is a little behind on his cognitive abilities. She exhibits the same behavior she sees in her most difficult patients and hates herself for it, but she can't help it. She wants to tell them to mind their own business, to just let James grow up, to stop studying him, to stay out of it, to leave the Woodrows alone.

Yes, he is shy. Yes, he is unusual. At home, he plays with his blocks all day; he builds the most elaborate structures, neighborhoods, towns, cityscapes—all of which belie his stunted growth. (Hannah would come home from work to behold his creations. "See," Justin points. "See. He's all right, my boy.") And then, at night, right before bed, he knocks his buildings down.

("James. James, let's keep that up for a day. James, that's so beautiful. James, I'm very proud of you. James, let's keep it up to show off. Let's keep it up to look at it tomorrow—Oh!—!")

James allows Greta, only Greta, to play with him and she—who in second grade can add columns of two- and three-digit numbers, who is reading at the fourth-grade level and learning songs in French—Greta says, *Coo keep de-bot coo*, and he responds, *Gurgle geep mew*, and then it is bath time and together they squeal, BOOM!, and knock the buildings down together, two gibbering Penelopes, ready for bed.

In June, Miss Rose called them in for a special conference. She talked to them so carefully. "At this age," she said, "you want to see a child be able to put together a puzzle and be able to recognize numbers, to at least try to write their name. There's a certain . . . curiosity that James has not yet developed."

"He's different at home," Justin said. "He plays so fiercely."

"He's not talking in complete sentences. He doesn't articulate well. And he doesn't play with the other children."

"You should see him with his sister," Justin said.

"The thing is, Mr. and Mrs. Woodrow, I don't think James is ready for kindergarten next year. I strongly recommend you do not send him yet."

"But," Hannah said, "he'll be five. You go to kindergarten at five."

"You also want a child to be able to express himself, express feelings and desires. James does not. I think you should also consider getting him checked out by a developmental specialist. I have a name."

"But—"

"Think about it. We all want what's best for James."

So James won't be going to kindergarten in the fall. He isn't ready. He's behind his peers. He's stalled, he withers in public, he's so shy, he doesn't have social skills, he's incurious at school . . .

At night, in bed, the parents lie next to each other and whisper: *What if there's something really wrong with James?*

They had obviously done something wrong. They had been too

lax in his upbringing. They didn't buy him enough educational toys. They didn't expose him to new ideas and challenges. They didn't set goals for him. Not enough anyway—all of the toys, the books, the games, the stimulation, the well-balanced meals, it all was not enough.

In the quiet of night, Hannah blames herself. Her own doubt and fear had somehow stunted James in utero. Her unborn baby heard all of her thoughts and is now trying not to bother his mother too much— be quiet, dear, don't disturb Mommy.

Meanwhile, Justin has put it on himself to make James better. If he works just a little harder, if he spends just a little more time with his son, if he plays the right games with him and reads him the right books and asks him the right questions and does the right exercises and sings the alphabet song enough, James will be okay. Justin can make his son okay.

So. They won't send James to kindergarten yet. They'll watch him. At home, Justin has been taking careful notes on James's behavior. He has come to hate Tuesdays and Thursdays when James is out of sight for three hours of preschool. What if something there is holding him back? What if James misses his father?

Hannah has been looking on her own. She has been spending her spare time at work looking through journals and consulting the Mednet. He has symptoms of so many things, but nothing jells. Hannah researches birth defects, developmental disorders, toxic exposures, allergies, rare diseases, everything she can find.

They got an appointment with the best developmental pediatrician in the city, Dr. Henry Lewis—not Miss Rose's suggestion, Hannah found him on her own. The three of them will go in the first of October—it's the soonest they could get an appointment. There must be an explanation for this smallness, this glass people language, this silent submission to life. They will find it, and then they will fix him.

But then, one day in late September, on his sister's birthday, James Woodrow decided to volunteer at the circus.

Once upon a time, there was a little boy named James Woodrow, who was the sweetest little boy in the whole world. He had a blue jacket, a blue sweater, and sticky little boy hands. James believed the world was magical, and he liked it that way—he liked the way the sky turned all different colors, how caterpillars transformed into butterflies, how yellow and blue made green, how his mom and dad always appeared when he wanted them. He loved how if you put two things together you got a bigger thing, that if you kept building, you could make new shapes with your own hands.

One day James Woodrow raised his hand at the circus. Everyone was very surprised because James was a shy boy who never raised his hand anywhere. No one realized that he was just waiting for the right time. And it worked: James Woodrow raised his hand, and the clown—the tall clown with magical eyes—picked him. And James was happy. And he did all the right things and all the people laughed and he sat in the chair and he went up, up, up, and then—

In the car on the way home,

Justin and Hannah do not speak. Something happened in that room with the long table, to each of them, separately. Justin and Hannah saw James disappear, felt their worlds shake, and then they saw that everyone else just kept right on moving. The blow to their foundations was so great that the current that has been running back and forth between the two of them for the last fifteen years ruptured, and suddenly Hannah and Justin forgot they were in this world together. There was nothing between them, no gesture, no glance, to say, "Yes, yes, I saw what you saw. I know it too."

So they sit in their seats in the car, alone. There isn't a single thing they can say to each other; there is an unbridgeable space between them now. Each parent is alone with his own new universe; neither is ready to tell the other what he now knows. How do you say?— The world is not the place you think, the rules do not exist, Justin, darling—Hannah, sweetie—James has not been kidnapped, James is not hiding, James has just disappeared.

I know nothing. I don't know this person sitting next to me. I don't know these shapes around me. I don't know if this is air that I'm breathing and I don't know if I really breathe at all, or if that is a lie, too. My hands are such funny shapes and this body feels so strange around my thoughts. There are slips and tears in the universe, and I did not know, James has fallen through and I do not know how, reality is a joke, James is gone, and I do not know where he has gone or if he is just *gone*.

How could this happen? Why did this happen?

And most importantly: how on earth am I ever going to get him back?

The cops think James is just missing. They are following their carefully honed procedures for missing children, and what good is that going to do?

The police are following them home. The flashing blue and red police lights color the air all around them. The car has been searched already. There are detectives in their house searching for clues, and, of course, for signs that the parents are somehow culpable. The police want lists of everyone who has been in contact with James. They want more pictures, samples of his hair, imprints of his teeth, they want his baby footprint from the hospital, his perfect perfect perfect little footprint.

It's twelve miles from the auditorium to the Woodrow house. The drive takes twenty-two minutes. The speed limit ranges from twenty-five to forty-five miles per hour. There are seven stoplights and six stop signs.

The neighborhood has never seen this many police cars before, and the flashing lights look so odd against the tidily sleeping houses. Justin pulls into the white two-car garage next to Hannah's green sedan. He's about to turn off the ignition, when it occurs to him he could just keep it running. He could close the garage door and keep the car running, just like that, they could sit there and wait—him grabbing the steering wheel, her staring at nothing—they could just wait, like they are doing right now. They could do nothing and soon they would go to sleep, and they would never again wake up to this world that allows malevolent clowns and swarming policemen and disappearing sons. Justin closes his eyes and breathes the possibility in. It's Hannah that speaks.

"What are we going to tell Greta?"

Justin opens his eyes, and turns off the car.

"Justin?"

He slumps forward. He sighs. He looks at Hannah, all bent and defeated. His lips reemerge and seem to try out the words before he says them. He speaks like a man weeks without water. "We have nothing to tell."

Detective Blair, Detective Henry, and two officers are waiting in the driveway. Introductions are made, *Mr. and Mrs. Woodrow, this is Carlos Artola and Tom Johnson, they'll be assisting us*. But Hannah can barely hear; she is floating above them, somewhere in the night. This is where she belongs, up in the black sky—is this where James is?—she's watching these strange bodies move through space, one of them belongs to her. Hannah has never been outside her body before, she never knew this was medically possible—

The bodies below her are moving into a house, her house, it's supposed to be her house, but as Hannah floats back into her body, she cannot believe it's true. The kitchen, which they decorated so carefully, looks soulless, contrived—like a movie set. That island in the middle, those hanging pots, all the precious woodwork, look like someone's idea of a kitchen. It doesn't look like the place where real people who have real children live.

It then occurs to Hannah that she must be in a movie. That's it, of course, that's the only explanation. In real life, tragedies happen; she sees it all the time. But not like this. Tragedies always have a cause; this one is only effect. So this is not real. She could never see it before because she was always trapped inside her body, but now she knows: Hannah is an unwitting character in a movie entering the carefully constructed set of a kitchen, designed by an art director consciously trying to express something about this character.

Hannah looks around to learn about herself. She is a woman of means, look at those nice pots, those up-to-date appliances. She is a woman of order—look at how perfectly everything matches, down to the range, the faucet, the refrigerator. The maple floor is spotless, the cream-colored cabinets look new, the marble counter provides the perfect accent. Does anyone ever cook here? The audience already knows she is a doctor, from an earlier scene perhaps, where they are led to believe she is a creature more of efficiency than compassion. No, she certainly does not cook—the kitchen is designed for show, not use. All this sterile prettiness leads Hannah's audience to the unmistakable conclusion that Hannah is a woman of surfaces.

Through the movie, Hannah's husband is shown to be everything she is not. The gender roles are reversed—oh, the irony!—but the woman must deal with the guilt, mustn't she? The husband is handsome in a friendly sort of way—he looks like your favorite history teacher—the audience members would like to have him over for dinner, take him out for a drink, and the actor's stock rises.

In the movie, the couple's boy disappears into thin air. There is no explanation. No cause. What will happen to the woman then?

Hannah wonders about this movie. She wonders whether the details of her life have been meticulous build-up to this crisis, or whether James's disappearance is just the beginning. Is this climax or plot point? Where will it possibly go from here? And more importantly—either way—can this story possibly have a happy ending? Can this family be saved?

But Hannah will not fall victim to the machinations of plot. She may be someone else's character, but she has come to life. She knows now. She has free will, and she will not be a party to this. She will tear the sets down, and all those high-end, decoratively placed pots and pans will fall to the floor with a resounding BANG!

Hannah breathes in, then kicks the wall, BAM!

Justin flinches. "Hannah?"

The wall does not fall. The pots stay where they are. "Mrs. Woodrow?" The police have moved to the living room to congregate with more police. It is like cellular division. "Is everything all right?"

And then, just like that, everything is real again. Hannah's spirit sits squarely inside her body and she shudders—this is her house, her body. She is a mother and her child has disappeared.

Her husband is here, right here, he looks at her desperately, as if begging for her to make this all better. Where is he? What is he thinking? She wants to tell him, "Sweetheart, it's not what you think," but how can she? Is this better or worse? At least he is not hurt, James is not hurt, Hannah could not live if James were hurt, she would break apart and die on the spot, she would rip her heart out and bleed to death if James were hurt. He is not hurt. Thank God. But how can she tell Justin, he won't even believe her, he won't understand, he still thinks the police can help them.

In the living room, someone from the phone company seems to be drilling into their wall. Two policemen talk on cell phones while the two detectives rifle through paperwork. There are plastic bags filled with objects piled up on a table. They look closer and find bits and pieces of James's life. A hairbrush. A pillowcase. A block he has chewed on. It's like they want to collect DNA and build them a new boy.

"We didn't turn up anything out of the ordinary," says one of the policemen, hanging up his phone. "We need the numbers of James's doctors and dentists so we can get his records. We need some more recent photos. And if you want to get started on making those lists of people who come into contact with your son . . ."

Detective Blair clears his throat, and glances at the officer. "Yes, we will need those things," he says. "But it can wait a few minutes. Why don't you change your clothes, get some water, do what you need to do."

At that moment, Hannah's sister appears on the stairs. "You're home. I didn't know—" She rushes down the stairs and puts her hands on their arms. "Greta is upstairs. In bed. I can't get her to sleep. I've been sitting with her."

At the mention of Greta, both of the parents snap to attention. "Is she all right?" Justin asks.

"Well, she's, um . . . She's not very . . . I don't know. She's in shock, I guess . . ."

Hannah and Justin look at each other, connected again for a moment, and rush up the stairs to their daughter. One of the police officers starts to call after them, but Detective Blair shakes his head. "Give them time. We have work to do."

There is crime scene tape around

their son's room. James's bedroom is a crime scene. Justin wants to tear the tape down and shove it down the clown's throat, but there is no time now, there is Greta first. Alone in her bedroom—Catherine left her there alone; what if she's gone now too?

She's not though, she's right there on her bed. Justin does not ever want to let her out of his sight again. The clown could come for her, and then there would be nothing left.

Every light in Greta's room is on, including the two nightlights and the closet light. Greta sits in her canopied bed underneath her pink comforter, staring at the wall. She has seven stuffed animals perched around her, protective beasts solemn in their charge.

The parents go sit on the bed, one on each side. Hannah puts her hand on her child's forehead while Justin grabs the girl's hand. Greta's face is heavy, expressionless—Hannah would call it "flat affect" in a patient—she seems used, floppy, extinguished. The only life is in her green moon eyes, which she fixes on each parent in turn. Her lip quivers.

"Are you okay, baby?"

(Neither parent is sure which one of them says it.)

Greta does not respond. Hannah fills with a very real despair. How she would like to make Greta a promise right now. How Hannah would like to say, "It will be all right. Everything happens for a reason. We'll bring your brother back to you. You have nothing to fear." And, for a moment, Hannah tastes the lies on her lips and sees Greta change shape before her eyes. But you don't make promises you don't know you can keep; you don't lie to your kids. Hannah swallows the words back and tries to find new ones. "We're going to do everything we can to find your brother. You have our word on that."

Greta nods.

"You need to get some sleep, sweetheart. It's important. Will you promise us you will get some sleep?"

Greta nods again.

"Can we turn out your light?"

Greta shakes her head.

"Okay. We'll leave it on. Do you want us to sit here with you?"

Greta nods.

Hannah and Justin sit in Greta's pink and white room for almost an hour, as glassy-eyed and still as her animal retinue. Hannah keeps her hand on her daughter's arm and Justin continues to hold Greta's hand as they both listen to her breathe, steady and real—

They don't stir until Catherine pokes her head into the room. Hannah and Justin had forgotten that she existed.

"I just wanted to, um, see if everything was okay."

No one answers.

"Can I get you anything? Some water maybe? Juice, Greta?"

Still no one answers.

"Hannah, Justin. The police are asking for you."

Oh.

Justin whips his head toward his sister-in-law. "Will you watch her?"

"Of course," Catherine nods.

"Greta, honey," Justin says. "We have to go. But we'll come back, okay?"

"You should try to sleep, sweetie," says Hannah. "Do you think you can sleep?"

Terror flashes through Greta's eyes and without a word, Justin picks her up and carries her out the door, down the hallway, into their room, and places her in their queen-size bed. "You sleep with us tonight, sweetie," he murmurs. "Aunt Catherine will stay with you until we're done with the police." Catherine nods, and Greta cries, soundlessly, in her dad's arms. Hannah goes back into her daughter's room to get every single stuffed animal she can lay her hands on.

"Sit down, please." Four of the police are left in the living room, Detective Blair, Detective Henry, and the two other officers they met earlier. Hannah and Justin sit side by side on the couch, on command.

"We want to let you know where we are. We haven't been able to turn up anything at the crime scene, but we will keep looking. Detective Henry and I are going to go down now to interrogate the clown."

The parents nod.

"Now, there'll be a story in tomorrow's newspaper. And it will be all over the television tomorrow. The TV stations are always excellent in cases like this. Everyone in the metro area will see James's face and be on the lookout for him."

Justin shifts in his seat. And everybody in the metro area will shake their heads and say, "How sad. How sad," and then they will go back to their lives. This won't help. Don't they understand that this won't help? Justin's hand is clenched around the armrest of the couch, it just might rip through the fabric.

Detective Henry leans in. "I want to be sure you know how much effort is going into finding James. Missing children are our first priority. We have the entire metro area police force working on this. James's picture has been given to the National Center for Missing and Exploited Children, who will disseminate it. The FBI will assist with the investigation. We are going to do everything we can to bring him home to you."

These are the procedures. This is the well-oiled machine. Why don't they see what Justin sees? They saw the videotape. But they don't know, and he can't tell them because if they didn't see it, they are not going to believe him. These are cops; they solve crimes, they look for evidence, they live in the world of logic and tangibility, whatever do they know about disappearing boys?

"Now, you've met Officer Johnson," Detective Blair says, pointing to the stocky young man next to him. "He'll be staying on-site."

The officer puts his hand out. "You can call me Tom."

"On-site?" Hannah asks. Justin looks at her.

"Yes, we like to leave an officer on-site in these situations. In the house."

"Oh . . . We don't have an extra room, really," Hannah sounds half-awake. Justin's wife isn't there, her soul is gone, what's left is a shell—is she real, is she fading before his eyes?

"Don't worry about him. He's not a guest, he's working. We'll be in constant contact with him. And you can always call us, of course. Carlos, here, will give you all our numbers."

More words are said, papers exchange hands, reassurances are given, and then, Justin and Hannah find themselves moving upstairs again. Catherine is lying down next to Greta on their bed, and Greta is sleeping. When Catherine sees them, she gets up and tiptoes out to the hallway. Justin asks:

"How is she?"

"She just fell asleep."

"Catherine," he asks, "has Greta *said* anything to you tonight?"

"Said anything?"

"Talked."

Catherine shakes her head slowly. "No. No. Not a word."

Hannah shifts. Justin says, "Oh."

There's a pause.

"We should call a doctor for her," Justin says.

"I am a doctor," Hannah says.

"Well, I mean—"

"She's in shock," Hannah says. "We need to give her time."

Catherine says, "Do you want me to stay? Tonight? I could sleep in—sleep in Greta's bedroom and help you guys out."

Justin and Hannah look at each other. Justin opens his mouth, he's about to say, "Yes, that would be nice, thank you so much," but before he can form the words Hannah has already said, far too quickly, "No, thank you." Justin is surprised, Catherine is surprised, but Hannah does not need her younger sister, she doesn't need that policeman, she doesn't need anybody. She wants them all out of the house, all to leave her with her husband and her daughter and this hole where her son is supposed to be—the others will just distract her and she needs the whole house to accommodate her sorrow.

In bed, the two parents lie on either side of their daughter, staring at the ceiling. They will memorize this ceiling tonight, all its bumps and cracks and discolorations.

This was all a dream, right?

That explains the blurriness of the past few hours, the half-remembered details, the explosion of images, the misbehavior of time. This was all a dream. It has to have been, because one salient fact remains, haunting the parents as they lie awake staring at the ceiling. It is a dream and only in a dream could it be true that—

There are laws in the universe. Matter behaves a certain way. Little boys behave a certain way. They do not, they certainly do not—

Justin is holding on tight to Greta. Hannah can barely look at either of them for fear they will disappear too. Hannah curls up around the empty James-size spot in her stomach. She curls in tighter and tighter but the space won't fill. She closes her eyes and whispers, like a prayer:

"James, James, James—"

The Saturday That Would

Have Been

In another universe, there is a
Saturday morning like any other, in which the Woodrows wake up
to an ordinary day, in which whatever happened did not happen, in
which the fates were looking the other way, in which the clown never
picked James, in which James did not raise his hand at all, in which
James got a tummy ache and stayed home with one of his parents
(probably Justin, who does not like clowns), in which they refused the
tickets, in which Stewart never offered them the tickets, in which
Stewart Martin and Justin Woodrow did not stay friends, were never
friends, never even met, in which Stewart was never born because his
parents never met. In this universe, James Woodrow lies safe in his
bed, in between two stuffed bears, right where he is supposed to
be, and Hannah and Justin wake up to another perfectly quotidian
morning.

It's Saturday in the Woodrow household, and nothing is out of
the ordinary. Hannah gets up and puts on a bathrobe and slippers.
She'll have at least one hour, maybe more, to sit in the breakfast nook,
sipping coffee and reading the paper, before anyone else is up. It's
nearly silent in the house, but the outside is filled with the sounds of
the world waking up for the day. The sun is just rising now—in a
few weeks it will be dark when Hannah wakes up, and it will be the
time of year that she begins to contemplate moving the family to Cal-
ifornia. This urge usually lasts until the first time she sees James in
his snowsuit, or Justin and the kids building a snowman, then she's

happy for a few weeks, or until the next time she has to dig her car out of the clinic parking lot when it's twenty below.

Hannah watches two sparrows skip around below the bird feeder among the red, orange, yellow, and brown leaves. Suddenly, a squirrel comes running in and the sparrows take off. Justin always puts some birdseed on the ground away from the feeder so the squirrels don't try to climb into the feeder and scare off all the birds. It has not helped. The feeder itself is weight sensitive; if a squirrel tries to eat out of it, it will close up. The squirrels have been steadily working on counter-measures. Hannah doesn't see the problem, anyway, you can't just put out food and expect only the things you like to come.

She flips through the paper. There's a review in the Variety section of the show they saw last night with the headline, "Razzlers Circus Dazzles." A Stewart review of course, typically effusive and inane. She pours herself more coffee and sits back. She should have at least a half hour, maybe more, before—

A door slams in the distance and feet come tripping down the stairs. Hannah blinks and Greta is standing in front of her in her pink nightgown, bouncing up and down, wielding her beloved stuffed sea otter, named Otter. "Good morning, Mommy!"

"Greta! You're up early."

Greta's eyes go wide. "We have so much to *do*!"

"Honey, all the decorations are already up. We have plenty of time. They're not coming for four and a half hours."

"FOUR hours?" Greta gasps and runs up the stairs. Hannah listens to her room door slam, and sighs as the sound reverberates through the house. Sure enough, a moment later another door opens, and plod-ding husband-like feet make their way across the hallway upstairs. Hannah takes a slow sip of her coffee as the bathroom door closes, water runs for a minute, and then the door opens again. The same feet begin to thump their way down the stairs. A few moments later,

Justin appears in the kitchen doorway in his pajamas, asking sleepily, "At what age do they stop yelling?"

Hannah smiles. "Eighteen, I think."

Justin gets a cup of coffee and then comes over and rubs Hannah's shoulder with his left hand. He sighs. "I was hoping to get up with you this morning. We've got to get moving. We've got a party to throw."

"We've got four and a half hours," Hannah says calmly.

"Four?" Justin drops his hand from Hannah's shoulder, gulps down his coffee, wincing with every swallow, and disappears out the door and up the stairs. The bathroom door slams.

All is quiet for a few more moments, and Hannah turns to watch a squirrel dangle from the tree, flailing his paws toward the bird feeder. A blackbird lands on the feeder's shelf, but is too heavy, and the feeder closes. Legions of sparrows watch apprehensively from the trees. The blackbird squawks. Hannah smiles slightly and turns her head, and then starts. James has appeared across from her in the break-fast nook. He's watching the birds attentively.

Hannah leans forward and strokes James's head. "I didn't know you were here! Good morning, sunshine."

"Hi, Mom." He smiles.

"You're up early."

James shrugs. "Everyone's *crashing*."

Hannah nods. "I know. Boom!"

James giggles. "Boom! Boom!"

Hannah whispers conspiratorially, "You know, we've got Greta's party today."

James whispers back, "I know!"

"It's in four and a half hours." Hannah watches him. He shows no sign of panic. She leans closer. "There are going to be lots of girls in the house."

"They pinch me!"

Hannah grins. "It's because they think you're so adorable. Tell you what: you stick with me. I'll protect you."

"I'll protect you!" James says, beaming.

Hannah nods. "Thank you. I know you will. Would you like some cereal?"

"Ohh-kay," James nods. Hannah gets up, makes a bowl of cereal (he likes flakes the best), gets a glass of orange juice and a chewable vitamin, and puts it all in front of James. She gets her coffee and slides in next to him as he eats, one arm around her son, the other firmly attached to her coffee mug. Together, they sit and watch the squirrel try to outwit the feeder, silently cheering him all the way.

Two hours later, Justin and Hannah sit in the breakfast nook stuffing purple bags with candy, animal-shaped erasers, stickers, bookmarks, little barrettes, keychains, gel pens, various shiny objects, and all sorts of things having to do with glitter. James sits in the corner, drawing a birthday card for his sister.

Greta is up in her room getting ready; she doesn't have to help because it's her birthday (observed), and anyway, Greta didn't want to see what was going in the goodie bag, she trusted her father when he said it would be the best favor bag of any party in the whole second grade. What she doesn't know is Justin has gotten the best balloon animal maker/face painter in the state to come to Greta's party (She is legendary, and impossible to get—but Justin bribed the scheduler.) so each girl will go home with not only a primo goodie bag, but also a pretty painted face and one top-of-the-line balloon animal. Provided there's no popping. (This is why the face painter/balloon animal lady is coming at the end; if the balloons are to pop, they can pop in the car on the way home—Justin really wants to get through this party without anyone crying. The first parent to accomplish that during a school year is usually held as a kind of a god by all the other mothers of the class. Last year, it looked like Justin was going to win the title until during the last game Gretchen Larson pinned a tail on Lisa Ann Heller instead of the donkey.)

"Do you want to go over the list of games?" Justin asks.

Hannah smiles. "I think I've got it."

"It's very important to stay on a strict schedule. This is just two hours, and they get bored easily. I'm going to start them off with a couple warm-up games, to get them loose, and then we'll play animal charades."

"Okay." Hannah drops a few stickers into one of the bags.

"Hannah!" Justin's eyes pop. "Honey, you can't just do that haphazardly."

Hannah stares at him.

"Everyone has to get the exact same amount. You should have seen what happened with the goodie bag at Ashley Anderson's this summer."

Hannah rubs her neck. "Um, okay."

Justin grins. "I know, I know. It's just a lot of *pressure* . . ." He sighs. "You know, we should have conceived her a month earlier."

"Why?"

"Because summer birthday parties are so much easier. We could go to the park, play Red Rover—"

Hannah pauses. "Do they still do that?"

"Yes."

"Wow, I thought children's games would have evolved." She counts out the gel pens.

"Hey, is Catherine coming?"

"Oh." Hannah stops. "I didn't call her."

"Oh?"

"Work. You know. I just forgot. She wouldn't want to come anyway."

Justin nods noncommittally and begins labeling the bags. The markers squeak against the shiny purple paper. "Hannah?"

"Hmmm?"

"Do you think we should have had a theme?"

"A theme?"

"For the party. Ashley had a princess party. Jennifer Miller had this whole mermaid thing. Greta wanted a ballerina theme, but she also wanted something to do with puppies, and I couldn't reconcile the two. It just seemed wrong."

Hannah shakes her head. "That's it. From now on, whenever anyone asks me why it is I love you, I'll tell them it's because you needed dramatic coherence in your daughter's seventh birthday party."

"Do people ask you that a lot?"

Hannah smiles. "Now you made me lose count. Hey . . ." She looks around. "Where's James?"

Justin looks behind him. "He was just in the corner. Hmm. Must've wandered off . . ." Some paper and crayons lie scattered on the maple floor.

Hannah shakes her head. "He's so quiet. I never hear him."

"You think he'll be okay today?"

"Well," she shrugs. "We'll just try to include him in the games. Maybe he'll have fun."

"Okay, I've got to set up the animal bingo. Can you get the camcorder ready?"

"Sure." Hannah looks at her watch. One hour left. And in three, this will all be over.

Noon. The doorbell rings.

Greta barrels down the stairs, wearing a pink leotard and a tutu, with a strand of tinsel stars in her hair. Her face is coated in amorphous sparkle blobs.

"Look Mom!" she says. "I did it myself!"

"I can see that."

"Do you like my tutu?"

"Yes."

"You said I could wear whatever I wanted. Because it's my birthday party."

"I certainly did. You look lovely, dear. Now, shall we get the door?"

"Okay!" Greta runs to the front door, and opens it to find a woman holding the hands of two girls in party dresses. "Julie! Nikolaaaaaaa! Come in!"

And so it goes. The doorbell rings and rings, girls fill the house, presents pile, giggles abound. Greta skips and dances, beams and floats, the girls gather around her, reflect her energy, party dresses fluff, streamers go taut, and balloons stand at attention for the birthday girl. Chattering fills the house, punctuated by an occasional shriek. Hannah watches her daughter, sparkling even underneath the cutaneous glitter outbreak, and something fills and bursts inside of her. She is a wonder, my girl—

Soon, Justin herds the girls into a circle—it's remarkable how he can do this—they recognize him as a kindred spirit and follow him where he leads. "Come on, girls, stretch up to the sky! Down to the ground! Up again! Do what I do, come on Gretchen. Omigosh, your foot has the shakes! Now your whole leg! Now your hips!"

The girls shake in unison and wiggle and giggle some more. Only Justin, Hannah thinks, could use theater warm-ups for a birthday party. They pass the energy ball, do sound-and-motion—

But somebody is decidedly missing.

Hannah walks behind Justin and whispers, "I'll be right back."

James's door is slightly ajar, like he always leaves it. He used to have a nightmare about having a monster stuck in the room with him; he'd wake up crying, and would slip in bed between Hannah and Justin so quietly they didn't know until morning. Hannah told him that as long as he left the door open slightly, he would be safe—then the monster could get out because monsters prefer wide-open spaces. When Hannah was little, she had a nightmare that she woke up and a monster was peeking into her room, through the crack in the slightly open door. She insisted on having the door shut then—a habit she would not break until she met Justin, who also prefers wide-open spaces.

Hannah knocks on her son's door. "James?" She pushes it slowly open, expecting to find James sitting on his bed. But he's not there. She steps into the room and looks around. Nothing. He could be in their room or in the den. From downstairs comes the sound of ten girls and one grown man barking frenetically, and then oinking. Hannah turns around and is about to leave James's room when she notices the closet door is slightly ajar. She creeps over and peeks in, softly asking, "Honey?" And there he is, curled up in a ball with two teddy bears, fast asleep on the floor, surrounded by four pairs of little boy shoes.

Hannah smiles to herself and gets down on her knees and strokes James's thin orange hair. "James? Baby?"

His eyelids rustle, then pop open. He yawns, and the yawn encompasses his entire face—he is all boy mouth. He blinks, and smiles sleepily.

"Hi, baby. Taking a nap?"

He shrugs.

"We miss you at the party, you know." A burst of mooing comes from downstairs and James looks at his mother skeptically.

"Now," Hannah says softly. "I really think it's a lot of fun. You can stay up here if you want, but it's a pretty good party down there. Later there's going to be cake. And your sister really wants you there."

James's eyes grow wide and he nods, seriously, determinedly. He gets up, brushes himself off, and offers his hand to his mother. She squeezes it. "It'll be fun. I promise. They're playing lots of games. You want to know a secret?"

James's mouth opens and he nods again.

"We've got someone coming who makes *balloon animals*. I bet she'll make something special, just for you." Hannah leads her son down the stairs.

When they appear at the door of the playroom, the girls are strutting around like roosters. One yells, "JAMES!" and the rest stand up and run toward him. This is to be expected; Greta loves James, so everyone loves James. Most of these girls have little brothers themselves that they don't care a lick for, but James—oh, James! Greta's brother! They gather around him, pounce on him, from the mass comes squeals of, "He's so CUTE!"

One girl says they should play dress-up with James, and that's when Justin says, "Come on, it's time for bingo."

The doorbell rings just when it's supposed to, right after Greta has opened her mass of presents. The girls have just begun to mix their ice cream, frosting, and pop to make all kinds of potions—Rachel St. John begins to loudly demand food coloring. The sound of the doorbell makes all the girls straighten and, for a moment, be silent—they've attended enough parties to know that this sound mid-party portends great things. Greta lets out an inhuman squeal, "What is it! What is it?" Justin smiles at her and says, "You'll see." Hannah winks at James, who has frosting all over his face.

Justin leaves the playroom and goes to the front door, but when he opens it, he finds not the Midwest's best balloon animal lady, but a man in a top hat, cape, and funny pants. Justin stares. The man clears his throat.

"Uh, hi. I'm Fantastic Fred. The magician."

"Magician?"

"For the party?"

"We didn't order a magician. We ordered Lila."

"Says right here magician." He thrusts out an invoice.

"Well, that's wrong. Can you get Lila here, please?"

"Lila's booked for months, are you crazy?" He clears his throat. "Look, it's a good act."

Justin looks behind him. Hannah stands in the doorway of the playroom, shaking her head. Squeals of inquiry emerge from behind her, Justin motions for her to stall, and she nods and shuts the playroom door.

"Do you know you're leaving me without the key favor that would make the whole favor bag?" Justin puts his hand on his forehead. "Okay, look. I know. Come in, and do your act, and then, maybe you can teach them how the tricks work?"

"What?" Fred draws back.

"So they can, you know, have something to take home with them? It'll be *like* a favor ..."

Fred straightens. "I'm sorry. I can't do that. I cannot show anyone how the tricks work. Magician's code of honor."

"Okay, listen—"

Justin hadn't noticed James come up behind him until he feels the tugging on his pant leg. He looks down, and James is staring up at him, wide-eyed.

"What is it, buddy?"

James looks to the magician and looks back at his father urgently. Justin understands.

"You want to see magic tricks?"

James nods solemnly.

Justin relaxes and smiles at his son. "Well, you're in luck." He turns to Fred. "Come in."

And it's just fine. It's Greta's birthday, after all, and so the day is perfect, just perfect, and Greta, who has never shown the slightest interest in magic, jumps up when she sees Fantastic Fred. "Oooh! A *magician*?!"

And Justin and Hannah settle back, and the girls sit cross-legged in a line to watch. And Fred begins, his cape twirls, bright colored scarves fly through the air, and his hat produces an endless variety of treats. He takes one of Greta's ballet slippers and sticks it into his top hat and then, POOF!, it's gone, just like that! Greta shrieks and he smiles and says, "Don't worry, everything that disappears must appear again."

And he winks and Greta rubs her foot, and the magician produces a bouquet of flowers from thin air and hands it to Greta, who shrieks with delight. The magician leaves amid cries of, "How'd he DO that?"

And then it's over, the process reverses itself, the doorbell rings and rings, girls empty from the living room, the pile of favor bags diminishes, streamers and balloons sag. Greta loses a bit of bounce with each exit, until she is left grounded to the floor. She stands in the front hallway, her family around her, and then, just like that, James makes an alarmed gurgle. The whole family turns to look at him; he is staring at his hand, in which sits Greta's missing shoe.

Two hours later, all evidence of a party has disappeared. Greta is fast asleep in her room, James in his. This seems like an excellent idea to the parents. Hannah throws herself on the bed and stares at the ceiling. "I'm never moving again."

"Sounds good," Justin says, changing into a T-shirt.

"I'm serious. I'm not moving until Monday morning. We don't have anything else this weekend, do we?"

Justin stops. "Hannah. There's the party at the Millers' tonight."

"There is?"

"They called us last week. You said it was okay."

She looks at him. "Do we have to go?"

"I've already got Jenny lined up."

"Jenny? I don't think James likes Jenny."

"Why not?"

91

Hannah shrugs. "It's just an impression I get."

"Has he said something? Did something happen?"

"No . . . no . . ."

Justin sits down and puts his arm around her. "Don't you want to go out?"

Hannah sits up. "Honey, I'm so tired. We had ten seven-year-old girls in the house this afternoon, which is nine more than any person should have to deal with at one time. I just want to rest. We can put the kids to bed, watch a movie—"

"Han . . ." Justin sits down next to her and grabs her hand. "I hate canceling on people. We do it too much."

"I know too many couples without children, that's the problem," Hannah grumbles. "They think getting together with people is fun."

"No, these are the people *with* kids. They're the ones who get together purely to get away from the children." Justin smiles. "We won't stay long, I promise."

Hannah wants to say no, to explain she can't possibly, to request some quiet time with her husband, but she cannot press this one anymore. This is the way they disagree, quietly, questioningly, until a compromise is reached, someone gives way. Hannah sighs heavily, comically. "What time?"

"Seven o'clock. Plenty of time for a nap." He touches her face, a thank you, an apology, an acknowledgment of what has passed. "Come on, I'll tuck you in."

The Millers live two blocks away. The party is for the neighborhood, and it is filled with like people, other families who wanted to live in the city, close to downtown, and still have lawns and good public schools and these well-sized houses. They know one another as parents—the kids play together, the parents carpool, cheer together at T-ball, soccer, gymnastics. The Posts are there, the Wilsons, the Larsons. There's a neighborhood party once every two months or so. Hannah knows that soon they will have to throw a party themselves or people will stop inviting them. She wouldn't mind, for herself, but Justin likes this. She understands; if she were home with the kids all day she'd want to be around grown-ups too.

Justin is the life of the party. This is always the case. (Hannah stays at his side, so she doesn't have to expend the energy to be a separate, sentient being; she holds on to his arm, as if gathering energy from him.) He is the one in the center of the crowds of people. He remembers everything about everyone; he remembers that Peter Tsao just changed jobs and Rod Wilson broke his leg playing basketball last month and that the Jacksons' kids have mono. He asks questions; he listens to the answers; he makes little jokes that are always appropriate. He glows, he warms Hannah's hand, and she squeezes his arm a little tighter. Justin is remarkable. She wonders, sometimes, what they say about her when she is not there. *Justin Woodrow is so generous, how did he end up with such a cold fish? And she works and makes him take care of the kids, can you believe it?*

Let them talk. Hannah doesn't need them at all; all she needs is her family and her husband, warming her hand.

Gretchen Larson's parents are telling Justin how much fun Gretchen had at Greta's party this afternoon and Justin grins. Hannah smiles and excuses herself for the bathroom, and on the way she's cornered by another of Greta's classmates' moms who wants Hannah to come talk on career day.

When she reemerges, Justin is engaged in conversation with Angela Post, who is listening to him with her entire upper body. Angie, who has children age five, seven, and nine, is the kind of mother that makes Hannah feel she is going to get her license revoked. She runs bake sales and silent auctions, volunteers for field trips, organizes car pools and phone trees, plays the piano for school concerts, makes costumes for the plays, acts as den mother, room mother, *über* mother, and never loses the shine in her hair. Angie always has lots of advice for Hannah. Angie makes Hannah feel like violating her Hippocratic oath.

Hannah comes up and takes Justin's arm again, and Angie turns to her and smiles.

"So," she says. "I was surprised that James isn't in Janie's class this year, I was sure he would be. Are you sending him to private kindergarten?"

Hello, Angie, Hannah wants to say. How are you? Oh, I'm good, thank you so much for asking. And thank you for saving this question for me, because I know you would never ask Justin, because you suspect the answer.

"No," Hannah says, straightening. Hannah has excellent posture. "He's still at Acorn—"

"Oh!" she says.

There's a bit of a silence. Hannah gets the same feeling she used to get when her parents would fight and she'd quietly slink away to hide in her room.

Justin winks at Angie. "I wasn't ready to lose my boy to regular kindergarten yet," he says. "I'd miss him too much at home."

Angie breaks out into a smile. "Of course you would," she says lovingly, then turns her attention back to Hannah. "So how is James doing?"

(On the way home from the party, Hannah will say, "I can't believe Angie did that. She knew James was doing another year of preschool, she just wanted to find a way to talk about him."

And Justin will say, "She means well."

And Hannah will sigh dramatically and Justin will laugh, because he always says people mean well, and Hannah always sighs dramatically.)

"James is terrific," Hannah says. "How's Janie?"

They talk a little more, Angie fills them with news of her youngest daughter's latest accomplishments—she can't help it, Justin will say later—and then, a burst of energy runs along the current that connects the parents. Justin casts a glance at Hannah and Hannah nods slightly. Justin squeezes her hand, and Hannah squeezes back. It's time to go home.

Nighttime.

The children are already in bed when Justin and Hannah get home. Justin drives Jenny home ("How was James tonight?") while Hannah takes a hot bath. Then, Hannah crawls into bed while Justin comes home and lingers in the kitchen, watching TV and foraging for snacks. Hannah turns off her bedside lamp and begins to drift off to sleep. Soon, Justin comes in and crawls into bed, kissing his wife on the cheek, and Hannah wakens just enough to appreciate it. Justin turns on a lamp and reads, while Hannah closes her eyes and listens to her husband breathe. She falls asleep, slowly, gently—then Justin too . . .

And this is the alternate universe, the one where James did not disappear, where Hannah and Justin had stopped it, hadn't done whatever they did wrong to make this happen, to cause the loss of their son—

What Actually Happens

Officer Tom Johnson has fallen

asleep on the Woodrow couch. It was not supposed to happen like this. He was going to stay awake all night, so when Hannah or Justin Woodrow emerged on the day after their son disappeared, they would find a competent-looking police officer, of moderate height but reassuringly bulky frame, in their house at the ready for whatever their needs might be. *Don't worry, we're on the case, we're in charge, see, we're so on top of things we even have someone in the house, there, at the ready.*

He's got his badge. He's got a belt with a cell phone, a pager, a walkie-talkie, a flashlight, and of course, a gun.

You are generally not supposed to fall asleep wearing your gun.

Nonetheless, on the day after James Woodrow disappeared, Tom Johnson wakes up to find himself prone on the Woodrow couch. His eyes are still blurry from sleep, but he can just make out the small girl in pink flannel standing next to the couch, holding some kind of elongated stuffed bear, staring at him accusatorily.

"Who are you?" she says.

"Gretche—Greta!" He sits up. "I'm Officer Johnson." She is still staring. He tries a smile. "You can call me Tom."

She tilts her head. "What are you doing here?" Her two front teeth protrude from her mouth like sentient stalactites.

"Um," Tom clears his throat. He has a pitch that goes something like this: *I'm a police presence in the house. We like to have an officer on-*

site. I observe. I prepare the family for stresses that will be involved. I see who comes to the house. I can help with the media, with con artists, crank calls, psychics. I can protect the family and be a liaison to the department.

The pitch is not, however, designed for six-year-old girls.

"I'm here to help the family and protect them," he says, "—you." He attempts to look reassuring. He notices the animal she is clutching is not a bear; it has whiskers and is holding a clam, and Tom can almost think of the right word.

She cocks her head, considering. "Okay." She scratches her chin and surveys the couch. "Do you want a blanket?"

"No. No, thank you." He sits up straighter. "Greta, are your parents awake?"

"No, they're sleeping," she says, looking around. "Is James back yet?"

"Oh." Tom clears his throat. "No. No. I'm afraid not."

"Oh."

"But we're doing everything we can." He tries to smile encouragingly—his cheeks feel like plastic. He has no idea what to say to Greta Woodrow; he hasn't talked to a little girl in ages, possibly since he was little himself.

"It was sad last night. It's weird." She looks around the room again, and says matter-of-factly, "He should come back now."

Tom feels wiggly. Please don't tell anyone, but he actually has no idea what he's doing in the house. He's never done home duty before. Actually, he's never spent any time with a family, beyond interviews. (He excels at interviews, he can read everything he needs to know in the syntax of face, gesture, posture.) Detective Blair said this would be good for him, that this is an important part of his training. (Tom really wants to be a detective, he wants to be the guy who solves the case, who puts the bad guys away.) But Tom's useless here—he's always been the guy who's on the street looking for things, not sitting around waiting for the things to come to him. They should have sent

Carlos; Carlos's wife is pregnant, so he must know how to deal with kids. Carlos is good at talking to people, whereas Tom is better with, well, criminals. He's on the verge of explaining this to Greta, that really, he shouldn't be there, there should be his partner Carlos, or someone else nice, someone with some kind of training in home duty and in six-year-old girls. Really, she shouldn't expect anything from him, he has no idea what to say to her; he'd rather be out working for Blair trying to catch the guy who did this. He'd like to do the interrogation of the clown himself, really he would, he could do it, too. Detective Blair lets him get in on it sometimes, he makes suspects nervous, they can tell he spends time on his strength, little guys with muscles set them on edge; they think Tom's got something to prove. There is no doubt in Tom's mind that Michael Simmons is guilty, somehow, that he is responsible for whatever has happened to James, and Tom would like to be the one to get him to admit it. Tom could do it. The clown would break, would be sent to jail where he belongs, and Tom would have done his job and done it well, and then he would go on to another case. But he cannot quite explain this to Greta Woodrow and her stuffed . . . sea weasel.

Was Tom ever this age? He regards his childhood mistily; he can't see himself as a kid, he envisions a version of himself as he is today, just . . . shrunken.

"We're doing everything we can," he repeats lamely.

Greta looks at him in a way that might be described as skeptical but is perhaps just confused, and then asks, "Like what?"

"Well—"

The sound of hurrying footsteps on the stairway above them saves Tom. Hannah Woodrow's feet appear, then the whole Hannah—she runs down the stairs calling hurriedly, "Greta?"

"I'm here, Momma," Greta says.

"Greta, honey, where did you go? What—?" Hannah turns toward her daughter's voice. "Oh. Hi . . . Tim."

Tom clears his throat and stands. "Officer Tom Johnson, ma'am, at your service."

The mother looks ghostly in her white nightgown and robe. Her face is various shades of blue and white, with some red in the eyes. She flies toward her daughter, pulls her in to her chest, whispers fervently in her ear. The scene is so intimate, private, Tom feels himself blush a little, and he looks at the ground. He coughs—

"I'm sorry, ma'am," he says suddenly, answering the question the mother has not asked. "I don't have any new information for you as of yet. I assure you, they'll call me as soon as there are any updates."

She looks at him and blinks a few times. "No. No, of course you don't," she says softly, as if to herself. There's a moment, a pause in which Tom thinks again about how good he is on the street. Hannah strokes her daughter's hair, then clears her throat, and asks, "Listen, um, is it really necessary for you to be here?"

This is not what Tom was expecting to hear. "Dr. Woodrow?"

"I don't mean to be rude," Hannah says. Her voice sounds like it belongs to another body, far away—the words don't have any connection to this ghost woman clutching the girl who clutches the stuffed animal.

"Well, we like to have an officer on-site." He coughs. "I'm a police presence in the house. I observe. I see who comes to the house, who calls. I prepare you for stresses that will be involved. I'm here to help you and protect you . . ."

Hannah sighs heavily, "And you're here to watch us. Justin and me." Tom opens his mouth. "It's all right," she says. "I understand . . . But you need to understand that neither of us would ever, ever do anything to hurt James. You have to believe that." She is looking him in the eye now.

"I—I really am here to help."

"I know. I know." Hannah sits down, settling Greta on her lap. Greta just watches, eyes wide, mouth slightly open. "But . . ." she looks at him matter-of-factly, clinically, her voice becomes clearer, "put yourself in my shoes. If something happened to a member of your family, if he had . . . disappeared . . . would you want a policeman hanging around your house?"

"Well . . ." Tom finds himself twitching a little, "*yes* . . . I would . . ." He cannot quite believe the question. "Mrs.—Dr. Woodrow. I'm here to help find James. That's my job. We really are good at this. There," he points to the new phone on the table next to the couch, "there's a phone where Detective Blair can reach me at all times. There's a fax machine, there. Here," he points at the sheaf of paper by his briefcase. "Here are transcripts of interviews, lists of evidence. I'll get more all the time. I'm here to work." He draws himself straighter. "Listen, um, I'm going to go home and shower and change, all right? I have my cell phone here, you can call me, and I'm going to transfer the calls from the extra line to it, all right? And I promise I'll call you if there's any news. I'll be back as soon as I can." He smiles competently, then moves toward the front door, leaving Hannah to study the new telephone perched next to the couch.

"Can I ask you a question?" she says suddenly. She doesn't really look at him, she's talking so dully, and Tom can barely hear her. He steps closer.

"Sure."

"Why did you guys install another phone line if you have a cell phone?"

Tom shifts. "It's procedure, Dr. Woodrow."

She's not challenging him consciously. Tom can tell. She doesn't have that look—in fact, she doesn't have any look; she is completely uninhabited. But Tom feels challenged *by* her, by her whole presence, by her embodied sadness. The house is sad, the air is sad, and Tom does not belong here.

Tom is a good cop. He doesn't claim this with pride, but rather he looks at it as part of the job description; he is an officer of the law, therefore he must be a good one. And he is learning how to be a better one every day. Complacency is the worst enemy of the police officer. People are your teachers, people are full of lessons. The minute you think you understand them, you are sunk. This is what he must remember. Hannah Woodrow has just lost her son. She is lashing out at him, perhaps because she needs to control something in an out-of-control universe. Perhaps there's another reason; he should just watch her. He can do that. That's all right. That's his job. It's okay.

"So," he says. "I'll be back in an hour. Maybe you two should try to get some more sleep. It's not even light yet."

She looks up at him strangely, as if he's suddenly started speaking Greek, and Tom shifts again. He realizes he could be there all day, and she would just keep staring at him like this. So he nods his farewell, and goes out the front door, but not before noticing Hannah is watching him every step of the way.

A few minutes later, Hannah still sits studying the door that Tom disappeared behind—maybe he's still behind it, listening to Hannah, watching her for clues—

He is a poor exchange for James.

Maybe he's gone for good. She hopes so. This policeman just appeared in her house, poof, to spy on her, to interrupt her thoughts, he is taking up the oxygen she desperately needs. She wants to be alone, didn't we establish this last night with Catherine? Wasn't anyone paying attention?

Hannah does not mean to be like this. But she woke up and remembered all over again that her son is gone, disappeared, without reason or rule. And then she found the empty space just where her daughter had been. And then she found her daughter talking to a policeman, in their own house, eye level with that gun in his belt. Hannah appreciates the need for procedure, and she can see, really she can, that if this were some kind of conventional case, if this were a kidnapping, it would be good to have a police presence in the house.

And she knows there are some sick parents in the world who might arrange the taking of their own children, and the police cannot assume the Woodrows are not like this just because they are loyal NPR subscribers. She can understand this, really she can, but the fact is that neither Hannah nor Justin did take James and hide him away somewhere. The police can't help. James disappeared, just disappeared, and Hannah would really, really like not to be watched right now, not to be suspected, because she has too much to deal with. What she would like, what she would really like, is her house to herself, her air to herself, herself to herself, she would like to be safe within her four walls, within her head and her body, so she can deal with this, think about it, try to figure out how to tell Justin, try to figure out how on earth to get James back—

Hannah sits on the couch holding on to her daughter. The thought has occurred to Hannah that if she were to let Greta go, Greta could disappear as well. The rules have changed, the sky has opened, the fabric that holds the world together has ripped, and the people that Hannah loves are falling through. This is not Hannah's realm. She is an expert at the organic, the way blood courses through the body, the way antibodies fight infection, the way cancer mutates a cell. She has no experience at something like this, she is absolutely helpless. The world is so big, everything seems to expand around her—walls fall, furniture disappears, Hannah is in a place of endless sky, clutching her daughter as close as she can. What is she supposed to do but hold on to what she's got left?

Greta is settling into Hannah's chest, blinking sleepily. Hannah strokes her head. Greta yawns and the yawn takes up her whole face, she is all child mouth and stringy orange hair. Hannah wants to attach her daughter to her chest, if she just holds her close enough she'll never go away . . .

Hannah sits like this for a half an hour, not even noticing the passing of time, until the phone rings, slapping her back into consciousness, out of the world made up entirely of the sound of Greta's breath. It rings again, and Hannah knows it will be her younger sister calling, who has been waiting all night to call again. But of course there's nothing to say, nothing but *I'm so sorry*, and that says nothing; it just affirms the emptiness, the helplessness of it all, and what good does it do anyone to be reminded of that? When their parents were dying (within six months of each other; the only thing they ever did in accord in their lives), Catherine called all the time, and Hannah didn't want to even answer the phone, she didn't have any words to make her sister feel better—all she wanted to do was hide in her room away from all the *I'm sorrys*, where she could cry in peace.

Nonetheless, Hannah has to pick up the phone, for the sake of her sister, who must say she's sorry.

"Hannah?"

"Catherine, hi . . ."

"Did I wake you?"

"No."

"I didn't think so . . ." There's a bit of a silence in which Catherine is probably trying to restrain herself from asking if there's been any word. Of course she knows it's a stupid question, she knows by her sister's voice that there is no news, all she will be doing is adding to the pile of stupid people in the world who call to ask grieving mothers if there is any word. Catherine wants to ask, Hannah can feel it, she is fighting the urge, but Catherine will win this battle, she will hear the deflation in Hannah's voice, she will understand that if there were anything to tell, Hannah would tell it. And of course, there is nothing, nothing, nothing.

Catherine clears her throat. "Is there any news?"

Ah. Well. "No."

"It's early yet." Hannah can practically hear Catherine shifting in her seat. Perhaps she would be saying the same things, perhaps she would be feeling just as stupid as her sister is feeling right now. Perhaps she would then clear her throat and ask if she could do anything, if she could bring something over, just come over to be in the house. Because that's what people do, when there's nothing they can do.

"Do you want me to come over?" Catherine asks. "Do you need anything?"

It's ridiculous. Hannah vows never to go over to anyone's house again. As if it helps. As if anyone would want her there. People want their houses to themselves, they want to be alone. Why does everyone want to come over? Why do people keep thinking that the more people that pile into the Woodrow house, the better off everyone is? There will be neighbor, casual acquaintance, fireman and plumber, window washer, carpet cleaner, interior designer, personal trainer, feng shui expert, all trying to get into the house. World records will be set, no one will believe the number of people that can fit inside the house, it will be like a clown car—it must be the last person, no, look, there's another! The carpets will be clean, the water will run, the windows will sparkle, and James will still not be back.

"Oh, no. It's really fine."

"You know, I can help. I can field phone calls."

"No. We've got the police to do that. There's an officer in our house."

"Really?"

"Yeah." Hannah says this in a voice that cuts off all future questions. She feels a little bad about it, but there are some times in life when you have every right to be a bitch.

"Hannah, you know, it's okay to . . ." Catherine stops, and sighs. "Please call me if you need anything . . ."

"I will." And Hannah hangs up.

She'll apologize to her sister, later say she was out of her mind, which she is, she really is, she'll explain this all when James—

When James comes back?

And how on earth, Hannah Woodrow, is that going to happen?

She hears the front door open, and for a moment, she thinks—but no, no, it's that policeman. Oh yes, him, he was going to come back. Has it been an hour already? Hannah blinks at him. He's short, but very stocky looking, like a good paperweight—what's a paperweight doing in her house? Did she mention he is a poor substitute for James? How did he get in? He must have a key. This shouldn't be possible, no one gave him a key, but maybe cops just have keys to people's houses so they can come in when the baby-sitter figures out the murderer is calling from *inside the house*. Cops should have keys, that's nice, it makes sense, they should have a giant key ring that lets them into every house in the city so they can get in, in case of emergency.

Of course, that wouldn't be so great, constitutionally—Hannah snorts out a little laugh. Officer Johnson looks at her, startled—

You see now? This is precisely why she doesn't want other people in the house, so she can make insane noises without anyone actually thinking she is insane.

"How are you doing, Dr. Woodrow?" Tom asks softly. He is being quiet, because of the sleeping Greta on her lap. He has no idea that it would take raining toads to wake her.

Hannah looks at her daughter, sleeping soundly, she is even drooling a little bit, and Hannah thinks what a very good idea this is, a very good idea. No one is asking Greta how she is doing, because she's asleep. "Um, I'm going to go take a nap, okay?"

"All right. Sure. Um. Look, did you see the article in the newspaper this morning?"

The article? "Oh. No."

"Do you want to?" He seems to be holding the paper in his hand, and if Hannah looked carefully, she could make out a studio portrait of her son smiling at her from the front page.

"No."

"Um, okay. Well, I'm here now. You're going to get a lot of phone calls today, people will see the article. But I'm going to answer the phone for you, okay? I'll take messages. And I'll come get you if there's any news. You can unplug your phone if you want to sleep or whatever, and I promise I'll get you the moment I hear anything." He smiles professionally.

"Thanks." Hannah hears how clipped she sounds, maybe if she is rude enough he will leave—

Tom nods to Greta. "She sleeps hard."

"Yes."

"It's impressive."

Hannah's mouth twitches. Is this how suspects act? Are they rude to the police? She doesn't want to act like a suspect; she doesn't want to be concerned about how she is acting at all—Hannah would just like to *be*, can't they just let her be?

Hannah wakes Greta up gently. She hates to disturb her, but she really doesn't want Greta to sleep on the couch with this guy watching her, and there's the special redundant police phone right there, and that gun, and anyway she has to keep her daughter close to her so Greta doesn't fall through the cracks like her son did.

"Come on, sweetie," she whispers. "Let's go upstairs and nap, okay?"

Greta nods, eyes still closed, and holds one hand out for her mother, the other firmly clasping Otter. She won't really wake up, she never does. Later, she won't even remember being moved. This is the wonder of Greta, one of the many wonders of Greta, the wonder that is Greta—

What if she is taken away too?

Hannah gets up and helps her daughter move one foot in front of the other. Stairs are no problem, Greta has mastered the art of sleepy stair walking. Hannah nudges her daughter, one step at a time, forgetting entirely about the police officer who is standing there, watching them go.

James has disappeared. This sort of thing happens in books all the time. Children disappear into thin air and end up in some other universe, some other dimension. There are tesseracts, tornadoes, and tears in time; there are looking glasses, magic wardrobes, enchanted castles, and rabbit holes. There all kinds of places for a young boy to go to—there is Camelot, there is Narnia, there is Never-Never Land, there is Oz, there is Wonderland. There are lions, Cowardly and Christlike, there are Wonderful Wizards, there are sorcerers, fairies, and knights, Tin Men and White Rabbits. But there are also witches, White and Wicked, Queens of Hearts, and Captains with a Hook. Be careful, James. Come back through the looking glass. Click your heels, James, come on. There's no place like home. There's no place like home. There's no place like home—

Why is it that nobody ever talks about the parents in these stories?

When he was a boy, Tom wanted

to be a superhero. There were too many shadows in the world, and Tom knew it was his destiny to fight them. He didn't think this would be a problem; over the course of his childhood, his mother frequently told him he could be whatever he wanted, ergo Tommy Johnson could be a superhero, just as soon as he could get his hands on some super-powers.

It proved to be more difficult than you would think. Try as he might, Tommy couldn't get a radioactive spider bite. There weren't any accident-prone chemical plants about, or hazardous waste dumps, and he wasn't allowed in the cabinets where the cleaning supplies were kept. No kindly strangers from mysterious foreign lands took an interest in him, no magic lanterns beckoned to him, no secret tombs unearthed themselves. It was made clear to him that no, he was not from Krypton. His mother was not an Amazonian, either, she insisted rather forcefully; she was just from St. Paul. He was beginning to lose hope. Enchantment was in short supply on Franklin Avenue during the Reagan years.

Well. Sometimes superheroes are born, sometimes they are made, sometimes they make themselves. Sometimes all it takes is will. Young Tommy had will. He had a desire to see truth told and evil eviscerated and justice justified. And therefore—

He began to prepare. He worked on refining his everyday alter ego so as not to create suspicion. He donned a pair of glasses he bought at the drugstore. He pretended to be frail and noncompetitive during Capture the Flag and began dropping the ball in Little League. He stopped letting Jenny Liao chase him on the playground, because a superhero needs to avoid entanglements of the heart; it would put Jenny in danger, and anyway love messes up your judgment— Tommy'd seen it happen over and over again.

One Saturday evening in October, he donned the red cape from last year's Halloween costume and a red mask he made with felt and a rubber band and a black T-shirt onto which he put a masking tape "T," and told his mother on the way out the back door, "I'm going to go out and fight crime."

"Oh, okay," she said. And then she looked up from her newspaper. "Wait! Where are you going?"

"Well, Mom, I just don't know. I'm going to patrol the city."

"You are?"

"Yes. I'm the TomCat." He put his hands on his hips and thrust out his chest. "I have to go on the prowl." And he began to strut toward the back door.

His mom stood up and stepped toward him. "Tommykins! Wait!"

"What?"

"You can't."

He sighed. "Mom. If I'm going to be a superhero, I need to go where evil goes."

"It's getting dark."

He looked at her. "Mom, that's when all the evil happens."

"Yes, but . . ." she stared at him. "You know, you really can't be a superhero. You don't have any real superpowers."

"That's okay," Tommy said. "You don't need superpowers. Batman didn't have any real powers. He was just a man."

"What . . ." She blinked. "Yes, he did. He was bitten by a bat."

"No, Mom. That's Spiderman. Peter Parker got a radioactive spider bite, he got the strength of ten men, and spider-sense. But Bruce

Wayne was an ordinary man, he believed that criminals were cowardly and superstitious, so he dressed up like a creature of the night to put fear in their hearts."

"Oh." She pursed her lips. She rubbed her forehead. She studied her son, who was watching her very impatiently. She sighed. "All right," she said finally. "You can fight crime in the backyard."

That's good enough for a start! So Tom ran out of the back door, cape flying behind him. He deposited himself in the center of the backyard, arms on hips, chest puffed. He knows what evil lurks in the hearts of men. He will be ready for it.

Adult Tom remembers none of

this, he doesn't remember the desire itself, or even the belief that there is any such thing as a superhero—he doesn't know he ever lived in that kind of world. This is probably a good thing, because now, in the Woodrow house, watching Hannah and Greta disappear up the stairs, he feels distinctly unlike a hero. "I hope you sleep well," he says lamely. He coughs a little. Tom is not used to feeling like a moron.

He's very glad they're gone. They make him nervous, they're watching him, like he did something wrong. He's just trying to help. Of course, part of home duty is to look for suspicious behavior on the family's part, but, really, no one is going around thinking that Justin or Hannah Woodrow had anything to do with what happened to James. It was obviously the clown, he had some kind of accomplice and he took James.

But why?

This is what's getting to Tom: he can't figure it out. The clown doesn't have any kind of record, usually when these guys are perverts you find a case history, something about hanging out by school yards, or at least the M.O. matches something you've seen before, which this most certainly does not. And there's no way he can get this figured out sitting here shuffling through reports and saying asinine things to Hannah Woodrow and cowering in the face of interrogation by that girl of hers.

He is a good cop—has he said that before? He can get into people's heads, figure things out, see things other people can't. There are
no heroes, there is just crime and the people who try to understand it.

He misses Carlos. He'd never admit this in a million years of
course. It's just for every case for the last four years he's had someone
to bounce things off of, and now there's nothing. Carlos will spend
the day with some new partner doing Blair's bidding, delving into the
clown's life, doing actual useful work, helping to solve the case.

Does it make a difference for Carlos now that Nina's pregnant?
Once, over a beer, Carlos admitted he was terrified over how this
would change him. Cops shouldn't have kids, he said, it messes up
your judgment. How can you ever stay emotionally distant from a case
when you have a baby at home? You get screwed up, you get angry,
you want to solve a case too quickly, you make mistakes. Carlos and
Tom always used to talk about how great they were together, free
from obligation, from attachment. Judicious. Careful. Then Carlos met
Nina (who pretty much made Tom's jaw drop, too). Nina almost
didn't want to marry Carlos because he's a cop. Now, she keeps trying
to talk him into quitting. Tom understands, it's not fair to anyone to
ask them to love you when any day could be the day when you just
don't come home.

They're going to name the baby Thomas, they've said. (With
Tom's luck, it will probably be a girl.) Nina's got four more months
to go and Tom can't believe how she's changed. He went over last
week for dinner for the first time in weeks and afterward told Carlos,
hesitantly, "She's so . . . different."

"I know, I know." Carlos nodded, wide-eyed. "Her breasts are
enormous now."

(Tom hadn't wanted to say it.)

Anyway, if Carlos were here, they could go over the notes together,
bounce things off each other, they could figure this out and get the

boy and bring him back to Detective Blair their own selves before you could say "commendation."

Tom sighs and looks around at the empty living room. The place is so nice. Tom feels like he should have put down plastic before he napped on the couch—this living room is not designed for actual living. Everything is shiny and white—how do they do this with kids? Tom grew up in a house with three rooms, and you could nap all you wanted on the rough mustard couch or the tan worn-out Barcalounger.

"This is bullshit," Tom says to the couch. He picks up his phone and dials.

"Artola." His partner's voice crackles on the other end. He still sounds like he needs some coffee.

"Carlos!"

A low groan. "Tommy, man, it's early."

"Don't you have a case to solve?"

"I'm going in right now. Blair just called."

"You got a new partner yet? Are they putting you with a chimp?"

(This is their running joke. They go to see every cop movie there is, from PG to NC-17. They joke that one day they're going to get separated and be partnered with a woman, a foreigner, an old guy, a kid, a dog, a monkey, an alien. Or they are the oddball couple themselves; they argue who is the hero and who is the partner, the supporting player, the one who will die one day before retirement and break the hero's heart.)

"No, I'm getting Nicosia," Carlos says. "I feel like I'm babysitting."

"Well, you're such a fucking geezer now," Tom says. (Tom is still twenty-nine and does not let his thirty-year-old partner forget it. Nicosia is only two years younger than Tom, but the job ages you quickly; two years is a long time.)

"Are you at the house?" Carlos asks. "How you doing over there?"

"Bad," Tom says. "I don't know what the fuck I'm doing. I can't talk to these people. The mom looks like she's going to shatter any minute, seriously. And she keeps trying to get me to leave. I feel like I'm fucking trespassing."

"You don't think—"

"Naah. They didn't do it. She's just—I don't know . . ." Tom rubs his forehead. "Carlos?"

"Yeah?"

"Have you ever done a missing kid before?"

There's a pause. "Once."

"Yeah?"

"Yeah . . ." Carlos trails off. There's a pause. "Hey, this is crap. You should be out with me. I don't know why they didn't put Nic on-site. She's got the psych background. We can nail the guy."

Tom nods. "Yeah. Okay. Okay. I'm gonna call Blair."

"Okay. Good luck. Call me."

Tom hangs up. He feels energized—Carlos is right, Blair just doesn't understand. If he just explains things—

Detective Blair takes up the fourth (desk) and fifth (cell) entry in Tom's cell's phonebook. Carlos is the second. Most of the rest of the entries are devoted to food delivery. His mother is still "One," he's never been able to change it—anyway, it's nice to see her still there, like he could call her, just like that.

The detective picks up before the phone can finish its first ring. He is in, it's eight o' clock on a Saturday morning, but of course he's in—he has a case to solve.

"It's Tommy."

"Tommy!" He can hear the detective leaning back in that chair of his, the way he always does. The chair costs more than Tom's whole wardrobe; the detective's wife got it for him, and no one else is allowed to sit in it. "How're you doing over there?"

"Well, that's why I called . . ."

The detective doesn't seem to hear. "I think we're going to have to let Simmons go," he says.

"The clown?" Tom says. "You're kidding."

Blair sighs heavily. "We're still holding him. But time's running out."

"Fuck. Nothing to keep him?" You'd think that disappearing a boy in front of five hundred audience members would be enough to arrest a guy, but—

"Nada. His record's clean. He performs around the Midwest as both a clown and a magician, calls himself 'Mike the Clown' and 'Magical Mike.' Apparently he's great with kids." The detective's voice drips.

"I'll bet he is. Finances?"

"Yeah . . . he could need money. His apartment's shittier than yours, if you can believe that. He's got a seven-year-old in Chicago that the mother never lets him see. He's funneling all his money to the girl."

"What a saint," Tom says. "What's he saying?"

"Oh man, Tommy, you're not going to believe this one. He's saying the kid just disappeared. Poof. Magic."

"What?" This is a new one. "Do you think he believes that?"

"I don't know. How could he? It's the dumbest-ass excuse I've ever heard. He's either crazy or a moron. He's not even taking credit, says it was an accident. God, I'd take the credit."

Tom leans forward. His heart is beating loudly. "Can you get psych in there?"

"We're trying."

Tom's head tingles. This is definitely a new one. It's a little fascinating, really, a great puzzle. Why would a man say this? He can't think they'll buy it. And it's not going to exactly defray suspicion from him. Is he trying to get publicity? Maybe that's it, maybe this is a deranged publicity stunt. That would be something . . . Tom's heart speeds—he needs to be out there—

"Listen, um, Detective, I was wondering—"

Detective Blair interrupts. "You want out."

"Come on," Tom pleads. "I can crack this. There's nothing happening here. Let me talk to Mr. Wizard."

"Don't get ahead of yourself, Tommy; interrogation's my job. Anyway, I need you there. You gotta do this. You work for me, remember?"

Tom looks around. He lowers his voice to a whisper. "I can't talk to these people. I don't know what to say. They're so fucking sad . . . I got dressed down by a six-year-old girl."

"Seven," Blair corrects. "Greta Woodrow was seven yesterday."

Tom blinks. His scalp stops tingling, his heart stops rushing. "It was her birthday? Oh man."

"Hang in there for me, okay? You're the one for the job. You're the most level-headed guy I got. Think of it as part of your training."

Tom is about to protest when the Woodrows' phone rings. "Shit," he says. "That's the phone."

"Okay, time to do your job. I'll check in later, Tommy. I'm counting on you, remember."

Tom makes a noncommittal noise then hangs up, exhales, and picks up the Woodrows' line.

"Hello?" This is all he's supposed to say. Don't identify yourself. Don't identify the house. Just answer the phone.

There is a hesitation. A woman's voice asks, "Justin?"

"Oh. No." He does this like he has been told. "Justin can't come to the phone right now. Can I take a message?"

"Um, this is Jan Miller." Tom writes the name down in his notebook, "We . . . we read the story in the paper. We're so sorry. We wanted to know if there's anything we can do—"

"I will," Tom says.

The woman's voice is rushed, frantic. "Tell them we're canceling our party tonight. Tell them if there's anything—"

"Of course."

She coughs. "Is there any word?"

"I'm afraid I can't discuss that. I'll tell them you called."

Tom hangs up. That went okay, although a trained monkey could do the job just as well. And he'll have to think of better evasions, he doesn't necessarily need to sound like he's regurgitated a police manual on the phone.

He puts it down. There's another call.

"Justin Woodrow?"

"No—he can't come to the—"

"I know you have the kid. You've killed him, haven't you, you sick fuck."

"What the—" Oh. This. It happens. Usually it doesn't happen this early; for some reason these people tend to sleep late. Tom would like to hang up, but he needs to stay on long enough for them to trace the call, even though there's no way this is the guy who did it, this is just, to borrow a phrase, a sick fuck with a phone book. "What makes you say that?"

Too late. The phone is dead. That's all right, Tom's not one for conversation. This will happen the rest of the day, it always does— you hear stories from the guys who have done house duty. There will be frantic calls from friends and neighbors, none of whom know any-thing. There will be cranks. There will be people walking by the house, staring in. There will be media vans maintaining a vigil. This is his job, then. Someone's got to keep the family separate from all this. Fine. He'll do his job.

So Tom sits for the rest of the morning, answering the phone, reading the newspaper article up and down, shuffling through notes, for three full hours. He sees no sign of any Woodrows. He hears some pattering, some distinctly male thumping around, a chronic pattern much like pacing. The noise is first a little startling, and then some-what soothing. *Pat pat pat pat pat pat. Pause. Pat pat pat pat pat pat.*

Pause. Tom answers the phone again and again, carefully taking down the names, evading questions. A couple local stations call for interviews, and Tom says he'll consult with the family, just like he's supposed to. The stations know the drill. *Pat pat pat pat pat pat. Pause. Pat pat pat pat pat pat. Pause. Ring. Ring. Hello? No, can I take a message? Pat pat pat pat pat. Pause. Yes, I'll let them know. Thank you.*

And then, a little before noon, the doorbell rings. Tom is ready. He unclasps his sidearm and approaches the door. He places his left foot securely behind the door to prevent someone from forcing their way through. As he opens the door, just enough to assess the situation, he wields his badge, which he promptly presents to two girls in party dresses who are holding the hands of a rather confused-looking woman.

Last night, Catherine cleaned up all the birthday decorations— wrapped up Greta's cake, popped the balloons, took down streamers, took out the garbage, filed away the cards from Hannah and Justin, and put away the presents. All the evidence of a party is gone. Nonetheless, Tom, with his fine investigative skills, is able to quickly deduce what's going on here. Greta was seven yesterday; this is her birthday party.

There's a story about this in the newspaper—the parents should have seen it, and then known not to come. Didn't they read the newspaper? Why doesn't anyone read the newspaper anymore?

Tom clears his throat. Perhaps a trained monkey would be even better. "I'm sorry. The party is canceled," he says.

There's movement behind him, from the stairs?—the thought that Greta might see this gives him an acid taste in his mouth; he motions the mother and girls backward, and he follows, shutting the door behind him.

"What is it? Where's Justin?" the woman asks, clutching the girls.

Tom clears his throat. The words are simple. "There's been an incident. James Woodrow is missing. You can get the details from the newspaper. If you have any information—"

"Oh my God. What happened? What can I do?"

"There's a number where you can call with any information. There's a volunteer hot line—"

"Of course, of course—"

"Now, could I ask you a couple of questions?"

Tom spends twenty minutes on the front porch, waiting for other people who do not read newspapers. Each of the mothers reacts the exact same way; each gasps a little, each takes a step back, each grabs on to her child a little more tightly, each rushes the girl to the car. Every time he tells a mother, the world shifts again; he watches it happen—they've been touched by something now, and they can never go back. Tom sees this all the time in his job, but it still surprises him every time; he already lives in the world these mothers are tasting for the first time. He gives everyone the volunteer number; they can make signs, make phone calls, canvass neighborhoods. You never know. Tom takes down every name, even though he knows in his heart that anyone who orchestrated the kidnapping of a boy probably would not show up on the family's front step the next day bearing birthday presents, but he is just doing his job, for chrissakes.

When the stream of mothers finally stops (they all ask for Justin, Tom notices, not the mother . . .) Tom goes back into the house to find Justin himself in the kitchen, reading the newspaper. Justin's reddish brown hair is sticking out around his head; it looks like every hair in his body, in fact, might be standing on end. His eyes are bugged out, his jaw is set, and he's twitching a little.

Tom is about to reintroduce himself to Justin, to try to say something both soothing and competent, but Justin speaks first.

"They ran a review of the show!" His voice is sharp, strangely bright. He waves Tom over in an almost friendly way and holds up the Variety section for him. A headline in the bottom corner reads, "Razzlers Circus Dazzles."

"Fuck." Tom exhales. "I guess they didn't think to cancel it."

"Now," Justin looks at Tom, full of expression, "don't you think that's just unprofessional? Is that any way to run a newspaper?" Justin is shaking his head disbelievingly; he sounds like he is having a water cooler conversation in some heavily caffeinated universe.

"My friend wrote the review." Justin points to the byline. "Stewart Martin. He *loves* the clown—you should read this, Tom, he thinks the clown is the best thing since sliced bread, since the wagon wheel. He thinks the clown is *astonishing*. 'Astonishing.' I mean, really, Stewart. Shakespeare is 'astonishing,' Mozart is fucking 'astonishing.' Landing on the moon, that's something to be *astonished* by. Who edits this crap?"

Tom gets a sudden urge to flee.

"This is what happens," Justin says, shaking his head. "Nothing means anything anymore. Words are all dead. It just pisses me off. And for the rest of his life this shit-bag clown is going to think he's *astonishing*. That's really discerning critical judgment, Stewart, big boy, and thank you so much for the tickets." He slaps the table.

Tom perks up. "This guy gave you the tickets?"

"Yeah," Justin waves his hand, "but don't think he arranged this or anything, he's too much of a moron, anyone who uses that much hyperbole can't be a fucking criminal mastermind."

They always tell you when you interview a family never to be surprised by the way people act after a tragedy. The human mind is wired to handle a certain amount of stress, after that, the wires just blow. Tom's seen it all, he's even seen something approaching this, this sort of hyperactive denial. He's always wondered where the energy goes, what happens when it all becomes too much for the body to hold. He doesn't really want to be there for the inevitable explosion this time.

Tom doesn't know how he'd react in Justin's shoes; his job is not to react. He can't get emotional, emotions impede judgment. Of course, if someone had done something to his mom or something maybe he'd be just like this. But that's personal. Now, he's at work.

Everything around Justin is pounding. There's blood singing in his head; he is electric, he is on fire. All the pounding got louder when he came downstairs and saw his boy's picture on the front page of the paper—stupid article, suspects in custody, blah blah blah, don't they know that that's James who's gone? It's not some empty boy, some picture, some story, some pretend news-boy; it's his son, it's James. And there goes his heart again—

Badumbadumbadumbadum—

This cannot be healthy.

The little cop is watching him. Can he hear it? What if he can hear it? The cop would think he has something to hide, and he does; he does, he has a terrible secret—not just about James, but about the entire nature of the universe. There has been a tear, a great big tear in the fabric of life—

Badumbadumbadumbadum—

Bing bong!

That's the doorbell! My goodness! There's someone at the door! Justin pops out of his seat, he bumps into the table, damn that hurts, the little cop is following him, saying something; Justin runs to the door, faster than a speeding bullet, he opens it, and—

"Hi! I'm Fantastic Fred!"

Justin has opened up the front door to reveal a tall rubbery man in a tailcoat and funny pants. The man holds a big black suitcase in one hand.

The man smiles and scratches his nose. "I'm Fantastic Fred? I'm here for the birthday party? Is this the right address?" He stares at Tom, who has come up behind Justin, hand on holster.

Tom clears his throat and steps forward. "Yes, but the party isn't happening, sir. I'm sorry for your trouble."

Tom is trying to edge Justin out of the way, but Justin won't move. He stays focused on the man at the door. "You're a magician?" he asks.

Fred looks around. "Um. Yes."

"We didn't order a magician," Justin says slowly. "We ordered Lila."

Fred shakes his head and holds up an invoice. "Says here magician."

"Wow!" Justin exclaims. He looks at the invoice. It does say magician. Would you fancy that? (*badumbadumbadum*—) And it hits Justin: This Is No Accident. "Will you . . . will you come in? I want to talk to you for a few minutes."

"Uhhh . . . Didn't you say there's no party?"

"Yes, yes, but I—I want to talk to you. Please. Of course, we'll still pay you what you were expecting."

"Uhhhh . . . okay."

Justin smiles at the magician and gestures toward the living room chairs, the ones they only use for company. "Sit down, please." The magician complies, watching Justin carefully, keeping his suitcase close by. Justin has forgotten all about Tom, who sits back quietly on the couch behind the stairs, and poises himself to listen.

Justin leans toward Fred. He speaks seriously, intensely, like a man with state secrets that are just itching to be sold. "I need to know some things."

The magician shifts. "What kind of things?"

"I need to know about magic."

"Oh." He clears his throat. "Listen, I'm sorry, I can't tell you how any tricks work. Magician's code of honor, you know—"

"I'll pay you double. Please." The words tumble out of Justin's mouth.

"I should—"

"No. Please. It's just one trick. Just tell me what you can, okay?"

"Well—double?"

"I can't tell you how much this means to me—" Justin smiles kindly, like a sane man. This is a game, all a game, and if he plays it right, acts the right role, if he solves the mystery, then James will come back.

"All right," Fred nods, "shoot."

"Well, I was just wondering. If you wanted to make someone disappear, how would you go about doing that?"

"Oh! Well, that one isn't in my particular repertoire, and of course I can't tell you how it works, per se—"

"Magician's code of honor—"

"Exactly."

"That's all right."

The magician rubs his hands together. "Well, now, in general, say, most magicians are going to have their different methods. There's no one way to do a trick like that. But let me tell you this. Magic doesn't exist on its own; magic is a form of communication between your magician and your audience member. Magic is all about psychology. People want to believe the impossible; they want to be fooled. All you do is show them the way."

Justin nods. "Go on."

"Magic is misdirection. There're no tricks; everything happens in front of your eyes, but the magician's job is to make sure you're not looking. You distract them so they don't see you pocket the ball or palm the coin or activate the lever or whatever. People trust magicians; they believe just what the magician tells them to, and they suspend their judgment, all in order to believe the impossible, you know? Magic happens in your head . . ." He pauses, and then clarifies, "Your head, not my head."

"I got it. But what does that have to do with making a person disappear?"

"Well, what I'm telling you. You do something, you distract the audience somehow, and then the person goes in a secret compartment, or a screen can come down, or else you use lights. Smoke and mirrors. There's always a way."

Justin leans in again. "But how could you make someone really disappear?"

"Huh?"

"I mean, really make them disappear. Into thin air. Poof."

The magician starts. "You can't do that."

"Not at all?"

"No! Magic isn't *real*, you know."

"Are you sure? Maybe it's possible and you just don't know about it."

"Uh, look. No. You put them in a secret compartment or under a trapdoor, or cover them with something."

"Oh."

"Or else . . . or else they are just right there. Before your eyes. And you don't see them." The magician smiles and points to his brain. "In your head, remember?" He smiles, then blinks and moves his hand so it points at Justin's head again. "Your head."

Justin nods slowly. "Thank you. Thank you. You've been very helpful."

"No problem."

"I'll get your check."

Justin writes the man a check for some amount, he doesn't really notice what, he makes sure it's more than enough because that's what you do when you're playing the game, never know when you'll need to call on Fantastic Fred again, better to keep him on your side. Fred seems to be pleased, though, whatever amount it is—he grabs it happily and hurries out the door.

And Justin sits, trying to slow his heart.

So Fred doesn't think it's possible. Of course, he's an amateur, a birthday party magician sent by mistake, the old card-and-coin man who warms up for the real magicians. Or else he's lying, he's an accomplice, sent by Mike the Clown to throw Justin off his track, the old plant who's there to confuse and distract. Misdirection, indeed. Perhaps Justin will call on him again, perhaps Justin will loosen his lips. Justin will not be played, he's the player, and what is he doing sitting in the house pacing around and being watched by the little bowling ball–shaped cop?

He has to go.

He has to take matters into his own hands. He'll start at the auditorium, the scene of the crime—the police don't know what to look for, but he does. He'll do his own search. He'll find the direction behind the misdirection—he can do it, that's his job, he's the father, he's the hero of this story. It's time to start acting like it. There are rules here.

He cannot tell Hannah. How would he begin? She doesn't understand what happened; she only believes in what's medically possible. She would act like he was crazy; she would shake her head at him. No, that's not true, but she would prescribe something for him, something to relieve the stress that he is so visibly under, something to stop his delusions, something to make him sleep. Things around the house are terrible enough without Hannah resorting to psychopharmaceuticals. He is the hero, he will bring James back, he will bring Mike the Clown's head on a stick, and everyone will live happily ever after.

Justin is a changed man. He knows, for the first time in his life, the possibility of murder. He will kill the clown unless he brings James back. He will hurt him until he brings James back. If they let the clown out of jail, he will find him, he will hurt him, and then he will kill him. Justin breathes in the thought and feels it expand in his lungs. He tastes it in his mouth, runs it against his teeth, turns it about his tongue. He is a different man now. He is a man who knows what it is to want to kill.

Justin heads out the door, backs out of the drive, conscious that there are men parked on the street watching everything he does. He's going to the auditorium, he's going to look for clues, there will be something there, something to guide him on his search, and the men parked on the street can't possibly find fault with that. When it comes time to kill the clown, will they try to stop him?

The clown has made James disappear, and he won't bring him back. He is trying to get publicity, trying to make a name for himself. The trick would be no good if James just showed up again, after all; everyone would think it was just a trick, like Fred said. But it was real. Justin knows this is true; he knew it when he saw the videotape: James is there, and then he isn't there. James disappears. Justin *knows*. Maybe the loss of his son has driven Justin mad, but the loss of James itself is madness; what other possible reaction is there? When your son is taken from you, anything becomes possible.

Hannah is creeping into James's

room. He's supposed to be downstairs, for Greta's party. The girls always love him; they treat him like a pet. Hannah understands his need to hide, of course; there are one hundred girls downstairs, and afterward they will go home and tell their one hundred mothers all about what kind of parent Hannah Woodrow is, complete with scorecards, but there's nothing for James to be afraid of. His door is slightly ajar; she pushes it open, expecting to see James on his bed.

But when she looks into his room, the bed is empty. And something stirs in her stomach. No, this isn't right. This doesn't happen, does it? Where is he? Where's James?

Hannah steps into his room, feeling the sky swirl around her. Somewhere, in the distance, she thinks she hears applause and cheers, and her stomach wrenches.

But then she sees the closet door is slightly ajar, too—that's how James always leaves his doors. She pushes it open, to reveal a massive empty auditorium. She looks around frantically; James isn't in any of the seats. But there, onstage, she notices a large immobile pile of fabric. She walks the long mile up the aisle and sees James at the very top of the pile, fast asleep.

"James, you're here," she says. "Oh James, I was so afraid."

Hannah leaps onto the stage and climbs up the pile of clothes until she reaches her son. She sits down next to him and runs her hands through his thin orange hair.

"My little James. My angel boy. Don't do that to me, okay?"

James gurgles a little in his sleep, and Hannah thinks she might just fall into the pile with him, wrap herself around him, and protect him for the rest of his life.

"It's your sister's birthday. You should come down," she says softly, a lullaby. James balls his hands into little fists and rubs his eyes. He smacks his mouth a couple of times. His eyes don't open. Hannah considers cuddling up around him on this pile of clothes in this empty auditorium and falling asleep with him. She should get up, they should go, but she sits, stroking his head.

"I'm glad you're here, sweetie," she murmurs. "Oh, Jamesie, I had the worst dream—"

Greta is free! She had to wait until

her mother was asleep just to get away. It took forever. Her mom has barely let go of her all day long, like if she did, Greta would disappear, too. But that's just silly, Greta's not going anywhere, not when she has a brother to find. Mom was holding her so tightly you wouldn't even believe it, Greta had to ever-so-carefully sneak out of there like a top secret spy to go to the playroom where she can think best. She has been in her parents' bed most of the day with her otter (Otter) and her bear (Bear) and her dog (Fred) and together they have been Thinking. Well, she hasn't been thinking all day, sometimes she has been sleeping, but Greta Woodrow, there's no time for that. She's seven now and she needs to begin to act like it.

Greta needs to help.

James wouldn't have gone away on purpose. He doesn't do that kind of thing. James likes to stay put. That was what was so funny about him raising his hand! James likes to stay near his sister, and if he was planning on going somewhere he would have told Greta about it and probably taken her with him. He doesn't go anywhere alone, and he sticks his hand out and looks up at Greta and she smiles and takes his hand and they go off together. It's going to be so fun when James goes to kindergarten because then they'll be in the same building and she can see him in the hallways and say, "Hi James!" and at recess she can take him over to play with her friends, because they all love

James so much, and like to pinch him because that's what happens with cute little boys.

Though, sometimes James just hides, he hides right in front of your face. She can't explain it but sometimes you look and you don't see that he's there but he is. But then he tugs on her sleeve and says, "Ge-ta?" and she says, "James! You goose!"

At first she thought that's what happened with the magician, but James would have tugged on her sleeve sooner or later. This was a trick! A magic trick! A super-incredible, amazing-duper magic trick! Did James feel it? What did it feel like? Does he know how the magician did it?

And then there was lots of noise and her parents were crying, and of course they were, and Greta got upset, and Aunt Catherine came, and Greta felt bad, but she just didn't have it figured out yet; she didn't understand. Greta doesn't like loud noises and everybody being so upset and so she wasn't thinking so good.

The thing is, the magician should have brought James back right away. Somebody should just find the clown and ask him, very nicely, to bring James back. If he doesn't know how, they should help him look. That's what worries Greta. Doesn't he know how? Maybe he doesn't know how, so then she has to figure it out herself. James is too little to come back on his own.

Greta doesn't know much about magic, really. She's never been interested in it before. Magic is mostly for boys and she prefers puppies. There's a boy at school, Mark, and he likes to go around with cards and he shoves them in your face and says, "Pick a card, any card," and Greta, if you want to know the truth, finds it a little annoying because he acts like he is super cool because he can do some tricks and usually he gets his cards taken away from him anyway. So, he was someone who Greta wanted to avoid, because she doesn't like to be with people who have things taken away from them, she's already being told to use her indoor voice all the time at school, and that she shouldn't kiss people, and that she needs to stay in her seat, and be very careful not to squeeze things too hard, she doesn't need any more trouble. Still, she could ask Mark about it when she goes to school on Monday, if the clown hasn't figured out how to bring James back yet. Greta doesn't know anything, she doesn't even know where people go when they disappear, and all the books she's ever read say something different.

She's got a bunch of markers and some paper. This is as good a place to start as any. She can imagine where he is. She can draw pictures of his adventures; he's in the jungle with lions and tigers and bears and dogs. He's under the sea with mermaids and funny fishes and otters and underwater dogs. He's in the sky with magic birds and flying dogs. He's on other planets with flying dogs and talking bears. Greta's read all about this sort of thing happening, except she believed the school librarian when she said those kinds of things couldn't really happen, they were just pretend, and Greta should stop pestering her. Anyway it doesn't matter, because James is littler than the kids in these stories and he doesn't do so well by himself. He needs his big sister to watch over him. He might be scared; Greta usually helps him when he's scared.

She thinks when he comes back she'll give him her drawings and they can talk about his adventures. She'll tie it up in a little book like they learned in school last week and he can have it. To James from Greta. She'll draw pictures of the family. She'll make him lists, too, of the stuff he likes and doesn't like and stuff. He likes peanut butter sandwiches a lot. He hates tomatoes because he thinks the seeds look like eyes. He likes otters because they are so cute and of course he likes puppies because everyone likes puppies. He likes macaroni and cheese, and hot dogs as long as they have *lots* of ketchup. He likes bunnies. It's important to remember these things.

She's going to write it all down. She'll have everything she can think of about James on paper, and maybe if she is sad, she can look at it. Anyway, this way when he comes back he'll always have something to remind him who he is. He should come back soon.

The rest of the day is spent like

this. Hannah dreams, Justin searches, Greta imagines. And Tom, Tom answers the phone.

No, they are not giving interviews. No, they can't come to the phone. Yes, I'll tell them. Certainly. Thank you.

There are three media vans on the street. The doorbell keeps ringing. People are bringing things; there's so much food overwhelming the Woodrow kitchen now. There are casseroles, stews, muffins, cakes, fruit. Tom just thanks them and takes the food; he keeps thanking and thanking and after awhile he begins to feel like they are bringing the food for him. He doesn't know how to deal with all the dishes and platters and tins—the Woodrows aren't eating. He spreads them all out in the kitchen to look appetizing and then quickly changes his mind and piles them up in a corner; it looked too much like a wake.

He's been stopping in to look at Greta once in a while. She's been by herself in this playroom of theirs all afternoon. Neither of the parents have even checked in on her; you'd think they'd be watching her like hawks. But the Woodrows seem to have forgotten all about their daughter.

But it's not Tom's place to judge.

Hannah wakes up to find the sun setting and her daughter gone from her side. She doesn't panic, there is no cause to panic, yet. She simply springs out of bed and walks through every room in the house, until she gets to the playroom and sees Greta, present and whole.

"Where's your father?" Hannah asks.

"Gone," says Greta.

Poof?

No. No. Just out. Of course. She should have known. Justin just slipped out, didn't tell her where he was going. But she knows exactly where he went; Justin went to run around the auditorium to look for James. He was looking for the secret compartment, the trapdoor, the hidden screen. He was looking for a clue, a dropped sneaker, a piece of fabric, a calling card with the killer's name on it. Hercule Poirot sees things the others do not.

This is fully within Justin's character. He means so well. There is no problem he cannot solve. You get up in the morning, you greet life, you take care of things. Everything will work out. Hannah has always admired this. She admires it now. He's trying to do something. And that is very, very admirable, that is just what Hannah should be doing, if Hannah knew anything to do.

This is outside her area of expertise. When James was just sick, she knew what to do, or at least she knew where to begin. She knew the questions to ask. There was no resource she would leave unmined until she got the answer. It's why she became a doctor in the first place. There are so many mysteries wrapped up in the human body; Hannah gets to solve them.

But now, medicine is no use; what is left? We are in the realm of wishes, here—and this is not a realm Hannah knows much about.

The day passes into night, and nothing happens at all. Justin reappears in the house after spending two hours in the auditorium—the security guard, the one who punched Mike, let him in, and together they walked around and looked and looked and looked and looked. The guard kept looking at him too, like he felt sorry for him, he didn't know Justin was a man on a mission, the hero in the story; you do not have to feel sorry for a man who is destined to solve the case. Nothing happened, really—and that's odd, it really is, you'd think there would be a clue, something to show him he was on the right path, something to help him in his search, but there was nothing nothing nothing—so Justin knows the key is with the clown, then, he will have to beat it out of the clown, and maybe he'll even break into the jailhouse to do it. Justin sat on the stage, on the site of his son's disappearance, and tasted revenge and death while the security guard watched with his eyebrows knit together and his lips pursed, looking . . . hopeless?

In the evening, Justin sits in the bedroom looking into the mirror trying to get the expression on the security guard's face out of his head. It is the nature of the hero that no one else understands him, or even what drives him in the first place—it is that which is bothering Justin, right? The fact that he would not be believed, that is what bothers him, not that hopelessness, not that hopelessness.

Hannah wanders around the first floor in a daze. She makes Greta dinner at some point, she won't even remember what she made an hour later, and perhaps she even eats something herself. Later, Tom summons them to the couch, where they sit side-by-side, again. Tom pulls up a chair and is talking to Hannah and Justin gently about how the police are working very hard and doing everything they can.

Everything in Hannah's body aches. Her head is filled with pudding. Her husband looks blurry. He's moving so fast his edges are fuzzy. That's probably not healthy—she should know, she's a doctor. He's in an absolutely different dimension than she; no wonder they can't talk to each other, they don't exist in the same plane of reality. Funny though, his voice should be sounding like a tape on fast forward, but it seems to come out normally—the translation matrix must be working. Hannah is way up here, outside her body, watching these two people together on the couch—one vibrating, one perfectly still. Are they really married? Are they really connected? Did they really get together and make children, did they make a disappearing boy? That's what happened, that's why the sky ripped open, that's why James fell through, Hannah and Justin are cosmically incompatible, they belong to different planes, and their boy could not hold together.

Or something like that.

Officer Johnson never did leave her house like she asked him very nicely to do. He's still here, he's been answering the phone all day, he's been keeping track of the people who call. Isn't that strange? He's like a private secretary, a private spying secretary, and he makes Hannah so very sleepy and pudding-brained.

"James's doctor called," he says. "A Dr. Lewis?"

"Fucker."

Ha! Who said that? Hannah looks around. Both the men are looking at her—did she say it? She seems to have said it.

Tom coughs. "Dr. Woodrow? Do you have some . . . concerns about Henry Lewis?"

"No. He's just a fucker."

She laughs a little. She doesn't really care at all about Dr. Henry Lewis, but she is very, very, very much enjoying calling him a fucker. It's a fun word, and Hannah never gets to use it. She should use it more often. Fucker. Fucker. Fucker.

"Okay, um. Justin, your mother called a few times."

"Oh!" he says.

"She was, um, a little upset. She'd really like you to call."

"She knows?" Justin says. "Who told her?"

"Well, of course, the police interview family members . . ."

Justin sits up. "Somebody thinks my *mom* took James?" He blinks. "She lives in Ohio!"

That would be funny, Hannah thinks. Justin's mom, the kids' only grandparent, uses a walker and can barely go grocery shopping. Maybe it's all a ruse though, maybe she's a dastardly child snatcher! Fucker! Ha!

Justin is staring at her, maybe he doesn't think any of this is funny. What would happen if she reached out to touch him, would he break apart or just ripple away?

"We need to talk a little bit about the media, all right?" Tom leans in. "Other reporters have called. All of the TV stations have called. Justin, they have nice footage of you coming in and out of the house now, and god knows what else. There will be a lot of attention focused on you, and I want you to be ready for that ... Also, Detective Blair feels—we feel—that the, um, unusual nature of James's disappearance could garner you some unnecessary attention. There will be crazies out there who believe he's just, POOF!, disappeared."

At this, Hannah and Justin utter the same noncommittal syllable.

"Listen," Justin says, leaning forward. "Can't we keep the media off this? I mean the clown just wants publicity. Maybe if he doesn't get any ..."

Hannah raises her eyebrows. So that's what he thinks. She hadn't even stopped to wonder what Justin was thinking, what his explanation was. But of course, he has to have a theory, Justin needs theories, that's how he gets out of bed, that is the secret to Justin—it's all so clear to Hannah now.

Tom shakes his head. "We couldn't even if we wanted to. But nobody really knows about the clown. He's not getting any publicity from this, at this point. He's our chief suspect, and we're doing our best to keep him under wraps. Don't worry."

Tom has decided not to tell the Woodrows that the clown was let out of jail today—that they had no evidence to keep him. He considered it; he would tell them that the police will be following him, and they hope he'll make contact with the boy, an accomplice, someone. But something in his instincts says to wait, wait, wait, don't tell them yet; Justin does not look like he'll be able to take the information, and Tom doesn't need a murderous father on his hands.

Tom can't even fathom what world these people are in. Justin is fire and Hannah is ice. It makes sense. The body has to set up some mechanism, of course, after such a great shock, or else it would break apart from sadness. Tom understands, it's human nature. Tom's not a parent, he can't judge. He can't imagine what he'd be like if he were a father—he doesn't know anything about kids. He can't even talk to their daughter that they're ignoring—

"Where's Greta?" he finds himself saying.

"Oh. She's upstairs," Justin says. "She's in our room. Sleeping."

"Okay," Tom says. "I want you guys to get some sleep too."

Hannah nods slowly. Sleep, she's been doing it all day. It's been wonderful—she closes her eyes, and there's James.

Justin has never fought so well

before. The sword flashes through the air, leaving a trail of steel. The captain of the guard is doing his best to keep up, but he's growing wearier while Justin seems only to be getting stronger. He's not trembling now; this is the control he is supposed to have. Justin cackles and says, "Enough of this warm-up! It's time to fight." The captain stares at him, then drops his sword, turns white, and runs away— that's his only choice. Better to live as a coward than die by Justin's merciless blade.

He can hear the princess's screams from the tower; he didn't know there was a tower, but it's right there in front of him. He understands; he only has a little more time before she is forcibly married. But he has no fear. He slices through the few guards with courage enough to fight ("Brave men," he thinks. "It's a shame they have to die.") and then, with a spin of his sword, he runs into the castle. BAM! POW! He pushes men away, one after another, he is almost at the door, and then he is face to face with the dastardly Count Fosco.

"You will not foil my plan," says Fosco.

"I can only respond with my foil!" Justin says, whirling out his sword. He slices! He dices! The Count is good, but not good enough and Justin has him backed against the wall.

"This will teach you to abduct princesses!" says Justin, blade at his throat.

And then Fosco starts to cry, "Please, Woodrow, have mercy! Have mercy!"

And Justin thrusts the blade closer, the point pierces his skin. "I want you to leave. If I ever see you here again—"

The blood trickles down from the evil man's neck. Justin does not budge.

"Okay, okay, just don't hurt me!" Fosco says, bleeding all over the place. He opens the door to the tower, then runs away, blubbering.

And there she is. Beautiful Hannah, tied up in the tower— porcelain face, red hair, willowy and white, with eyes that betray nothing, except when they betray everything. Beautiful Hannah: difficult, infinite, precious, his.

But—

This isn't a room in a castle. It's just a room, painted all in black. Hannah sits dressed all in white, tied to a rickety wooden chair, a gag on her mouth, blood all over her front.

Justin says, "I've come to rescue you. I've come to rescue the princess."

But then there is a sound like fingers snapping, and Hannah is free. The bonds and the chair are gone, and they're just alone together in the black room. She grabs his arm. She is shaking.

"No, we're not looking for the princess," she says desperately. "You have the princess. We're looking for James."

"James?"

"Our son. He disappeared."

The sword is gone. Justin is wearing a T-shirt and jeans. He feels his throat begin to tighten. "Where did he go?"

"I don't know. But we have to find him. I can't live without him. Please."

"How?"

"That's your job. You're the white knight." Hannah begins to cry, she wraps around him. She feels so small. "Please, Justin. I'm so afraid. I'm so afraid we'll never get him back."

Hannah is awake. Of course she

is, she's been sleeping all day. Now her circadian rhythms are off and she won't be able to sleep. Greta is on a mattress on the floor, and the man to whom Hannah has pledged her troth is in bed next to her. He's twitching; he's dreaming, she can tell. Dreaming—he's so lucky— he can dream of James.

She's lying there and all she can think about is the great lack at the center of her universe, and how if she cut open her stomach with a knife, maybe James would crawl out. And maybe he wouldn't, but the pain would take her mind off it, and anyway, it would hurt so much less than this.

What will happen if her whole family goes? They all break off into the ether, and Hannah is left, alone. How many body parts can she cut open? Could she travel back in time, cutting their memories out from the film of her past, so that all that is left is Hannah, alone? It might be the only way to bear this.

She is completely helpless. She is awash in her own helplessness. Her muscles atrophy from it, her bones ache with it, her blood thickens, her brain fogs. How strange this is. Always, for Hannah, there has been something to do, *something*, and now there is nothing nothing nothing, now when it matters most of all.

She can't sleep anymore, she's slept too much, but she can't be awake either because when she is awake, James is gone, and there's nothing nothing nothing she can do, except cut herself open.

Hannah gets up and goes to the bathroom. She unlocks the medicine cabinet and peers at the top shelf. She rummages through the samples and finds what she wants. She takes a pill. She drinks it down with a full glass of water. She brushes her teeth, puts the package away on the highest shelf, locks the medicine cabinet back up.

This sleep medication works by targeting a neurotransmitter called GABA—it assists GABA in dampening electrical activity in the brain. Hannah prescribes it for insomnia occasionally. It can cause dizziness and nausea, hypersomnia and rebound insomnia. People react very differently to the drug; it's difficult to get the dosage right. Hannah's usually very careful with these things, pills are such an easy solution and sometimes the problem is much more complicated. Too many doctors are lazy; they don't want to get in and find the cause, but Hannah likes problems, she likes to figure things out, at least she used to, until the problem got very very hard and very very personal, and Hannah just wants to sleep, all right? She just wants to sleep.

She knows this is how it works. It's this way in all the movies. The child disappears and the mother lies in bed with stringy hair and mismatched sweats. And Hannah always thought, no, that's not what I would do, I would do something, I would do research, I would look up cases, I would do interviews, I would shadow the cops, I would search the ends of the earth, I would do something. Now, it makes perfect sense to Hannah, it's the thing to do, the world stops and you stop with it; finally Hannah Woodrow is acting like a mother.

Hannah crawls back into bed, checking on her twitching husband from outer space. He doesn't wake up, and she wonders if he's even aware of her at all. It's fine if he's not, she feels invisible to herself, too. She closes her eyes. She counts to one hundred, slowly, and then one hundred and fifty—

That's better. That's so much better. The numbers are fading, Hannah is falling asleep. She has set her mind to respond to one alarm and one alarm only—until she hears the words, *James is back*, Hannah

Woodrow will keep sleeping. She has enough pills to last her a couple weeks, which isn't long enough for the body to become dependent; Hannah knows pill addiction has nothing to do with willpower or inner strength and everything to do with chemicals, and if people just understood that there would be far fewer addicts in this world.

This is what she thinks as she dozes off, that and, "I am dozing off, thank God—"

And soon, Hannah falls back into the dream-touched universe where James was never gone—

Greta is sitting on a puffy cloud

in the bright blue sky. Everything is the color of magic markers. She can grab onto wisps of cloud and stretch them out like cotton candy. She's pulling on a strand now, twisting it around her fingers. The gigantic red bird squawks at her but she just squawks right back, SQUAWK! She winds cloud around her arm and she wonders if she can dress herself in it. And that's when she hears the voice in the wind:

"Ge-tie?"

She looks at the big red bird. The bird looks back. They both look around, trying to see the source of the noise, but there is no one there. The bird squawks again—SQUAWK—but does not offer any clues. Greta is about to give up and go back to playing with her cloud arm, when she hears it again:

"Ge-tie?"

There is no mistaking it this time. "James!"

"Yeah!"

Greta leaps up on her cloud and looks around. "Where are you?"

Actually, it's not so much like hearing a voice anymore. It's like the words just appear in her head. "I'm right here."

Greta climbs up on the bird's back. There is a good place there for a little girl to stand, so she stands up and looks around. "Where? I can't see you."

"I can't see me too."

151

"Where did you go?" Greta stamps her foot. The bird squawks—SQUAWK!

"Up."

Greta looks up. She doesn't see anything but more clouds and more gigantic red birds, one next to each cloud. The birds must pull the clouds along, that must be how they move, Greta notes, before getting back to the matter at hand. "Why?"

"These things just happen," the not-voice says.

Wait. "Is this really James?"

"Maybe not."

Greta scrunches her face. "Is this a crank call?"

"No." The gigantic red birds all stand perfectly still. Is the voice in their heads too? They seem to be waiting for something, like Greta's been waiting. Did they lose their brothers too?

"Where's James?"

"Maybe he ran away to join the circus."

"That's stupid. Where's James?"

"He disappeared." There is a sound like the snapping of fingers and then all the gigantic red birds are gone, just like that. Greta falls from her perch. It's a good thing there is a cloud there!

"Where did he go?" She stands up. It is hard to get a very good footing on a cloud. "Tell him to come back. I want him to come back."

"Really? You should—"

And then the finger-snapping sound and all the clouds disappear, and Greta feels herself lurch and fall. Why did that have to happen? They were just about to tell her what she should do.

If you asked Tom, he'd say he

never dreams. This is, as Hannah would tell him, impossible. Everybody dreams. They just don't always remember. It's part of the brain's natural function, but nobody knows for sure why. The ancients thought dreams were sent by the gods and contained prophecies. Freud and Jung called dreams wish fulfillment, the expression of the unconscious mind. Neurologists hold up PET scans and say that dreams are meaningless, a response of normal electrical activity from the cerebral cortex.

What we know is this: dreaming occurs during desynchronized, or REM, sleep, which is generated largely in a region of the brain stem known as the pons; there are neurons in the pons that are only active during REM. Infants spend fifty percent of their sleep in this phase, while for adults it's more like twenty percent. When the body is deprived of REM sleep, its owner becomes irritable, foggy, unable to concentrate, and clumsy, and the next sleeping period contains longer, more intense periods of REM. The evidence is clear. We need to dream.

Often, this description of the biological process is given as explanation for why we dream, which Hannah finds completely ridiculous. As if it explained anything. Hannah understands what these scientists do not, that the body is not just mechanistic, but poetic as well.

If Tom told her he never dreams, she would explain all this to him (in another universe, in the universe where James did not raise his hand, was not picked . . .) and she would silently accuse him of thinking he is too macho to have an unconscious. And she would probably be right.

Tom dreams, of course; he's dreaming right now. But he will remember none of it. It's too bad. He'd like it, at least the first part. He misses his childhood home, and right now he's standing in the backyard, watching his childhood self across the span of two decades. The fence is not white picket, but chain link. The grass is light green and shaggy—it's time to cut it again, but Tom isn't quite old enough, and his mother has to hire a neighbor boy this year. There are dandelions everywhere and Child Tom knows their secrets. He knows if you rub one against your face and it leaves a yellow mark, it means you like butter, and he knows that you can blow on dandelion seeds and make a wish, and if you catch one of the seeds, the wish will come true. Tom the watchful adult knows nothing about wishes, or about the way yellow feels against your face, and he is only beginning to understand what his childhood self is doing. He is beginning to remember:

Tommy Johnson spends a better part of a year patrolling, stalking the neighbor's dog, who stalks him in return. The superhero and his arch nemesis eye each other as they pace back and forth on either side of the fence. The dog issues a challenge, the TomCat responds with a witty retort. Where will it end? Who will win? The TomCat, eventually, of course, because that is the way of these things. Good triumphs. This is why we have superheroes, after all—otherwise what would the world be like?

Tommy knows things now. You do a lot of thinking when you are out in the backyard waiting for evil. His father felt like Tommy; he was a champion of good. He went off every day looking so important in his blue uniform and Tom's mom said he was making the world safer. Then one day, something happened. At first, Tommy thought he was really gone. How silly, how silly of him—his father is strong and brave and keeps the world safe—how could he be gone?

He staged it. He is a genius. He is in hiding. Tommy should have known. Because Tommy's dad is a superhero too. And soon, he will come out of hiding and he will see that his son has inherited his superpowers and they will be a team, father and son. (Will he have to change his name? He doesn't know what his dad's superhero identity is, and he'd hate to become the TomKitten.) They will keep the world always balanced toward good. They will help the helpless, protect the people, fight fear, conquer evil.

But for now, Tommy must wait. His dad is still in hiding and he can only play at his destiny, puffing out his chest, hands on hips, cape fluttering in the breeze, trying to anticipate the corgi's next movements—

Child Tom plays happily on, while memory turns back to dream. There's a shadow falling over the house, Adult Tom can see it, can taste it, but Child Tom does not notice—he thinks he's a superhero, protector of the galaxy, defender of the innocent, champion of the good—

Adult Tom opens his mouth, tries to say something, to warn him about the shadow, but the words don't come out. And then everything changes, and Little Tom is no longer alone. He's playing with Greta Woodrow, her orange hair in braids, she's leaping and giggling with him. They take turns rescuing each other, completely oblivious to the danger that approaches. And then the scene freezes, both Child Tom and Greta are perfectly still, eyes wide, mouths open slightly, like a photograph, a still moment caught in time. Tom can't move either, they are all frozen, but the shadow still encroaches. And suddenly, the shadow thins out, takes shape and meaning—a head, arms, torso— and it swallows Greta Woodrow, and then she is gone, all gone, and Tom is alone.

It's nine A.M. the next morning.

Justin is in on the bathroom floor doing push-ups. He hasn't done any in years; he's been so neglectful. He's a father, it's his job to be strong. How else will James be able to tell other kids on the playground, "My dad can beat up your dad"? How else will Justin be able to defend his children? How else will Justin be able to murder a clown?

But it's going well—surprisingly well. He's good at this. Better than he remembered. He was never an athlete, but now, but now! Look at him go! He could go on like this forever! He's a push-up master. He could enter competitions, destroy worlds. He is going and going and going and going and going. Justin barely notices his wife and his daughter standing in the doorway. He glances up to see Greta's face all scrunched up and Hannah with her hand over her mouth. She might be thinking that he looks very strong, yes, indeed she might be thinking that. She might be thinking that he is ready, now, ready to go defend the family, ready to win back his son. She might be thinking that she can hear his heart, that nothing should ever beat so fast, that he is a medical miracle. She might be thinking any number of things. And Greta—"Greta! Greta!" he says, "Come on, Greta, get on Papa's back! Come on! It'll be fun!" Greta doesn't move, but soon Justin can barely see her. The longer he goes, the less he can see; he can only see what's straight ahead.

· · ·

Tom has nothing to do. Nothing. There are no new leads. No information. Nothing. The phone and doorbell are fairly quiet—it's ten A.M. on a Sunday, two days after the disappearance of James, and early, yet, for the calls—so he can't even do his secretarial duties. He has papers, which he can continue to shuffle if he must. He can pace around the house, but from the sound of things on the ceiling above him Justin Woodrow is already doing that. He can read the back of his antacid bottle. He can go to the window and stare ominously at the media vans for a while, but he's already done that this morning. He can call Detective Blair and beg to be relieved, he can call and ask for every detail of the investigation so far from the arch of an eyebrow to the inflection of a word, but he has already asked too many times.

He didn't sleep well. There's something nudging at his brain, a strange sensation, a footprint with no owner. Was it a dream? Impossible, Tom doesn't dream. A memory? A wish? One thing is clear: Tom has too much time on his hands.

He already talked to Carlos earlier on Carlos's way into the station. Last Christmas, Tom got him one of those little headpieces you can plug into your cell phone so you can talk on the phone and still keep both hands on the wheel. Nina was very grateful. Next Christmas, he might help Carlos get the thing sewn to his head. Carlos said Nina felt the baby kick for the first time yesterday—which must be quite something—and Tom would like to call Nina and go over and sit there with his hand on her belly until Tom Jr. kicks again. (Carlos might not like that though—when the baby kicked, he was at the volunteer HQ doing surreptitious background checks on the people there, and he wants to be the one with his hand constantly monitoring his wife's body parts.)

Tom has no chance of being the partner who is killed today, at least it's very unlikely. And he is definitely not the hero today—or if he is, this is an extremely boring cop movie. There's nothing for him to do here; there's a missing child and Tom is sitting on his butt.

He reads today's article on the case again. The Woodrows haven't seen it, and Tom doesn't want them to. Most of it just runs over the details, but the reporter managed to turn up some audience member to give a quote; "I can't believe they didn't go backstage right after the act. I mean if our son didn't come back right away we'd go looking, we wouldn't wait until the show was over."

This always happens, something happens to a kid and there's always someone out there who wants to go on record blaming the parents. Tom supposes it's comforting for them; if you say the Woodrows are bad parents, then it's their fault, there's someone to blame—and then what happened to James can't possibly happen to your kid because you are an excellent parent. Your kid is safe.

Tom finishes the article and sighs. There's nothing new, now, the eighth time through the newspaper story. He pops an antacid and flips through the files. There must be something someone hasn't seen. He looks through the sheaf of this morning's faxes. At least he can color code the interviews—he does that sometimes; he has a system down, it helps him find things, though Carlos makes fun of him for it. Anyway, he can do that, that'll be something—

Tom goes to the playroom door and clears his throat.

Greta Woodrow is sitting at the little maple table, chomping her lip and slowly forming letters on a big sheet of drawing paper. The room is chaos. Brightly colored kids' books are scattered everywhere. Playing cards are spread out on the floor. A pile of building blocks has overtaken one corner. Big sheets of paper with marker drawings cover just about every inch of floor.

She hasn't noticed him. "Greta?" he says. She looks up. "Um," he shifts, "can I borrow some of your markers?"

Greta looks at him. "You gonna color?"

"Um, well, I'm trying to do some work, and—"

"Me too," she says, nodding earnestly. Everything about her is earnest, she is dressed earnestly, she is sitting earnestly. Are all children like this? Tom has no idea. And despite the brightly colored child's chaos around her, the room filled with toys, the bright purple shirt and green pants, there is nothing colorful about Greta Woodrow right now, she seems the grayest little girl in the world.

He takes a step into the room. "Oh, you are?"

"I'm writing down stuff James likes and stuff. I'm making him a book. So he doesn't forget when he comes back."

Tom moves a little closer. "You are? That's nice." He looks at what she's working on. There's a little stick figure standing next to a huge red bowl with purple and orange squiggly things in it and a big black stick sticking out. Greta is adding more squiggles. There's a caption that reads, "JAMES LIKES SEREEOL."

"Yeah," she says, "it's hard though. Sometimes I don't spell so good."

Tom blinks. He has no idea he is going to say this until after it has been said. "Do you want help?"

At the words, Greta Woodrow transforms, she beams, her smile takes up her whole body, her freckles shine. "Okay!" And something inside Tom softly shifts, and he smiles a little too. He puts his arm around Greta's chair.

"Okay, listen," he says, "I can help for a little while. But I have to answer the phone when it rings, okay?"

"Okay!" Greta nods.

Tom pulls up a chair and sits down, his legs sprawling over to either side of the table. "Now, what can I help you with?"

A half hour later, Tom has taught Greta how to spell "puppy" and "otter" and "macaroni," and it strikes him that she will remember now; she will spell those words right for the rest of her life. That's something. She's given some of the drawing over to him; she wants him to fill in the details, but she, only she, draws James. He's currently working on a peanut butter sandwich, with the fixings in the background, when the phone rings.

Tom bursts out of his chair, practically knocking over the table. He brushes off his pants and straightens his shirt. And then he notices how alarmed Greta looks, and he forgets about his clothing and straightens up the table and whispers, "I'll be right back," to her.

It's Catherine Bennett on the phone, Hannah's younger sister. She lives twenty minutes away and sees the Woodrows only occasionally, but always comes with presents for the children. She is thirty-four, works in advertising, and lives with a real estate lawyer named Greg Miller who she's known for three years. She doesn't seem particularly close to her sister, but is not considered a suspect.

"Officer Johnson?" she says. "Good, um, Detective Blair isn't answering his phone. I have to talk to you . . ."

Everything in Tom goes on alert. "What?"

"Well," she says. There's a moment, and then she asks carefully, "Isn't Michael Simmons in jail?"

Tom stops still. "Ms. Bennett, why do you ask?"

"Someone followed me today . . ."

Tom sits down, gets out a pad, and poises himself. "Tell me everything—"

Catherine Bennett is in the gro-
cery store standing dumbly between the oranges and lemons. She's
doing this for her sister—not the standing dumbly, but the whole
grocery store thing. It is her pathetic way of trying to make things
better.

It should be noted that Catherine has a complicated relationship
with her older sister. The sisters never were great friends; each girl
seemed to respond to the tension in their childhood house by seques-
tering herself. So they evolved separately and live separately now
(though Catherine thinks Hannah has changed since Justin came into
her life; she's become much softer around the edges).

But all of this heavily weighted past falls away when something
terrible happens to your sister. When her son goes missing, it doesn't
matter whether or not she let you play in her reindeer games when
you were young. The world alters, and you realize that perhaps you
could have done more, that life is short, that family is family, and that,
no matter what, you love your sister very much, because she is your
sister, and that is as good a reason as any.

And you want so desperately to help, and you want it all to be
better, and you don't have any words, and you don't have a magic
wand (and your sister refuses to believe that it's okay to experience
emotion in front of other people) so, with guilt and grief and helplessness you do the only thing you can do for your sister. You buy her
food.

But now, as Catherine stands dumbly between the oranges and the lemons, she realizes that she made a terrible mistake. Grocery shopping requires a certain level of emotional stability that she just does not have right now. Other people are squeezing produce around her, consulting lists, obeying/ignoring whims, making decisions about nightly meals, considering food pyramids and recommended daily allowances, and Catherine is just standing, holding a half-filled basket limply in her hand. Mist sprays over leafy vegetables, bananas ripen, shopping carts roll along, and Catherine cannot move.

She thinks she might collapse right there, dissolve into the shiny floor among the shopping cart skids—what happens to people who cry in supermarkets? Do people stop to comfort you, or do they look the other way, scurrying their children along? Does a pimply stock boy politely ask you to leave because you are frightening the normal people?

There are pictures of James in the grocery store. Catherine couldn't believe it when she saw them, little "Missing Boy" posters all over the front wall and in the parking lot. She'd heard vague talk of volunteers—did they do this? She can help, too, that's something, she can call the number and hang up signs and do whatever she has to do. She could come back to Hannah with all the reports of the countless people lining up to help, and maybe then Hannah would understand—if only Catherine could move from her spot in the produce section.

James is everywhere. She can feel it. The story is all over the newspaper and the television, the air hums with talk of it: *Did you hear about the little boy? Isn't it awful? I can't believe this could happen here. Is there any word? Do they know who did it? Are there any leads?* Everyone around her in the produce section knows and has been touched by the story; she can tell by the way they eye strangers and keep their children close.

Catherine herself is quoted in the newspaper—James's aunt, area resident Catherine Bennett, making a plea for her beloved nephew's safe return—"What would you like to say to the kidnappers?" the reporter asked in a voice dripping with sympathy. And Catherine could not tell him to fuck off, that wouldn't be appropriate, so she said something cliched and inane that will do nothing to save James, but it's too late, and all she can do is try to buy Hannah food.

This is ridiculous, she could be here in the produce section for the rest of her life; she could age and die here amid the oranges and the lemons and the Muzak and it's doing no one any good. Catherine grips her basket a little tighter and mutters, "Come on, Cath," aware the whole time that she is now a woman who talks to herself in the supermarket.

And then—BAM!—one of the carts runs into her. It catches Catherine off-balance and she stumbles back and nearly lands in the oranges.

"Oh, ma'am, I'm so sorry!"

It's a man. She should have been able to tell by the projectile shopping cart, which is filled with frozen pizza and endless boxes of cereal. She regains her balance and smiles reasonably politely, which is the best she can do given that her hip is throbbing. "No problem," she says, in a way that shows it really is.

"No, really," he says. The man is extremely tall and extremely thin, and Catherine has to turn her head up so she's not staring into his rib cage. His eyes are brown and nondescript. His face is long and rough. "I just wasn't watching where I was going."

"You must have been driving that thing awfully hard," Catherine says dryly.

"Don't tell, they might revoke my license," the man says, smiling gently. He is so soft-spoken Catherine can barely hear him. It's the only thing that keeps her from finding this whole thing creepy—the voice is so harmless.

Sometimes men flirt with Catherine in strange places. It's something about her—her short stature, her round face—that makes her look accessible somehow. And she has no ring, of course. She has a theory that these features make her attractive to divorcés, who think she looks like a nicer person than their first wives. Catherine, though, is not in the mood to be flirted with, even if it weren't in a vaguely weird way. So she smiles politely and dismissively, like you do to crazy people or native speakers in foreign countries, and moves away.

She goes through aisles picking things off shelves. Granola bars. Soup. Peanut Butter. Pasta. Sauce. Coffee. Yogurt. Eggs. Cheese. Bread. Juice. She has no idea what they need. She gets bagels from the bakery and premade dinners from the deli; she has to change her basket for a shopping cart to fit it all in, and it still doesn't help her feel any less inadequate.

But she's made it through without dissolving, and she might even be able to check out and drive to Hannah's without causing any seven-car pileups if she keep focusing on her breathing like this, and that is something at least. Catherine gets in line. The woman in front of her is sorting out coupons for her cartload of canned food and Catherine digs her heels in for the long haul. Her hip still aches.

There is a soft voice behind her. "Hi again."

She turns. The man from Produce is there, in line, with all his bachelor food. She had forgotten all about him. He has a massive scar right below his left eye, she wrote a paper in college on how scars in fictional characters are always used to signal some inner deformity; the external scar is the only way we can safely identify malevolent intent. It is fiction's way of comforting us, assuring us we can read a person's external features and discover all we need to know about the internal. But that is in books, not in grocery stores.

"Hi," she mumbles noncommittally. She is about to turn back, but her eye lands on the newspaper in his hands. And there is James, staring right back at her.

"Sad, huh?" The man nods toward the picture.

She swallows and composes herself. "Very."

"Cute kid."

"Yes." How many coupons does this woman have?

"Have you been following this story?"

Catherine shifts. "I guess so."

"So, what do you think happened?" he said.

Catherine decides she was right about the scar. She could just leave her cart right there and run off. She could do that, but then she wouldn't have any offerings for Hannah at all. What kind of man would turn a boy's disappearance into fodder for conversation?

She bites her lip. "I really don't know."

"You think the clown did it, don't you? That's what everyone's saying."

This isn't what Catherine was expecting to hear. She straightens abruptly. She is no longer having a casual conversation; she looks him straight in the eyes, she cranes her neck up, and says very slowly, "Everyone who?"

"Well . . ." he shifts slightly. "You know. People. What if he didn't do it? What if he's just as surprised as anyone? Maybe they're looking at the wrong guy. Maybe nobody took the kid . . . isn't it possible that this is nobody's fault?"

It's extremely clear to Catherine at this moment that none of this is an accident. She should have known from the beginning. This is the grocery store equivalent of a crank call. It happens; people are freaks. Someone knows who she is from the newspaper and is following her. She turns around, head high, and stares directly ahead. I will not be harassed. Not today. On another day I would tell you that you are pond scum, I would give you several pieces of my mind because that is who I am and what I do. Today I wish you away.

And it works, for a moment; he is quiet. And then, is that a hand on her shoulder? Is he touching her? She whirls around, but he is backing away.

"I'm sorry," he says. "I'm so sorry." He shakes his head and wheels his cart away.

And only then does it occur to Catherine who he might be—

Justin is standing on the stairwell,

listening to Tom talk on the phone. He is still, absolutely still, a predator in the bushes. Tom's words come wafting up to him: *It sounds like him . . . No, we didn't have enough evidence . . . We had to let him out . . . He's being followed constantly . . .*

A trickle of sweat forms at Justin's hairline. It falls down the side of his head, past his temple, onto his cheek, and then it slithers down his face and falls off his jaw. Some combination of blood and bile is swelling up inside him, and he feels like he's made of fierce red and sickly yellow. He knows, now: the clown is free.

The cop hangs up, and Justin springs down the stairs and lands, in a single bound, in front of the couch. "Why didn't you tell me?" He's staring at the cop, staring him down; the cop might be muscular, but Justin can do push-ups without end, and he is in a fury, superpowered by blood and bile.

Tom stares right back. "Tell you what?"

"Why didn't you tell me they let the clown out of jail?" Justin speaks very slowly and clearly. "When was he out?"

Tom sighs heavily. "Yesterday. We didn't have enough evidence to hold him. Now, Mr. Woodrow—"

Justin turns. "I have to go."

"Mr. Woodrow!" Tom stands up. "Where're you going?"

Justin might as well tell him. He'll find out soon enough. "I'm going to go kill him."

"Mr. Woodrow!" Tom is behind Justin, Tom's hand lands on his shoulder. "I can't have you doing that. I understand your urge, but killing Mr. Simmons won't bring your son back."

Justin turns. He is toe to toe with Tom, and he stares pointedly down into his face. "How do you know?"

Tom is caught off guard a moment, but soon recovers. "Because that's just not how it works. Mr. Woodrow, I can't have you taking the law into your own hands, and I can't let you leave this house right now. Come back with me and sit down."

Justin finds himself being steered by Tom back to the couch. The bile settles, the fury sits down; he can't get out now, that's clear, it's okay, he can wait, he can wait.

"Listen, Justin. We're using every available resource, we really are. You have the police force of the metro area at your disposal. Every department in the state has officers looking for James. We're tailing the clown all the time. If he has James, he'll go to him eventually. We have his phone tapped. We're taking care of this."

Justin doesn't say anything. Tom's tone changes. He sits down across from Justin and leans in, "You must understand that interfering with our investigation in any way will seriously hamper our efforts. It won't help, it will only hurt. And if you do hamper us, I'll arrest you without hesitation. Is that clear?"

Justin nods. Sure, sure. He'll get out somehow. This little cop can't watch him every minute, can he?

An hour later, Tom is back on the phone with Detective Blair discussing Catherine's grocery store encounter. He had to wait until he was sure Justin Woodrow was calm—at least calmer. He can imagine what simmers inside Justin, of course—Tom would be the same way; this isn't time for rational thought. What would his mom have done if someone had taken him—she probably would have tried to rip out the guy's throat if she thought it would bring Tommy back to her.

But of course it wouldn't, it doesn't work like that, and Justin just needed to be calmed down. Tom had to talk him out of it, reason with him. No one can do this job better than the police, it's their job to do, and when he calmed down, Justin would realize that, and he could just go back to pacing and let the professionals try to get James back.

Not that they're doing a great job.

"Goddammit, aren't there guys on his tail?" he asks into the phone. "How could they let him near the aunt? Who the fuck is on him and can you get someone whose head isn't up his—"

"Tommy," Detective Blair says. "Come on now, you know they're not going to approach him unless they absolutely have to. We want to find the kid."

Something's bugging Tom, and he can't quite put his finger on it, but there's something very wrong here, he can feel it. There's something encroaching—

"I just—I don't like the idea of him harassing the family. He's done enough."

"Tommy, we don't even know for sure the guy's guilty—"

"Well, of course he's guilty. Who do you think took him, the fucking tooth fairy? Oh God," he stops. Greta Woodrow is standing in front of him. "Hold on—"

Greta is looking at him accusatorily. "You're not supposed to swear," she scolds. "Mom doesn't like it."

He puts his hand over the mouthpiece. "Greta, I'm very sorry." What did he say? God, he could have said anything and she would have heard. He's got to watch himself. Dammit.

She relaxes. "Aren't you coming back?" she asks impatiently. "I don't know how to spell 'sandwich.'"

Tom leans in and whispers, "Give me some time, okay? I've just got to do some more things, and then I'll come help you." He has a strange urge to put his hand out and muss up her hair, which he controls. He wishes he could tell her he's sure her brother is coming back soon, that he's working on bringing him back, but really he is doing as much good in the playroom as he is doing at his post on the couch.

"Okay. Hurry," she sighs, "we've got lots of work to do."

She disappears then, and Tom puts the phone back to his ear.

"What was that all about?" Detective Blair says.

"Nothing," Tom says. "What was I saying?"

They talk for another fifteen minutes, then Tom calls Carlos to yell some more. Carlos is much more sympathetic. The phone has started ringing again—more cranks, more media, more family and friends. Tom makes the best excuses he can to Justin's mother; he can't quite explain that her son can't come to the phone because he's recovering from a murderous rage. She would be on the next plane, she says, but her health—but she's about to come anyway and are they going to find her grandson? She asks one thousand questions that require one thousand answers; what she doesn't know, and what Tom doesn't know, is that her son is standing right at the staircase, listening, waiting. Justin can't get out yet, but he will. He knows that. He just has to wait.

And he finds his chance, the next morning, when Tom is just like this, talking to Carlos, who finally got to feel his baby kick, while Justin creeps down the stairs behind Tom, into the kitchen, and out the back door.

The address was in the phone

book. Of course it was, of course Mike the Clown is local and of course he has a listed address. Because it's fate. Justin doesn't even consider that it might be a different Michael Simmons on Emerson Avenue South; if it were a different one, Justin couldn't go beat the life out of him and get James back. And that's just not how the story works.

His dad would be so proud. Finally, Justin is a man of action.

He did such a good job creeping down the stairs and out of the house. Nobody even knows he's gone—Hannah is still fast asleep, Greta is busying herself with something or other, and the cop—his dramatic foil—was too engaged on the phone. He knew it would happen sooner or later; he just had to wait. He was going to do it at night but Tom put another cop in the house, as if he didn't trust Justin or something.

He'll have to be careful at the clown's. There are policemen watching Mike, and they probably won't like Justin beating him into a pulp. But a father's got to do what a father's got to do.

Justin finds himself feeling strangely calm as he drives to Mike's apartment building. This could be it. This could bring James back. His plan is simple: threaten Mike, beat him up until he brings James back, and then kill him so he can never do this to another family again. Justin has not brought any weapons with him, he is strictly against guns, and anyway he thinks that under these circumstances it would be better to use his own bare hands.

He will probably go to jail. The jury will be light on him; his lawyer will make sure the jury is made up of parents. They will understand. They know this could have been their kid; they would have done the exact same thing, they know Justin has done the world a great service. And it is worth time in jail to get James back—it is worth every last bit of time that there is. Getting James back is worth anything.

Justin parks a block away from Mike's apartment. He gets out of the car and purposefully walks to the building. He notices a blue sedan with two men in it parked across the street. He tries not to draw attention to himself. *I am just an ordinary man*, he telegraphs, *not a man on a mission*. Is he being followed himself? Will he be stopped? They won't stop him, they don't want to blow their tail, and anyway, this is fate.

The building has a secured entrance, but someone is walking out just as Justin approaches. Ah, Justin thinks, the world is with him. Apartment 42. How calm he is! Justin hasn't ever felt this calm. He could jump off cliffs, out of airplanes, solve pi for millions of digits, compose a sonnet, make the sound of one hand clapping. He could do it all without blinking an eye. Everything is clear to him now, so clear.

He's in front of the metallic blue door. The morning paper is still there. Good. The clown's not even up yet.

Knock, knock.

Nothing.

But he's home. Justin knows he's home, he can feel it.

Knock. Knock. Knock.

A pause, and then, "Yeah?"

And then—oh!—here's where Justin's nerves get to him a little—he hasn't really thought this part through. He's never beaten anyone up before, though he did teach his students stage combat one year. He has three seconds to come up with a plan, but he can do it, he can do it. "Mike?"

"Yeah?"

And then, just as Mike starts to open the door, Justin kicks it. This proves to be a good idea. The door slams into Mike, and Mike stumbles backward. Justin rushes in, grabs him by the collar, kicks in Mike's feet, and pushes him with all his strength. Mike topples down on the floor, sprawled flat. Justin takes three steps and kicks him in the face. Then he kicks him again. He places his foot on Mike's throat. This is all going very well.

Mike is sputtering between spits of blood. What comes out is something like, "What the HELL!"

"Bring my son back!" Justin says this fairly calmly.

"Get off me, man!" Mike keeps spitting and spitting, so blood is getting all over his face and on the floor. Justin has never seen so much blood in real life; it's so much drippier than it is on television. Justin loses the ability to solve for pi, but he can say this:

"Bring my son back. If you don't tell me how to bring him back, I will kill you." Yes, that's right. That's good. The clown is pressing himself against the floor, panting and bleeding and spitting and sputtering. Justin kicks again. He's never kicked someone before—it's surprisingly effective, even when you are losing feeling in your legs. He kicks again.

"Are you . . . fucking . . . insane?" Mike yells.

"Possibly," Justin says, this is like what they would say in the movies, all cool and collected and saucy-like. Only in the movies they do not pant, and Justin seems to be panting, and maybe shaking a little, and they certainly don't do that. Wasn't he calm? Just a moment ago, wasn't he calm?

"Man, *(cough)* come on, *(spit)* get off me!" Mike tries to catch his breath. "Just . . . get off me . . . and we'll talk, okay?"

Justin looks down at Mike, who is becoming blurry. "I want my son back." He can feel sweat and tears running down his face. When did that happen? His heart is about to explode. His control is gone. It isn't really supposed to happen like this.

"Okay," Mike says, in a just-hand-over-the-gun kind of way. He raises his head the tiniest possible bit. "Okay, listen. You've—you've got to believe me. I don't—I don't know how to bring him back."

"Then why'd you fucking do it?" Justin is trembling now. Just keep your foot on the throat, he tells himself. That's all you have to do. And don't pass out, you have to do that too.

"I didn't, you've got to believe me. I don't know how to...do something like that. I have no idea how. Please."

"What the hell do you mean?" Justin yells. "You expect me to believe it was an *accident*?" Breathe, Justin. In and out. Like that.

"It just happened. I didn't do it, I didn't. I'd bring him back *(cough, spit)* if I could. I don't know how it happened, please you've got to believe me."

Justin can't help it. His leg relaxes and then the clown is up, snap, like that. He is oozing blood all over his bathrobe. He doesn't spring at Justin, he just stands there, slightly crouched, hands to the sides, like he's talking a person from jumping off a very high building, and says, "Okay? Okay?"

Justin's knees give way, then he falls to the ground. And then he vomits, and vomits some more, he is vomiting every last bit of moisture in his body, he vomits up what can only be parts of his insides. And then Mike the Clown does something extraordinary, something Justin wholly did not expect. While Justin is vomiting pieces of his body, Michael Simmons kneels down next to him and puts his arms on Justin's back. He says, "I'm sorry, I'm sorry," he says it again and again while he bleeds all over Justin, and Justin vomits out everything.

"Pick a card, any card. Don't show me what you've picked."

Greta has spread some cards in front of her. Otter stares at the deck, unable to decide. When he does, Greta will take the card, put it back in the deck, shuffle the deck, and then magically pick Otter's card from the middle. Otter will be duly impressed.

It's really not magic though.

Greta knows; she has been reading. Mom and Dad don't know it; she reads in secret. She's reading about magic. She has a book she got for Christmas last year from Gramma Woodrow. She's going to have to get more books though, because this one doesn't mention how to bring someone back when they disappear. Probably because the book is for kids, and kids probably shouldn't know how to make people disappear because they'd probably do it when they weren't supposed to. Some of Greta's friends would want to make their little brothers disappear, but not Greta. Anyway the book doesn't need to show how to make someone disappear, just how to bring them back. That would be okay for kids.

But it doesn't. The book just shows magic tricks with coins and cards and paper clips and stuff. And handkerchiefs, which the book tells her to borrow from her dad, but her dad doesn't have anything like that as far as Greta can tell. The funny thing about all these tricks is they are just tricks; there's always a secret to them and there's no magic at all. It's just about fooling people and lying. Why is everything for kids so dumb?

Greta needs some more grown-up books, that is all. Books with real magic in them. She can read them, she bets. It's not so hard, and she's a good reader, that's what Mrs. Olson says, even though she's not very good at sitting quietly in class and speaking only when she is called on. She can't tell her parents to get the books for her, because she doesn't want to get their hopes up, but she can maybe order the books off the Internet.

In the book she has, there are tricks in which you think something disappears, but actually it doesn't. You just hide the thing in your sleeve or your hand or under the cup or in the handkerchief. But none of those things would fit James anyway; he's a boy, not a coin, and couldn't go up anybody's sleeve. And anyway, James isn't being hidden somewhere, he disappeared, even Greta could see that.

Lots of times when there's a mystery, there's a clue, too, and it's up to the girl to figure it out, because adults just don't.

So she works on figuring out where James went and making sure everything's nice for him when he comes back. So she makes her drawings—her book is growing quite big, it has ten pages now! Tom's good at drawing. But lots of times he can't help because he has to sit on the company sofa, and he's always answering the phone! That's okay. It's nice that he helps when he can. He's been on the phone all morning. Mom's asleep and Dad went out, so Greta has to wait for Tom to get off the phone if she has any spelling questions.

When she's in school and she has a question, and she has a lot of questions, they're always telling her to go look it up. This is stupid because the teacher is supposed to know everything because she's a teacher, and she should answer Greta's questions about stuff, because it would save a lot of time. Mrs. Olson says that she's trying to teach Greta how to do things for herself, but Greta already does plenty for herself; she knows how to use a library because they have shown her a million times. Sometimes she wants to know things, like how come there are clouds, and why feet smell, and how gum works, stuff like that. She has a feeling her teacher wouldn't like it very much if Greta asked where people go when they disappear, because Jon Weinstein asks questions like that all the time and she just looks out the window. Anyway, Mrs. Olson doesn't have very much imagination.

So this time Greta is doing research and they would be very proud of her for it and she can tell Mrs. Olson she did this all by herself.

Greta read a story once where a girl had a magic fairy watching over her. The girl didn't know she had a magic fairy, but whenever anything bad happened, like a dog was going to bite her or she was going to spill some very hot soup, the fairy stopped her and so the girl always came out okay. A lot of bad things almost happened to this girl, her name was Marie. Anyway, the girl was always drawing pictures and it turned out the fairy was talking to the girl through the pictures, though it took the girl a super long time to figure it out. It turned out at the end that the fairy was actually the girl's mom, who had died when the girl was just a baby. Marie kept drawing pictures of moms and it turned out one of the pictures looked just like her mom, who she had never met, and that's how they knew. It was a sad story, but kind of happy too.

Greta thinks maybe James will talk to her through her drawings. It's worth a try at least. He always likes to watch her draw. She would draw him pictures and tell him stories and stuff, while he played with the blocks.

Yesterday she drew a picture of a man in a funny hat. Her dad looked at it and said, "It's a clown..." Her mom looked at it and said, "It's a magician..." They were both half right.

She draws a lot of pictures of her brother, but her mom and dad don't know who it is, though they keep guessing. But of course it's James; why don't they remember what he looks like?

"Greta?"

Oh, that's Tom in the playroom door. She can call him Tom even though he's a grown-up. He's a police officer, and you can trust them; they help kids. Girls can be policemen too, and airplane pilots, and President.

"Hi!" she says. "You ready to color?"

"Um, maybe in a bit. Have you seen your father?" His face is all tight and scrunched, like he's worried or thinking too hard or something hurts.

"Daddy? He left."

"He did?"

"Yeah. I saw him go."

"Oh, f— oh, okay. Um, listen, Greta, I have to make a phone call, but then I'll come sit with you."

"Okay! You're a good colorer."

"Thank you." He smiles a little. "And um . . . how long ago did your dad go out?"

Greta shrugs.

"Okay, okay. Thanks, Greta."

And he disappears. She hopes he comes back soon.

Hannah has been asleep for three days. She gets up occasionally . . . to check on Greta, to get a glass of water, to take another pill. In every dream she's looking for James and then she finds him. Sometimes she's just coming home from work and he's there, waiting for her in the kitchen, rosy, healthy, and whole. She kisses him on the cheek, he puts his arms around her. She wishes she could pick him up, she'd lift him to the sky, carry him everywhere, but he's too big now; he has to stay earthbound. Justin has dinner ready—chicken for them, hot dogs for the children, peas for everyone. Greta does most of the talking, and James concentrates on his eating. The hot dogs are already in little pieces, but James likes to saw at them even more with his child's knife. His brow wrinkles, his tongue slips out of his mouth just a little, and he works away at the pieces. He bunches them all up in a pile on the right side of the plate. He likes to squeeze out the ketchup himself; he turns the bottle upside down with both hands and clenches with all his might, he squeezes his whole face tight, his eyes shut, and he just sits there waiting until the ketchup oozes out. It's a great act of faith for him, if he tries hard enough, if he waits long enough—eyes closed, arms steady—the ketchup will come.

Suddenly, it's almost bedtime. Justin and Hannah bathe him and Greta, like they do every night. Justin likes to use this time to acquaint the children with Shakespeare, he's taught Greta to yell, *ONCE MORE UNTO THE BREACH, DEAR FRIENDS* every time she gets into the bath. This causes James to burst out into giggles, every time—tonight he squeals with delight and Greta squeals too. Justin sits on the edge of the bath while Hannah fills a bucket in the sink. James especially likes the bubbles; he likes to build sculptures with them and then bat them at his sister, who giggles madly. By this point, Justin is sopping wet. He scrubs the children, and Hannah pours the bucket of water over their heads. Soap is too slippery for James's taste; he wiggles when it gets on his skin. Hannah refills the bucket again, and Justin washes James's hair. Greta puts the shampoo in herself, she scrubs her head and piles the hair high in a sudsy pompadour. Hannah rinses them both, and Greta springs out of the tub and out of the bathroom. Justin chases her while Hannah helps James out of the tub. She wraps him in a big towel and dries him off.

Soon, it's bedtime. Tonight Justin reads to Greta and Hannah has James. She picks out a book about a baby dragon who is best friends with a boy named James. He gurgles while she reads, and he's asleep before the book is done. Hannah puts the book down and sits, looking at her boy, she looks at his chest rise up, at his eyelids fluttering, and she's filled with a tremendous warmth. Hannah is light, she is life, she lies down next to her son and cuddles him. It's just a day, an ordinary day, a perfect, magical, ordinary day—this is enough, just this—

Hannah wakes up with the smell and feel of her son still on her, a warmth in her arms and against her belly. She squeezes her eyes shut and holds the feeling close, she lies there, not moving, for fear something will startle this phantom away.

And something is coming. Police sirens are approaching the house. They get louder, and then they stop, right in front of Hannah's eardrums. Hannah bursts out of bed and looks out of the window. A police car has pulled up. Policemen get out of either side of the car, slamming the doors behind them at precisely the same time. They stalk to the rear door and poise at the ready. The one closest to Hannah opens the door and leads a man out. They take him by either arm, lead him up the walk, and knock on the front door. The man in between them looks quite a bit like Hannah's husband, except he's incredibly pale, and his shirt and pants are covered in blood—

Hannah gasps and runs down the stairs—*Justin? Justin?*

Hannah and Justin sit side by side

on the couch. Hannah is clenching Justin's hand so hard both of their fingers are white. Justin reeks of blood and vomit—the smell of vomit usually makes Hannah want to vomit too, but now all she knows is that she should be holding on to her husband's hand as tight as she can. Her eyes are shut, clenched with the intensity of prayer, so she does not see Tom pacing back and forth in front of the couch as he sputters to her husband, who is shaking and silent.

"I told you not to do that, I told you," he says. "I didn't want to call the police on you—do you think I wanted to do that? Those are officers that could be out looking for James and I have to send them after you, because you decide to take the law into your own hands. Dammit. Goddammit. What the hell were you thinking? It's a crime. He could press charges. I can't believe he's not going to press charges. I would press charges. What does this do for our case now? What the hell does this do? Jesus. Dammit. I'd like to press charges myself. We're the police you know. We know what we're doing, but instead of letting us do our job you have to go charging off. What were you thinking? Are you crazy, is that it? You think this is some sort of movie where you can solve the goddamn case by killing the principal suspect your own goddamn self? What in the hell were you thinking? He probably knows he's being followed now—"

"He didn't do anything," Justin mumbles.

"What?" Tom stops. He's breathing heavily.

183

"He didn't do anything," he repeats. Hannah opens her eyes.

Tom sighs heavily. "I see. I see. Is *that* what you think now, in your professional opinion?"

"Nobody did it," Justin says quietly. "It was an accident."

Hannah freezes. Tom stares at Justin. He seems about to speak and then stops. He blows air out of his mouth. He shakes his head. He disengages from his ranting posture and lifts his hands in the air. "Okay. Okay. I'm done now. But if I ever catch you doing something like that again, I'll punch you my own damn self, do you hear me?"

Justin nods slowly. He has not stopped looking at the ground since he sat down. Pieces of Hannah are breaking apart, but that doesn't matter; it's her husband she needs to put back together again.

Hannah looks at Tom. "Is that all?" she asks softly.

"Yeah," he nods at her. "That's it."

Justin isn't moving, so Hannah stands up and reaches out her arm to him. "Justin? Honey? Come on. Come on, sweetheart, come on, honey, let's clean you up."

Downstairs, Tom is pacing. He's

still trying to calm himself down. He's such a fucking idiot. How could he let his guard down like that? He just assumed it would be okay, that Justin Woodrow had calmed down—it just never occurred to Tom that Justin would really, truly do this. How could Justin Woodrow not have seen reason? How could he not have understood that he was just hurting the investigation? Did Tom not make that perfectly clear?

Who does he think he is, some kind of superhero?

He forgets that people are irrational. He forgets that people do not always make decisions based on what is best, that emotions get in the way. This is why there are police; this is why there are laws.

He should have known that a man who is too crazed to call his elderly mother back during a time like this is not thinking right.

And what would have happened if Greta had seen her father like that? After he got off the phone with Detective Blair telling him to get the guys into Simmons's apartment *now*, Tom convinced Greta it would be an excellent time for a nap—he was thinking of taking one himself, he said, and then maybe later he could help her out. And her otter—it's an otter, not a sea weasel he knows now—was looking pretty sleepy too. And it worked, she said it sounded like an excellent idea and Otter was certainly due for a little break, and Tom can't believe it, but maybe being a parent isn't that hard, especially if the kid is as good as Greta Woodrow. Acting in loco parentis was not part of the job description, but the parents have gone loco and Tom is doing the best he can. Someone has to protect Greta.

Tom is pacing. He can't stop. He's almost out of antacids, and something is burning through his stomach. He shouldn't be as angry as he is; something's wrong, something's making him want to strangle Justin Woodrow himself for fucking things up like this. The investigation isn't going anywhere. It's been three days and they haven't been able to turn up anything on Simmons. Even Carlos doesn't seem to be working as hard as Tom would like. There's no sign at all of James Woodrow; it's like he disappeared into thin air. The more time that passes the more difficult it will be. And something's wrong, wrong, wrong—Tom could spit, could scream, could pace all night like this, his heart is going too fast—and Tom's not really like that, he's not, but there's something wrong . . .

First, Hannah leads Justin into the bathroom. She takes off his shirt and his pants and shoes and socks and throws them all down the laundry chute, even the shoes, which clunk their way to the basement. She brings in a chair from the bedroom and sits him down. She fills the sink with warm water and folds up a towel, and begins swabbing his hair, his face, his neck, his shoulders, his chest, his stomach. She reacquaints herself with him, stroke by stroke. She doesn't speak, not yet; everything she has to say to him is in the softness of the towel, the warmth of the water, the motion of her hand. Justin just sits, slumps, stares, while Hannah tries to bathe him back to life.

This is a new world, my love. I'm baptizing you into it with water and blood. Here, everything changes in the space of a moment. We are not safe. We have no control. I hate to do this, I want you to stay in the other world, but there's no choice anymore. Shh, my love, shh—

Eventually, a voice emerges from Justin's body. Hannah doesn't speak, doesn't interrupt, she just lets the words come:

He lives in a dirty apartment. His furniture is all torn apart. He has a daughter he never gets to see. She's named Molly. She's six years old. He gives all his money to the girl. He'd never hurt anyone. He has no idea how it happened. He's tearing himself apart. He didn't do anything to James. He's just a man. I could have killed him . . . I could have killed him, I could have killed him—

"Shh—" Hannah says. "Shh, sweetie—"

I could have. I would have. He's just a man.

"It's okay—"

I thought it would bring James back. But he can't bring James back. No one can. I can't even bring him back. I hated him so much. And you know what? Now I hate him even more because he can't bring James back—

"Baby—"

And then, there, something moves through Justin, he wakes up from wherever he's been; he looks right into his wife's eyes. There's a conversation that happens silently between them—we can't be quite sure of the words—but it goes something like this:

You know. You know about James. You've known all along. Of course, of course. Of course you know. You're my husband/wife. You are me. And I am a person again. I am human again, I am back and you are back and we are together, and where in God's name do we go from here?

Where We Go from Here

Today, James is being held captive

in a secret underground lair of dwarves. They aren't mean to James, though; he lives inside a hut and they are feeding him cake. But he'd still rather go home. (Greta doesn't have any toy dwarves, but she has little plastic guys with square bodies and round heads that will do quite nicely. She has littler guys as a part of her Tiny Town set and there's a boy with a baseball cap that will do for James, even though he doesn't like hats.) The clown was working with the dwarves, he was raised by them. Once when he was younger he made it to the mermaid kingdom and he stole treasure and the secret of the sound in seashells and that's how he got his magical abilities. He knows the secrets of things, he knows why clouds float and why water is clear but the ocean is blue and he knows how to travel in between the worlds, but now he can't go swimming in any kind of ocean or big lake because he's wanted in five mermaid counties—that's what Tom says.

Anyway, dwarves are fascinated by little boys. They raised the clown and he grew up to be so tall, like a giant! They thought he must be part tree! And they want to be tall too—it makes it easier to get stuff down. The clown was already all grown by the time they realized how much they still had to learn, so the clown, who was so grateful to them for rescuing him from that dandelion bed and raising him up, promised he would send them a little boy so the dwarves could watch him grow and they could learn too. The clown can't promise that the dwarves can be tall too, sometimes you just are the way you are and you should like yourself that way, but he couldn't blame them for trying.

So James lives inside a great cave. He's got a nice bed, dwarves like it very comfortable. He's got a lot of toys too. They're trying to do everything like it would be done normally, but they sing a lot more because they are dwarves after all. (Greta sings a dwarf song.) But they don't understand about things like sisters that may help a little boy grow.

So James is there. It is okay there, but he can't leave. It's Greta's job to rescue him.

But when she sneaks into the secret dwarf lair she realizes she doesn't have any kind of plan at all! And all the dwarves are there looking at her! She thought she could just get there, untie James, and go home. But she ends up in front of a whole dwarf meeting!

Dwarves have never seen a little girl before (dwarves are all boys, you know) and they do not really know what to do. "What is it?" one whispers to another. A few look scared.

"I'm a girl," she says.

"What?" the dwarves murmur.

"I'm a girl," she says. "And you took my little brother. And I'm very, very angry."

The dwarves look around, trying to decide what to do.

"I don't think she can harm us," one whispers. "We are many and she is just one."

"Oh yeah?" says Greta. "I know magic!"

"Magic?" the dwarves whisper. They know all about magic from Mike the Clown because he took all the magic secrets from the mermaids. He never used it against them, he wouldn't because they were his family after all, but he always told them he could stop anyone from coming near them, and they sure believed him. Anyway, they're not quite sure what to make of Greta as she stands in the middle of the dwarf circle, but they're listening to her now.

"Maybe she's lying!" one dwarf says, his name is Frank.

"Lying?" says Greta. "Then let me show you!"

She goes up in front of Frank and takes a deck of cards from her pocket, and fans them out, which is usually hard for her because she can't hold them all in her hands, but now she does it perfectly.

"Pick a card, any card," she says.

He squishes his eyebrows up and takes a card in his hand and looks at it.

"Don't show me!" Greta says. "Show everyone else." And all the dwarves crowd behind Frank to look. Greta is a little nervous, if you want to know the truth, because she's never done magic in front of an audience like this. And she doesn't really know magic, not like Mike, all she knows are tricks from that book, what if they figure that out?

But the dwarves are watching her very carefully, and Frank puts the card in the deck, and Greta has flipped the deck over so Frank's card is facing the other way, but the dwarves don't know that, that's the trick, see! So she does some shuffling and some magic-like stuff, and then she pulls the card from the deck and shows all the dwarves!

"Is this your card?"

A gasp from the dwarf crowd! "Yes," Frank says, trembling. "Yes, it's my card."

Just like that, all the dwarves take a giant step back from Greta. They huddle in close to one another.

"Now, get me my brother!" Greta says.

"We will! Just don't hurt us!"

"And if you ever steal a little boy again I'm gonna come after you. Anyway, growing tall isn't a secret, it's just the way people are. You have to be happy the way you are." (Stories are always better when there's a moral to them.)

And then a dwarf, his name is Bob, comes in the room holding James by the hand. And Greta is so happy! And James smiles soooooo big. And he says "Ge-ta!" And the dwarf lets go of James and James run to Greta and she hugs him sooooooo hard, and she introduces him to Tom, and James hugs Tom, and they go home and have strawberry ice cream, and they live happily ever after.

The end!

There's another moral to the story and that moral is that Greta will always find James. Maybe she should make that clearer. What is James's story? When James comes back he'll tell her all about his adventures, that's for sure. And she can't wait. That's the thing, stories get dangerous sometimes, but the kids always come back, and everybody learns something, and everything is better again.

Greta's setting up a new adventure—now James is in a tree surrounded by giant monkeys and she and her flying dog and her friend Tom have to rescue him before the monkeys take him to their giant monkey world. This probably isn't what happened either, but maybe one of these days Greta will imagine what did happen and then she'll just know, and then she can tell everyone, and then they'll get James back, and then they'll stop being so sad. Greta misses him, but she knows he's okay, because everything always works out all right in the end.

Tom is standing in the doorway, not in the story, but in real life. Hi Tom! She waves at him with the Tiny Town policeman. She tells him the story of what happened with the dwarves. He listens closely and seriously. He says she's very brave. She likes that so much, really, Tom is the one who's brave because he's a policeman. It makes Greta so happy! Tom sits down with her and starts helping her draw and he seems happy too, not like when he's on the company couch talking on the phone when he uses a real grumpy voice. Tom likes Greta, she can tell, and that's good because Tom's her favorite grown-up ever, and she tells him so—and he smiles and says, but what about your parents, and then she says those aren't grown-ups, they're my parents, and he grins and he likes it so much, and that makes Greta happy.

He'd so much rather be in here with her than on the company sofa, Greta knows that, and she likes it a lot.

She explains to Tom that the dwarf story is mostly an adventure one. Sometimes kids get sent places and they have too much adventure and then when they come back they realize life at home isn't so bad after all. Sometimes you think things inside your head that are true, but they really aren't, sometimes those things seem more real than stuff that's really real, but then you realize that they're not, that they're just in your head. Not that life for James is what you call bad, at least Greta doesn't think so. If someone sent Greta somewhere she wouldn't realize anything of the kind when she got home; she would be happy to be back with her dad and her mom and her James. But the point is usually when the kids go off to another place they have some kind of lesson to learn, but what kind of lesson could James have to learn?

It seems strange that James would be the one to go, he's not quite old enough, really, to realize stuff. And anyway he might be afraid. If Greta sent a little boy somewhere, even if there was some kind of point, she would make sure that he was never scared. She would say, "It's okay, little boy, you are inside a story and sometimes things get pretty scary inside stories, but they always work out okay."

That's the nice thing about stories. If they sent Greta, she wouldn't be afraid. But maybe James would miss her too much, he would be worried she wouldn't come back, and that would be too awful. Now, Greta is learning a lesson, really, really, she's learning that she misses her brother and she should never ever let him out of her sight again.

In the morning, it's Justin who

does not want to get out of bed. Hannah lies with him, smoothing his skin. *Shh, baby, sleep, baby, shh, my love* . . .

Justin lies on his side, his body curled into itself, protecting itself against the world. Hannah's hands run over his arms, his shoulders, his back—they slowly, carefully remold the last remnants of yesterday's vengeful, violent man back into Justin Woodrow.

Shh, my love, I'm here, my love . . .

Hannah slides herself over and presses her body against Justin's back and wraps her arms around him. Her eyes close, her body sinks into her husband's, she feels his breath rise and fall in his body, his heart beat. She buries her face in the base of his neck, her own breath surrounds her, acrid, sleep-filled, and real.

I am human again.

Her husband needs tending to, and Hannah needs to tend. She is real again, she is awake now, and finally there is something she can do.

Should they be like this? With James missing, should they still be able to touch? Aren't they supposed to break apart, their marriage shattering into bits? Isn't that how it always works? The marriage is unable to take the strain of the missing child, the wedge is too great. How is it possible that something so tragic happens and they still can love each other?

"Justin?" Hannah props herself up.

"Hmm?"

"Maybe we should get up . . ."

A pause, then Justin comes to life. He rolls over to face his wife—sometimes he forgets how beautiful she is, is he allowed to remember now? Husband looks at wife, wife back at husband, while they wonder what they are allowed to feel. Hannah shifts and Justin says quietly, "We can stay here a little longer."

And Hannah nods, thinking of how well her husband knows her. They settle back into each other—Hannah still tasting her dreams of James, Justin trying to fight off the memory of the taste of blood. Who was he? What had he become?

I am human again.

"Han?"

"Hmmm . . ."

"Greta. How is she?" He motions to the empty mattress at the foot of the bed. (Her parents don't even know, but she's been up for hours, imagining James.) Greta is gone, Otter is gone, Bear and Fred are gone.

"I guess she's awake already . . ." Hannah says. "I haven't been . . ."

"Me neither. We should find her."

A look flashes between the parents. A realization. Hearts sink, guts clench. They have failed. They are failures, complete and utter failures. The worst happens, and Hannah goes to sleep and Justin goes insane and they entirely forget about their six—no, seven—year-old daughter, just when she needs them most. (Is she really seven already? How is that possible? Where did the six-year-old go?) They are terrible, terrible people, they should be locked away, they should have stones thrown at them on the streets. What on earth have they been doing? How dare they? James disappears, the parents sink into themselves, and who on earth has been tending to Greta?

The answer, they will learn, is Tom. Tom has been tending to

Greta. The policeman sent to spy on them, the one who called the cops on Justin, the one who keeps them from feeling at home in their home, is Greta's new best friend. She bubbles over with talk of him. *James will like to be his friend*, she says. *When he comes back.*

Does she understand what happened? Does she know why Tom is there? They don't know how to tell her—what to tell her. They can't explain anything, because there's nothing to explain. Greta has James in some sort of story-land—normally that would be denial, but now, who's to say she's not right? She has remembered seven years' worth of bedtime stories and she holds them now as travel guides to her brother's journey.

Greta spends her day in the playroom, studiously drawing pictures or quietly playing with her figures. There's a steadiness, a certainty to her. The parents sit by her, touch her shoulder, her hair, not to comfort but to be comforted by. Their daughter knows a secret they don't; it warms her skin and gives her life. But whatever the secret is, she's not telling.

Is she safe?

Of course she's not. Nothing's safe. In the afternoon, Hannah stands in the doorway to the playroom and something creeps up to her and whispers in her ear.

I could take her away, too.

Poof.

Just like that.

I could mutate a cell, I could hit her with a car, I could stick her finger in an outlet, I could feed her poisonous chemicals, I could push her head under water, I could crack her skull, I could pick her up in a mall, there is so much I could do, I could just take her away from you—

And Hannah Woodrow knows, she has known all along. She knows she can do nothing. She stands in the threshold staring at her daughter, with fear whispering sweet nothings in her ear, and her whole body freezes. *Just back away, Hannah. Stay out. Back away now.*

And she can only shut her eyes and silence the voice and step into the room. *You will not stop me.*

Later, it's Justin's turn. He stands in the playroom door fighting the urge to watch everything Greta does. Things can go wrong. She could be taken away any moment, and there's nothing Justin can do. If he could, he would assign Tom to Greta for the rest of her life, he would never let her out of the house again, he would place her lovingly inside a bubble. He dares not turn his back. *I could take her away, too, at any moment. Life teems with dangers. One moment she will be here and the next she will be gone forever. Accidents happen—*

Justin stands in the playroom door for what seems like hours, frozen, watching his daughter while fear whispers in his ear. *Watch her every move. As soon as you turn your back, she will be mine.*

And he can only shut his eyes and step back and say, *I can't let you control her life.* His heart breaks, he knows what this means; for the first time, Justin Woodrow is stepping back from his child.

Why is it that Greta seems to know how to act and her parents just don't? There is nothing they can do, but they have to do something. *James, my little baby boy, James, please come back, James, I miss you so much—*

Everything is still so strange. Hannah is still foggy from her sleep, from her dreams, from her GABA assistants. Justin is still in a stunned submission to the world. He approaches the air apologetically, shaming himself for disturbing the dust. He closes his eyes and he sees Mike's bloody face. Time floats by, moments drift into each other, and every minute is another one in which James is gone.

At least there are things to take care of. You would not believe how many things there can be; it has been five days since Justin and Hannah engaged with the world, and all the things have piled up. Justin does not want to deal with them; he eyes the things in terror. So Hannah calls work and then calls Greta's school—*a few more days. We'll let you know. Thank you for understanding. Of course, thank you, thank you.*

There are so many messages. Hannah sits in the kitchen and goes through the notebook Tom has kept for them. (Tom has the neatest handwriting; it's small, clean, and precise, like that of a seventh-grade girl who worries too much about upsetting the teacher. She wouldn't have expected that.) Everyone they know has called—even people they don't know. Everyone from James's preschool, from Greta's class. Teachers, principals, doctors, the dentist, all of Hannah's coworkers, old schoolmates, Justin's octogenarian barber, their dry cleaner, Justin's legions of assorted friends. And the mothers, all the mothers have called and called again. *We are so sorry. Our thoughts are with you. Our very best. If there's anything we can do. Would Greta like to come out with us today; we're going to the zoo. Can we get groceries for you? We left you some muffins by your front door. Please call us if there's anything else we can do. Would you like to use our cabin? Would you like Greta to stay with us? Whatever, whatever—*

Hannah feels something tickle inside her, her heart, her throat. She swallows and closes her eyes tightly, then opens them again and finds herself focusing with tremendous intensity on the word "muffins."

It never even occurred to Hannah to think about where all the food came from. It's true that one corner of the kitchen has been packed for days with all kinds of dishes that Hannah does not recognize, she just didn't really consider it. Things appear and disappear so easily. But there they are, next to the refrigerator—bags and baskets and platters. And there, indeed, is a basket of muffins—Hannah walks over and takes the plastic wrap off the basket and unfolds the napkins and picks up one of the muffins. Blueberry. She regards it carefully. There's sugar sprinkled on top, a demure paper wrapper framing the bottom, and just enough asymmetry to prove it was handmade.

"Tom?" she calls suddenly. "Tom, are you there?"

And, just like that, Tom is there, in front of her, looking so concerned, looking small, clean, and precise. "What is it? Are you okay, Dr. Woodrow?"

"Yes, I just...um, who sent all this food?"

"Oh!" he says. "Well, I have a list." He reaches into his back pocket and pulls out a notebook and begins to flip through it. "Okay, well, those muffins are from the Gellerts, this basket here," he points, "is from the St. Johns—they're cranberry and banana nut. The big fruit basket here is from your office *(flip)*, and this smaller one is from Greta's teacher. It looked a lot nicer before," he says apologetically, "but I had to refrigerate some of it, I was afraid the grapes would go bad. And, um, there's a lot more in here," he opens the fridge. "The cheese lasagna is from the Rothblatts, um, *(flip)* cook it for thirty minutes at four twenty-five. This here is a plate of enchiladas from the Millers, and this one is macaroni and cheese from the Larsons— they say it's for Greta, and this..."

And Tom keeps talking and flipping. There is so much food. The kitchen is filled with offerings; the refrigerator is bursting with microwave-safe plates. They could feed the families of one thousand disappearing boys on the food.

And Hannah realizes: she would not bring food. If this were another neighborhood family, it wouldn't even occur to her to bring food. It's not that she wouldn't feel terrible for the Larsons, it's not that she wouldn't want to help, it's just she'd assume they wouldn't want her to call, to interfere, they'd want to be alone, all the muffins in the world would just be a monument to their loss and to the utter helplessness of life. But the muffins do nothing of the kind. The muffins are handmade and full of blueberries, and that is something beautiful.

Hannah finds herself sitting in the breakfast nook, clutching the muffin and staring at Tom's careful documentation of empathy in the form of reheating instructions. There are notes, too—gentle messages on index and recipe cards. *Freeze after four days. My mother's chicken noodle soup. Cook for twenty minutes. Defrost for ten minutes. Tuna Casserole from a Friend. Some treats for Greta—refrigerate until ready to eat.*

And, at that moment, it occurs to Hannah that she does not want to cry in her room with the door closed. She wants to take all this food in her arms and hold it to her. She wants to invite over all the other mothers and listen to all their opinions. She wants to surround herself with mothers, she wants to prepare every single dish according to the cooking instructions, she wants to eat up all the food and write long thank you notes telling them how good it was.

Almost.

And for now, that's good enough.

So Hannah picks up the phone and calls her sister.

"Cath?" She feels her voice crack a little.

"Hannah! Hannah what is it?"

"No, there's nothing. I just—um. Would you like to come over tomorrow? In the morning or after work?"

"Y-yes. I'd love to. Can I bring anything?"

"No," Hannah says. "We have a lot of food."

"Okay, listen, why don't I take the day off? I don't have much tomorrow. I can help you around the house, take care of things for you . . ."

And Hannah is about to say, no, no you don't have to do that, but then she looks at her muffin, and says, "That would be nice. Thank you."

In the playroom, Justin is also holding a notebook. This one is blue, and it is covered with his large, messy writing—Justin found it in the back pocket of his pants. It's the James notebook, the one where he has been writing down his son's behavior for Dr. Lewis. Justin had forgotten the entire existence of such a thing—what a strange thing to have. Who does this? Who takes notes on their child? They've never done this with Greta—despite any number of suggestions that she might be hyperactive. They never observed her, they just let her be a kid. What were they doing with James? *September 2: James was so quiet today.* Now, James has fallen out of existence and all they have is this record of his food intake and daily interaction with the world. *September 3: James wanted toast instead of cereal for breakfast. One piece, with raspberry jelly, and orange juice. Lactose?* It is woefully inadequate. *James said he had a good day at preschool, he got to use the clay. He seems happy. Did he talk in class at all? Ask Miss Rose?* Perhaps they wrote him out of existence, perhaps when you observe something too much, all you have left are the observations.

"What are you looking at, Daddy?" Greta asks. She is surrounded by her own block village, and if Justin just closes his eyes, he can almost see James in there. Maybe if she arranged the blocks in just the right way, his son would come back. James can play with blocks for the rest of his life, they will let him do nothing but sit in the playroom, he will be thirty and making building block cities, and that would be fine, just fine, as long as he comes back.

"Nothing Greta. Nothing important. What are you playing?"

Justin puts the notebook back in his pocket. He can't decide whether or not he'd like to flush it down the toilet—he hates it, he hates everything about it, but at least it is a document of his disappearing son. It is something to hold on to, until it disappears as well—

Justin used to think the world was full of *things*, objects you touch, hands you shake, wind that blows against your skin, smells, sounds, tastes, all affirmations that there is a tangible world enveloping you every moment. Now Justin knows that is all just an illusion, everything is undetermined, formless. But here he has his wife and his daughter, and his family is the only thing in the entire world that is real. At night, he will sleep with a hand on each of them to keep himself from floating away.

Justin is at a small table in a
kitchen he's never been in before. There's a girl sitting across from
him. It's not Greta—the hair is black and the eyes are brown, but the
braids are the same, the juice stain on the collar is the same.

He's not himself, literally. He's somebody else—he's taller, thin-
ner, and he can balance large objects on his chin. His face is bruised
and broken. This is his daughter across from him—Justin has seen
Mike's daughter's pictures, and now in his dream she is present and
whole.

"Molly, honey," he says. "Pick a card, any card. Don't show me
what it is. Now . . ."

He loves doing tricks. He's been doing them ever since he was
six. He did them on every kid in school, and they always wanted to
know how, and he'd never tell. He loves doing them on kids now, at
parties and fairs—it leaves them with a taste of mystery and wonder,
a suspense never quite resolved. This is good for them. But with his
daughter, it's different—you do the trick and she giggles and bounces
and cheers, but then, this is very important, you show her how the
trick is done.

"You can flip the deck, like this, so no one notices, see? There are
all kinds of ways. Let me show you another one." And he does. He
shows her trick after trick. The cards fly in his hands. She watches
carefully.

"Don't tell anyone how this works," he says. "You're never supposed to tell anyone how the trick is done. Magician's code of conduct. Do you promise?"

She looks at him. "But you're telling me."

"That's different. You need to know these things, someone could do a trick on you at any moment."

"What happened to your face?" she asks.

"I got attacked," he says. "But that's not important right now. You've got to focus."

"I can do the trick," she says. "Watch." And she can, she does trick after trick, the cards are flying in her hands. He watches. He loves this, he loves her, he teaches her all the tricks. That's what fathers do.

"There's nothing I can do, you know."

"I know," she says. "If there were, you'd bring him back."

"I thought I was the hero of the story," he says. "Can it end happily?"

"It doesn't matter," she says. "It's not how it ends. It's what you do in spite of everything." She pauses, and picks the seven of hearts from the deck. "Is this your card?"

Justin shudders awake. He sits up and looks around. He's back in his own bedroom. His wife and his daughter are there, sleeping. His body is his own. But the taste of the dream still lingers. He closes his eyes and can see Mike, as he might be, alone in his box of an apartment with its dusty blinds and cracked walls. Is this what Mike dreams? Of course it is, at night all he can do is think of his daughter. It's what Justin would do.

Justin is right. Mike dreams of her every night, but now the dreams are more complicated. Mike still tastes the night in jail, the smell still will not wash from his hair. He has nightmares; he's doing his trick and his own daughter is in the chair, he's holding the chair in his mouth (it's the mouth, not the chin, everyone thinks it's the chin but it's an illusion) and everyone is applauding and then he stumbles and the chair falls and Molly falls and then all there is is an empty chair.

At first Michael thought he actually did it; he disapparated James through his own magic. He gets like this when he's in front of an audience—five hundred people are in awe at your every move and it goes to your head a little. Michael's own euphoria lifted James up and took him away—it could happen, anything could happen. And the applause and cheers had never been so loud and in that moment all those disparate pieces of Mike came together and finally made sense. The blurry became sharp, the ethereal tangible. Mike was *there*, he existed, he sounded his barbaric yawp—under those lights, in front of all those eyes he was made whole.

That lasted until he was arrested. He began to dissipate again and the world with him. Everything was blurry and wrong. Boy missing. Your fault. Where is he? What did you do to him? Pervert. Freak. Where's the boy? We'll let you get off easy if you tell us. Where's the boy?

Where's the boy? Who's the boy? How did this happen? He was there, in the chair, and then he wasn't. Poof. Mike almost dropped the chair, almost fell over flat. The boy is missing now? Parents? Everything blurs and the next thing Mike knows he's in a jail cell, and all the applause is gone. Where did it go?

Boy missing. James Woodrow. Five years old—near Molly's age. Something unnatural happened on that stage—he has no idea what, but the boy is just gone. And Michael can't bring him back. Molly is gone, now this boy is gone too and there isn't a single thing Michael Simmons can do about it.

The world is so full of these bright empty spaces. They pop up everywhere. Michael lives inside one of them now. He looked up the aunt from the newspaper and followed her because he wanted to explain, apologize, make contact, something. He wanted the family to know he was grieving too. But everything came out all wrong, and the spaces only got brighter and emptier. Now, the Woodrow family grief has broken his body and Michael still has not paid enough penance for the act he did not do. He wants to do more, more, more—there is nothing to be done, but he wants to do it anyway.

Mike sits on the futon thinking of the father, Justin Woodrow, there, in his bed, with that beautiful fragile-looking wife of his. Molly is gone, but she is not *gone*—Mike can't even imagine the grief. What must Justin's dreams be like—

Justin is sleeping again, dreaming—he has stepped away from his wife, his daughter, and something terrible is happening—he's driving; a red ball trickles into the street, a girl runs after it, he doesn't see her until it's too late. The brakes don't work and afterward no one will let Justin kill himself. Justin shudders awake. He holds on to his family for dear life; he has a wife, a beautiful, infinite wife—and a girl, a little girl, with red hair and green eyes and freckles, trembling from the lack of her brother.

Mike is sleeping again, dreaming—he is back onstage, balancing a chair on his face, everyone is applauding. There's a man in the wings, watching him. It's Justin Woodrow and he has a gun. He'll kill Mike if Mike drops the chair. There's something else, there's a shadow flickering behind Justin Woodrow. A person. A child. A girl, there's a girl hiding behind his leg, staring at Mike, crying, terrified. Of him. She has nightmares, like the kind Molly used to have, a man steals her away from her bed at night. For the little girl standing behind Justin Woodrow's leg, Mike is that man. And Mike stumbles and the chair begins to fall and Justin Woodrow pulls the trigger—

And Mike shudders awake. Somewhere, in the corner of his mind, he has remembered. James has a sister. He heard the cops talking about it. The poor girl. Molly-age, Molly-size, heartbroken from lack of a brother. What was her name? Greta. It is Greta. Mike closes his eyes and sees a girl, his mind draws a picture of his own daughter with James Woodrow–like red hair; the girl is dreaming of him and she wakes up screaming.

Tom, too, is in bed, thinking of

Michael Simmons. Simmons lingers behind Tom's eyes; he's sitting in his dirty apartment with its broken blinds and cracked walls dwelling on the lack within himself. The lack is so strong it threatens to enter Tom as well.

Tom is growing to understand this man, this kidnapper, this criminal. He has been thinking about him for days, and a profile is forming. Simmons gets power from performing, from being the master of spectacle. It is intoxicating, addictive, he is manic, euphoric—but at the end, it just isn't enough. He needs more.

His popularity grows. The shows get larger. The stunts more outlandish. The laughs bigger, the applause louder, the paychecks fatter. The phone rings and rings, the press sings—he is Mike the Clown, he is Magical Mike, he is the master of your ceremony. Pay attention. And they do, they all do.

And it still isn't enough.

He comes up with a plan. A stunt. A magic trick like no other. Magic has always been reassuring; it's the man who takes away your quarter and then plucks it out of your ear. Someone is in control. Uncertainty is just an illusion. Everything is manageable; everything is going to be all right. This is the covenant between magician and audience, and Mike will break it spectacularly.

Poof.

Did he pick James by accident or had he known about him for

some time? Did he collude with the theater writer? Had he been studying the family? He must have; it's the only explanation for how he found Catherine. Simmons has a growing obsession with the whole-ness of others. He was out one day—at the grocery? in the park?—and he saw the four Woodrows—Mom, Dad, Girl, Boy—happy, healthy, complete. And the great lack grew, it hurt so much at that moment, it consumed his insides. He followed them, he learned every-thing about them. He saw their future—broken, empty—and his own, finally complete.

He did it. It is done. The boy is gone.

And, still, it isn't enough.

(Where is James now? Tom can't see that far. He strains but can't discern the truth. How far does this perversion go? Maybe Simmons wants to raise the boy himself, maybe he found someone else with a burning lack where a child once was, maybe he killed the boy so he would never come back and destroy the illusion.)

Mike is a master villain, is Tom's nemesis, and Tom is beginning to understand him. Tom looks into Mike's soul and sees the empty shape of the wife who walked out on him and took their daughter with her. (She lives in Chicago now, she's remarried to a lawyer. She says—according to the interviews—Simmons is a man who hates him-self because the mountains do not come to him.)

And now, of course, it's still not enough. His obsession with the family keeps growing, even now, tonight, as Simmons lies in his rat-trap apartment. He has wounded them, but not broken them, and he still has a tremendous empty space to fill. There is another chance; there is the girl.

Tom peers right into Mike's imaginary heart, and he sees a form trapped inside. A girl, with braids and freckles, cowering against the encroaching shadow. Tom stares into Mike's soul and finds himself staring right at Greta.

Night ends, the sun rises—it's

Thursday morning now, almost one week since James disappeared. He would have preschool today, where he would have a turn on the glockenspiel, and Miss Rose would be pleasantly surprised by how much he seemed to enjoy playing. Justin would have those three hours to himself, and he would finally get to replacing the showerhead, which has been leaking for a month, driving him nuts. Today Greta's classmates will be introduced to subtracting double-digit numbers and the concept of mammals, and in drama they will act out fairy tales—if Greta were there, she would give a rousing performance as the Giant in an improvised Jack and the Beanstalk, but today the role will be interpreted by Jimmy Sanchez, in what will be a breakthrough role for the shy second-grader. Tom would be on patrol with Carlos; they still patrol sometimes, Blair says it keeps them on their toes—they'd respond to a three-car accident, a gas station break-in, and a domestic disturbance. (Tucker and Malloy do the route instead, and Malloy will be so angered by what he finds at the domestic disturbance call that he accidentally breaks the boyfriend's wrist while cuffing him, giving the defense lawyer enough ammo to reduce the sentence to six months. Lieutenant Moran will grumble to the D.A. that Tom and Carlos never make those kind of mistakes.) Michael Simmons would be made an official member of the Razzlers today, with a one-year contract, a spot on the tour, and an adequate bonus that he would funnel directly to Molly.

That is another universe. In this one, the day begins with Tom waking up after a night of thinking about Michael Simmons. He arrives at the Woodrows' at seven, and sits on the company sofa compulsively eating the scones that have been left on the doorstep, counting down until eight-thirty when he knows Detective Blair will be in. (The detective gets very cranky if you call his cell and interrupt breakfast with his wife.) At eight twenty-five, he dials.

"Blair!"

"It's Tommy. I've got to talk to you."

He hears the detective settle back in his chair. "What's up?" he says cheerfully. "You want out again?"

"No—no—it's not that . . ." Why exactly is he calling? He didn't quite have a plan, more of a loose idea, an urge really, if you want to be precise. "I just want to know what the hell's going on here."

A pause. Detective Blair says, "And by 'here' you mean—"

"In this investigation. It's been six days. Six days. And we've got nothing. We're no closer to figuring who did this than we were on Friday."

"I'm well aware of how long it's been, Tommy," the detective says dryly. "But everybody's working their asses off, you know that."

"Why can't we get anything on Simmons? We know he did it—"

"We *suspect* he did it."

"—and it's obvious what happened. He has an accomplice, the accomplice took the kid during the show. So why can't we get anything from him? What kind of monkey squad do you have on this case?"

"Careful, Johnson. You're talking to the head monkey."

"I didn't mean—" (Didn't he?) "It's not that. I just can't believe he hasn't made contact with the guy, with the kid. It just seems like the guys on him are missing something. They have to be. I can't believe no one can figure this out."

"I told you before my decision on posting you to the house is final, so—"

"No, no, it's not that. I should be here—"

"Okay, Tommy." The detective exhales loudly. "What's your problem?"

This is an excellent question. "My problem is that this guy is just out there, on the streets, running free, and he's dangerous."

"Dangerous?"

"He's a kidnapper, how much more dangerous do you want him to be? Can we pick him up for something? For harassing the aunt?"

"Catherine Bennett? That was three days ago. And in the meantime one of your charges went all Deuteronomy on Simmons's face, if you recall."

Tom clears his throat. "I know. I know. I'm just worried he'll bother the family again . . . I think he's going to come after Greta."

"Why?"

"Call it a hunch."

"Well, that's what you're there for, remember? You're there to protect them."

"I know, but—"

"But nothing, Tommy. You do your job, and let me do mine. Don't go weird on me, I'm counting on you. All right?"

"Okay. Okay."

"And try not to let Justin Woodrow beat anyone else up, okay?"

"Okay."

There's a pause. The detective's chair squeaks. "You know, Tommy," he says, "I think this is the first time we've ever had a conversation where you haven't said any variation of the verb 'to fuck.'"

"Well," Tom says defensively, "there's a kid here . . ."

Another pause. Then a little exhale from the detective. "Okay, Tommy," he says. "Talk to you later."

John Blair has the disturbing ability to calm anyone down (which in the past, Tom has only observed—he's never needed calming down himself before). But pretty soon all of the unsaid worries come flooding back to him. Tom can't watch Greta all the time. And if these guys don't get their act together, if they don't figure this out, they'll rotate him out of the house. And then what?

Greta has practically forgotten

what outside is like! She hasn't left the house in a bazillion years at least. It's like when she's sick or something. She forgot it was cold out, she expected it to be summer because of how there's no school now. But Greta has to wear her orange puffy coat, which she likes because Daddy calls her his little orange marshmallow. She likes it in fall, because the leaves smell so good, and you can put them in big piles and jump in them. But you should never hide in the piles they make in the street because the cars might not know you are in there and when you play in leaves you should always be supervised.

Now she's not outside for anything like jumping in leaves. She is trying to make James come back, and it's not working inside. She had to beg her dad to let her go out at all. She's never had to do that before. He always lets her play outside when she wants to, not like Rachel's mom who freaks out whenever Rachel leaves the house, and Greta hates going to play there because she's always watching them.

Now, Aunt Cathy is sitting on the back step watching her. She says she just wanted some fresh air too, but Greta knows better. It's okay, Aunt Cathy is usually fun and when she baby-sits she doesn't try to make up crazy rules like some other baby-sitters do. Aunt Cathy is Mom's sister like James is Greta's brother, isn't that funny? Only when she and James are old like that he'll come over lots more, and he'll live closer too, like next door maybe.

So Aunt Cathy's here, and not to baby-sit, really. She's been hanging out with Mom. They talked all morning, and it wasn't with that funny company voice her mom usually uses. Now she's on the back step, pretending she's not watching Greta. Greta can wave at her, just like this, see? Aunt Cathy has a boyfriend. His name is Greg. They aren't married but they live in the same house. Greta barely ever sees him, because Mom thinks he is a blowhard, and some other things Greta isn't supposed to hear. Greta thinks Aunt Cathy should marry Tom instead, then he'd be her Uncle Tom and that would be cool.

Anyway, Greta's in the backyard sitting. She's sitting on a blanket because the ground is freezing cold! But if she didn't go outside soon she was going to go crrrrrrrrrrrrrrrrrrrrazy. She brought her cards outside. She wants to practice more tricks on Otter but he doesn't like it outside because the leaves get all over his fur, so she's just practicing stuff by herself.

There's all sorts of magic tricks you can do with cards. Some of them you're supposed to have trick decks for. You can glue cards on top of other cards and cut them up and the cards look they are something else than they really are. But she doesn't like those as much, especially because she gets the glue all over her fingers. It's too much of a trick that way, anyway. It's just fooling people. If you use a regular deck of cards then it's just like magic, almost.

Greta is practicing forcing a card. That's when you make a person pick a certain card, but they think they've picked it all on their own. So you can guess seven of hearts because you've known all along, and they think you are amazing. You can do it lots of ways. One is by cutting the deck and having them count off a certain number, but you already know what card is at the bottom. Also you can keep your thumb on the card they pick and bend the other cards, and when you shuffle you keep your finger there. You can memorize the bottom card and make them pick it. There's all kinds of ways. See, if you don't know what card they've picked in the first place, you can't do the trick. It's not really magic, you see, even though you are pretending it is. When they say it's magic they're just hiding something. It's really more like cheating.

It's hard because you are supposed to be pretending you aren't fooling them, and you are supposed to talk all the time, it's called "patter," so they don't look at the stuff you are really doing, like trick shuffling and stuff. Greta has always shuffled by putting the cards on the floor and swirling them around with her hand, but you can't do that in magic, really, because you can't keep track of the forced card that way.

"Greta?" Aunt Cathy says all of a sudden. Greta looks at her. She's standing up and rubbing her arms, pretty dramatically Greta has to say. "I have to go inside, Greta, honey. It's too cold here. Aren't you cold?"

A little. "No."

"Come inside, okay?"

But Greta does not want to go inside, she just got outside and she's very happy there. Did she mention she hasn't been outside in *ages*? Grown-ups are supposed to like when you go outside and get fresh air and stuff instead of being cooped up in the house on such a beautiful day. Greta looks up at her aunt. "But I like being outside. Can I stay out?" Aunt Cathy is about to say something, and Greta quickly adds, as sweetly as possible, "Pleeeeeeaaaaaaaaaaaase?"

Aunt Cathy smashes her lips together and stares at Greta. Adults are always looking at her like this. She sighs. "Okay. I'm going to send Officer Tom out, okay?"

"Okay!" Greta says. She considers a moment, then adds, "He's nice, isn't he, Aunt Cathy? He's not a blowhard at all." Greta smiles innocently. Aunt Cathy stops and looks at her again, and then she blinks about a billion times and then goes in the back door.

Greta shrugs, and goes back to her cards. She's trying to get the thing right where you leave your thumb on the card and shuffle around it. It's so hard, and her hands are too little. She's concentrating so hard she barely notices the tall thin man come up to her until he's standing right there. His shadow is so long! She looks up at him.

"Hey," she says. "What happened to your face?" She can't help it. The words just come out of her mouth. This happens sometimes. But his face is all smooshed up and bruised and gross. It's probably rude to say so out loud, these are usually the things Greta is supposed to think but not say, but it's also rude to interrupt Greta while she's trying to learn to force a card.

The man squats down next to her. He's got the longest legs Greta has ever seen, longer than a giant's even. "Hi," he says.

"Hi," she says, in a manner designed to cut off further conversation.

It doesn't work. "What's your name?"

Greta bites her lips. She looks over her shoulder for a grown-up. She's not really supposed to talk to strangers at all. And she tells him so.

He looks really surprised. "Don't you know me?"

No, she does *not* know him. She doesn't know anybody who has a smooshed face; sometimes she forgets her mom and dad's friends, but she would remember that for sure. He looks like the guys on the movies Dad watches when she's supposed to be in bed.

"My name is Mike," he says. "Are you playing with those cards?"

Greta shrugs.

"Do you want to see a trick?"

Oh! She looks at him carefully. "A magic trick?"

He nods.

Greta chews on her lip. Is this going to be a real trick or a cheating trick? Maybe he knows real magic. He's so tall that he looks like he might. If he does, maybe he can help, because Greta is certainly getting nowhere here. This is an exception to the stranger rule: when someone can help you bring your brother back, it's okay to talk to them. She nods slowly and hands him the pile of cards.

And—you wouldn't believe it! You wouldn't believe it was the same deck of cards! The cards go flying through the air—woosh, woosh, zoooooooooooooom! Greta could watch it all day. They make the prettiest shapes. Greta can practice for a jillion years and she'll never be able to shuffle like that! This giant man is so amazing!

"Wow!" she says. "You're so good!"

And he smiles at her, like she's made him really happy, like no one has ever told him how good he was before, which is silly because if you're that good at something someone is bound to let you know once in a while. But anyway, that's the way he looks at her, like she's made his whole year.

"You like that?" he says. "That's nothing. Let me show you—" And the cards go so fast Greta can barely tell that they are cards anymore. Colors blur through the air in lines and arcs, up, down, back, forth. It's like nothing she's ever seen. She squeals in delight and he laughs too, and then he spreads out the deck, and asks her to pick a card, and she does, and then—

A sound comes from behind her, a muffled noise, like someone is yelling with their mouth closed. It's Tom! He's behind her. Hi Tom! She wants him to come watch the trick and stand next to this tall tall man, but before she can say anything he *yells*—

"Greta, get inside."

He doesn't even sound like Tom, his voice is scary and cold and yelling and Greta can't move from where she is and might possibly cry, yes she might—

"Greta! Go!" He is very, very scary when he says this, and the noise makes Greta's head whirl around to look at him. But he isn't looking at her, he's looking at the man, staring, and Greta doesn't move, she can't move, and he doesn't even seem to notice. She's just watching him, frozen to the ground. He is growing, shaking, growling, he takes a step forward and hisses, "What are you doing here?"

Greta hears the giant man say, "I—"

"Stay away from this family!" Tom says.

Mike takes a slow step toward Greta, holding out the deck of cards to give them back to her, and she would reach out to take them if she could move. But before she gets a chance to do anything Tom reaches down and grabs something from his belt, and then sticks his arms out.

Greta can't believe it. Tom has a gun. Guns are very, very dangerous and very bad and are not toys. If you are ever at a friend's house and you see a gun you leave the room and tell a grown-up and call your dad to come pick you up right away. Greta's never seen a real gun, just pictures. And she certainly couldn't tell you what it was that is so scary about it, but nonetheless when she sees it she opens her mouth and screams.

Justin and Hannah come running

out of the house to see their resident policeman holding Michael Simmons at gunpoint. Greta is screaming like she's never screamed before. Michael Simmons has his hands up in the air and is not moving at all, not one single tremor. And Tom, Tom is still and hard, but something is wrong, he's sweating, he's white, his cheeks are bright red. He's looking at Mike with such hatred.

Justin knows this look.

In the blink of an eye, Justin and Hannah mentally calculate the distance between the gun and their daughter—she's sitting to the left of Tom, she's nowhere near a bullet's trajectory, but that doesn't mean they aren't both about to pounce on Greta, cover her with their bodies, drag her away. They look quickly back and forth from their daughter to the man with the gun. Their vision telescopes from the man to the gun then to the trigger, and then focuses on the finger slowly squeezing in.

Tom is not himself.

Without a word, Justin moves toward Tom and Hannah toward Greta. "Tom," Justin says softly. "Tom. He's not going to hurt her." "Greta, come to Mom," Hannah says urgently, and Greta just sits there, crying. Michael Simmons is looking back and forth from the gun to the girl, and he leans down a bit toward Greta and whispers, "Greta, go to your mo—," and that's when Tom shoots.

Their New Policeman Is

Named Carlos

Everything happens so quickly.

There is the moment of stillness, the only motion a wisp of smoke and a nine-millimeter lead projectile buzzing through the air at about 975 feet per second toward its target. All else is silent. The hollow-point bullet hits just a little above where it was aimed, making contact at Mike's thigh, bursting through the skin, through the subcutaneous fat, through the muscles, and into his femur, blasting bone and rupturing the femoral artery.

Then: a rip of a yell from Mike, and a tumbling sideways. The sound touches Greta, who begins to scream. Justin dives for his daughter, picks her up, and runs her into the house—yelling over Greta's wails at Catherine to call 911. Hannah registers that her husband and daughter have reached the house safely, and then finds herself at Mike's side. She pulls off her shirt and presses it to his leg. She's just in a bra now and her bare skin begins to pucker. She looks around for something to prop his good leg on to keep blood flowing to his brain, but can't find anything so she squares herself around and puts his good leg on her back while she presses the cloth against his wound—the thought slips into her mind, this is the last person to touch James, and it slips back out again—all the while using her own brand of patter; "You're going to be okay, Michael. There's no sign the bullet has ricocheted. There are no vital organs in the area of the wound. It's going to be fine. I need you to breathe deeply for me now, okay? Come on, Michael, breathe deeply—"

Everyone is animated but Tom. He just stands there, frozen.

The ambulance comes quickly; the paramedics confer with a bloodsoaked Hannah. Catherine comes running out with a blanket for her sister while Mike is laid on a stretcher and loaded into the back of the ambulance. A police car pulls up, followed by a blue sedan. Two young officers get out of the squad car—one is Carlos—while Detectives Blair and Henry come slamming out of the sedan. The detectives and one officer whisper with Hannah while Carlos heads straight for Tom. He puts his arm around Tom's shoulders, and the two men stand there like that for several moments while the ambulance doors slam shut. Finally Detective Blair comes over to Tom and takes him by the arm. He nods to Carlos and the men silently lead their wordless friend to the sedan, where he gets in the backseat and puts his head in his hands.

It takes some time to calm Greta. She doesn't understand what happened, really—if she were a little older, when guns and bullets and triggers and wounds would mean more to her, maybe it would be worse. What she knows is the terrible sound of Tom's voice, the loud pop of a firecracker next to her head, the heart-stop stillness, the tumbling over of the man, and her father's rushing and yelling, and the very certain sense that something awful happened. There was running, grabbing, and noise noise noise. She cries recklessly, tucked in her room with stuffed animals all around her. Her father sits next to her, holding her hand, stroking her hair, "Everything's okay now, sweetheart . . . everything's okay."

Catherine puts her arm around a shivering Hannah and leads her back into the house, just as a van filled with press pulls up to sniff for blood in the backyard. "I have to go check on Greta," Hannah says.

"Wait," Catherine says. "Let's take care of you. You're freezing."

"No, I should go—"

"Hannah!" Catherine stops her. "You're covered in blood."

Hannah looks down. "Oh," she says. "Okay."

Catherine puts on the teakettle and helps her sister up the stairs, watching for Greta with every step. They go into the master bedroom, and Hannah unwraps herself from the blanket. She shudders visibly.

"Keep that on a minute," Catherine says. "I'm getting your tea."

Hannah nods obediently and sits. Catherine studies her for a moment, wraps another blanket around her, then goes out the door. Two minutes later, she's back with a steaming cup that she makes her sister sip from. "Okay," Catherine says. "Let's get you out of these clothes."

Hannah nods. For the first time in their lives, Catherine is in charge. It's fine with Hannah. She stands up and takes off her jeans, they hang limply in her hand. She stares at them. "Maybe we should just throw these away," she says softly.

"Okay." Catherine reaches for the pants.

"No!" Hannah says quickly. Catherine stares at her. "The blood. You shouldn't touch them."

"Oh . . ."

"Why don't you get me a trash bag? There are some under the bathroom sink—"

"Sure, okay."

"And I better take a shower . . ."

They go into the bathroom. Catherine holds the bag open and Hannah dumps her jeans and bra inside. She stands naked in front of her sister, still with spots of blood on her body.

"I have to wash my hands," Hannah says.

"Of course." Catherine does not stop to ask why Hannah would be washing her hands when there's a shower right there. She keeps a palm on Hannah's back while Hannah scrubs her hands, working the soap underneath the fingernails. She scrubs and scrubs, all the way up to her elbows, looking for cuts in the skin.

Catherine turns and starts the shower, getting it steaming hot like

Hannah used to like when they were young. She guides her sister in, sets out a towel for her, and then goes back into the bedroom, sits on the bed, puts her head in her hands, and cries.

Hannah watches Catherine leave, then leans up against the wall of the shower while the hot water beats down on her skin. No one has ever been this tired before in the history of the world. The wall isn't enough support; she sits on the tile floor of the shower, leaning back against the wall, while this fiercely hot water beats down on her. Her skin is turning pink. She thrusts her face up to the water and lets it hit her eyelids, her mouth. She finds that she's sobbing, her whole body is shuddering, quaking, she gasps and heaves—

All right. There. She's done. She's pink and clean, and still. She climbs out of the shower and towels herself off. She puts her wet hair in a ponytail. She goes into her bedroom and puts on some sweatpants and a sweater, then kisses her sister on the head. Then she goes to tend to her daughter.

She sits on one side of the bed while Justin sits on the other. Justin holds Greta's hand, while Hannah rests her hand on her daughter's arm. Greta's stuffed animal retinue stands watch, glassy-eyed beasts, solemn in their charge. They have all been here before.

An hour later, Catherine knocks on the door to Greta's room and gently tells Hannah there's a new policeman to talk to them. Catherine goes to sit by Greta and stroke her hair and the parents slowly walk back downstairs. Hannah and Justin whisper to each other about their former policeman and what happened to him and what will happen to him. Then they find themselves back on the sofa, where their new policeman sits across from them, shuffling some papers and eyeing them with a sort of bewildered terror.

"I'm Officer Carlos Artola," he says. "I'm going to be T— Officer Johnson's replacement."

Hannah and Justin nod. That seems to be all the man has to say. All three sit quietly for a moment, staring at something invisible in the center of the room. Thoughts settle and resettle, throats are cleared, breaths pass lightly around the room.

"How is Michael Simmons?" Hannah asks quietly.

"They're going to have to rebuild his leg, but he'll be okay." Carlos clears his throat. "He would have been in a lot more danger if it hadn't been for you," he says, nodding at Hannah.

She shrugs a little.

"Now," he takes out his notepad. "Did you see what happened between your daughter and Simmons?"

Both parents shake their heads. They are so glad they don't have any information; they've answered far too many questions like these lately. It's so tiring, anyway, all these people who ask all the wrong questions.

Hannah looks at her husband, who nods, and says, "Um, Officer? What's going to happen to T— Officer Johnson?"

Carlos coughs. "Well, he'll be dealt with, you can be assured of that. And of course," he shifts, "the department is extremely regretful that this happened, and wants to assure you that this is not the sort of action that we make a habit of taking . . ."

"Oh, no," Hannah says. "We know. We're not—we're not looking for him to be punished. We just want to know what's going to happen to him."

"Oh." Carlos blinks. "Oh, okay."

They look at Carlos, who doesn't seem to know what to say. Finally Hannah asks, "Is he all right?"

Carlos looks at the ground. "I don't know. He'll be suspended. I don't know for how long. Nobody really expected this from Tommy."

Justin nods. His mouth fills with the taste of blood. He remembers—

"I probably shouldn't—" Carlos's voice changes, "Well, anyway he feels awful. He says he just thought the guy was going to hurt your daughter, and—well—"

Hannah understands everything. Things had changed for Tom. He went from being a man who was fascinated by the complexity of cases to a man who could help people. She knows; she has been through something similar herself. She does not know about the dreams, about the forgotten childhood wish, but in a way she understands—Tom wanted to be a hero. "He fell in love with our daughter," she says quietly. "That's all."

It's Thursday, still, even after all that; tomorrow will be exactly one week since James's disappearance. Then what? Time keeps trickling along, one moment leads to the next—it's been a week already and it's only felt like a year. Where has the time gone? What happens now? They'll break in a new police officer, they'll try to keep down this awful numbing. The media has stopped calling. Don't they care anymore? Is there some story that's more important than this one?

At some point, decisions have to be made. There will be a weekend, and then a Monday soon. When will Hannah go back to work? When will Greta go back to school? Does that mean that they're giving in, that they've accepted James's loss, that they are going to try to return to "normal"?

It's not fair. Time should disappear, too.

At some point, Greta emerges in search of food. No one is there when she comes out of her room and heads down the stairs toward the kitchen, where Hannah, Justin, and Catherine are whispering quietly among themselves. On the bottom stair she notices a flurry of movement to her right, on the company sofa. There's a man there. Alone. She approaches cautiously.

"Who are you?"

Carlos looks up from his folder to find himself stared at suspiciously by a seven-year-old girl. He clears his throat.

"Um. I'm Officer Artola . . . You must be Greta?"

She doesn't answer, just starts looking around the room. "Where's Tom?" she asks.

"Oh." Carlos rubs his cheek. "Well, he had to go."

"Oh!" Her eyebrows knit together. "Is he coming back?"

"Um. He might be gone for a while."

"Oh," she says quietly. "Okay . . ."

She keeps looking at him, like there is much more to this conversation. Her lower lip is protruding and her cheeks are flushed. Her eyes are red and Carlos really, really can't put his arm around her and tell her it's going to be all right.

But she doesn't cry. She chews on her lip for a few moments and says, "Do you know Tom?"

"Yeah," Carlos says. "He's my friend."

"Oh," she says. "He was my friend too. But I don't think he is anymore."

"Oh!" Carlos bends into her. "No, no! Why do you think that?"

"He didn't like that I was playing with the magical man. He got really mad. He yelled."

"Oh, Greta," Carlos says. "He's not mad at you, I promise. He's just worried about you. He wants you to be safe."

He looks at Greta imploringly, but she's already moved on. "Is the magical man gonna come back?"

"The—the clown? No, Greta. He can't hurt you."

Greta blinks, using her entire face. "Huh?"

"I mean he won't come back," Carlos says. "I promise."

"Oh," Greta says dejectedly. "I thought maybe he could help."

Carlos is having a hard time keeping up here, so it must be a relief to him when her father appears behind them.

"Greta, honey," he says, "why don't you come into the kitchen? I'll make you some dinner."

Greta looks at him. "I want hot dogs."

"Hot dogs it is."

"And cheese!" A pause. "Please."

"Okay, Greta . . . You go in and talk to Mom and Aunt Cathy. I'm going to talk to the police officer."

"Okay!" Greta turns away without another word and blurs her way into the kitchen. Justin watches her go, then turns to Carlos.

"What did she say to you?" he asks seriously.

"She wanted to know about Officer Johnson," Carlos says. "She thought he was mad at her . . . I tried to explain he wasn't."

Justin nods. "Thanks . . . I don't think she really understands what happened. All right." He turns to go and then stops. "Officer?"

"You can call me Carlos."

"All right, then, Carlos—" Justin exhales. "Are you armed?"

"Yes. In order to protect the family—"

Justin rubs his hands together. "I would appreciate it," he says softly, steadily, "if you would get that gun out of my house."

Carlos and Justin apprise each other for a moment, then Carlos exhales and sits back on the couch. He nods. "All right," he says. "All right."

Night. Catherine left an hour ago with the promise to come back on Saturday, and said to call her at work if they need anything, anything, anything at all, and she'd come right over. Hannah bathes Greta while Justin sits in the kitchen and stares at nothing, then the parents tuck their daughter in. They move about the house for a while, Justin stares at the television while Hannah does not read her magazines. Justin finds tears running down his cheeks; Hannah, who has already cried everything there is to cry, just sits. Carlos leaves for the evening, another police car pulls up front for the night watch, and then Justin and Hannah resign themselves to bed—grimly knowing that they will only have to wake up, again, tomorrow.

They settle into the bed slowly, with long breaths. Justin touches

Hannah's shoulder lightly and Hannah leans into him. There is nothing more real, and nothing more surreal, than a gunshot. This did not clarify their situation any.

"So, how is she?" Justin whispers.

Hannah does not need to ask who. "She's jumpier. She cried in the bath because shampoo got in her eyes. She hasn't done that in a year I don't think."

Justin nods. "She told the new policeman that she thought Tom was mad at her."

"Ohhh." Hannah sighs. "She didn't tell me that. Anyway, I don't think she saw any blood . . ." She rolls all the way into her husband. He puts his arms around her and pulls her close. They lie there awhile more, her hand on his chest, his in her hair.

"Michael Simmons got through the operation just fine," Hannah says. "They're going keep him there for a few days."

"Hmmm," Justin says. Perhaps they can look at the damage Justin did to his face, too—they can look at everything that has been done to this man, this ordinary, ordinary man.

"I gather they're going to suspend Tom," Hannah says.

"I guess so . . ." Justin curls a piece of hair around his finger. "I don't know if I can really forgive him, you know."

"What?" Hannah props herself up on her arm. "Really?"

"I mean he could have hurt Greta. Something could have happened, his arm could have been jostled. Something. He was trying to protect Greta, but he wasn't thinking. He could have hurt her. Just like that." He closes his eyes and sees Michael Simmons bloodied on the ground, he sees him slowly bleeding to death; he sees his blood all over his own body. At night he will dream and dream and in each dream he will be the one that shoots.

Hannah nods. "It's just . . . it's different for you to say something like that."

"After what I did?"

Hannah looks surprised. "No, no, I mean—you just usually . . . forgive."

"Well," he looks at her. "Things are different now."

"Greta's okay," Hannah says softly. "She's okay."

So they lie like that for some time, wrapped up in the dark and grounded by touch, until they each fall asleep. Hannah is awoken an hour later by a tentative knock on the door—it's Greta, who's had a nightmare involving a short, sharp explosion and a plume of smoke. The trees kept falling and Greta couldn't stop them. Her mom leads her and Otter into bed, where she wraps around them both and soothes her daughter to sleep.

Friday, 9:46 P.M.

Lindbergh Performing Arts Center

has been empty for a week. The Razzlers were booked for two weeks, but all the shows were canceled after the incident on opening night. At first, the producers thought they might be able to do shows again after the boy's disappearance, after a respectful break, but it soon became clear that no break seemed respectful enough. The media coverage has been enough to assure that there is no way any family is going to bring their little ones to the Razzlers Circus Stage Show, "Where we steal your kids!" as some performers mutter to each other. Moe, the Lindbergh security guard, certainly wouldn't bring his children there. After everything happened on Friday, he went home and told Lois and they both decided they would never take the kids anywhere ever again. Moe's been working here all week, afternoons and evenings, with no one else but a box-office person and the janitors. The place is probably hemorrhaging money this week, but Moe is pretty sure it's got enough to spare. Moe can tell you a thing or two about money hemorrhage.

He's got two kids. Girls. Suzanne and Shannon. They're nine and seven and they are his entire world. He works two jobs for them—he'd work six if he had to. And if anyone ever, ever, ever hurt them, he would rip the guy apart, piece by piece. His wife reads them extra-long stories at night now, and when he comes home he creeps into their room and kisses them, and then lingers, watching them sleep.

Why would anyone ever take a child? How could you be that

sick? For a while, Moe hoped the police just missed something. The father came in once and Moe helped him look. Moe looks himself, he looks every day, everywhere he can think of, and everywhere again. Maybe nobody took him, the world can't really be like that, can it? Maybe James just got . . . misplaced. Every time he opens the trapdoor under the stage he hopes he'll see a little orange-haired angel-faced boy there.

And that's why, tonight, when he comes into the auditorium for a walk-through, he thinks the small form on the stage is his imagination. It must be. He blinks, and looks again. It is still there. He moves closer. There is no mistaking it; there's a little red-haired boy in a blue sweater, blue jeans, and white sneakers sitting cross-legged on the stage, tracing the floorboards with his fingers, and making car sounds.

"Hey!" Moe shouts. "HEY!"

The boy looks up at him. Moe runs down the aisle and up the stairs, as quick as he's ever run in his life. "James? James?"

The boy looks around and says cautiously, "Hi."

"Are you James?"

The boy nods solemnly.

And then and there, Moe Nelson, who has not cried since he was seven years old and saw *Bambi*, begins to weep. He picks James Woodrow up and holds him to his chest, and cries in his hair.

In the Woodrow house, the day passes like the rest of them, but slower. Carlos worries about his partner and stutters around the family. The phone rings less and less. Justin and Hannah spend every moment with Greta, who tells them a story about James and some aliens, and then another story about magic dogs. They start to look at her book for James, but it makes Greta think of Tom. The parents watch Greta carefully—she seems slightly altered; she is herself, but more so. More

mercurial—louder, quieter; more frenetic, more tired; needier, cooler—
and they cannot be by her side enough.

When the phone rings at 10:02, Greta is in bed. Carlos is sitting
on the couch looking at his watch, the parents are in the kitchen—
Hannah is mindlessly scrubbing some cabinets while Justin sits on a
barstool wielding the remote control and flipping through channels
with no attention to what's on—both watch the night fall and dread
the moment when they must resign themselves to bed, again—the
eighth time since their son disappeared. It's the police hot line that
rings—the Woodrows have stopped jumping every time it makes its
high-pitched trill; the police details have numbed them into submission. But it is very late for that phone to be ringing, and Justin and
Hannah can't help but perk an ear up.

It's just a low murmur they hear at first, but something in the
tone makes them both stop short. Justin mutes the television, Hannah
stops her scrubbing. They hear a loud, "What? Where?" from the
living room and the two parents exchange a look and burst out of the
kitchen. Carlos is standing up, staring into the phone. He looks up at
the parents, stunned. They gape back, ready to pull the information
out of his throat if they have to. They lean toward him and Carlos
says, quietly, intensely, "They found James. He's just fine."

They're going to the station in a squad car, sirens blaring. Carlos drives
and Justin and Hannah are in the back. A neighbor is in the house
with Greta; they didn't want to wake her, get her hopes up, in case—in
case—in case what? That it's a trick? A lie? In case they see him and
he just disappears again?

Hannah sits perfectly still. She is afraid if she moves, she will
shatter the air and she will fall back through to the world where her
son is still missing.

Justin stares at a point on the seat in front of him. He stares and stares. He has his wife's hand. She's still there. Does he get to keep them all now?

Carlos doesn't know too much. James was just in the auditorium, onstage. The security guard found him like that. He was playing, really, he was playing cars on the stage. He seemed all right. He's at the station now. There are pediatricians and child psychologists examining him. They don't have any details yet, Carlos doesn't have any information on where he's been or how he got back to the auditorium, but they're working on it, he assures them, they're working on it—

Can't the car go any faster?

Hannah sits and watches the world whiz by. It is twelve miles from the police station to their house. The speed limit ranges from twenty-five to forty-five miles per hour, but they're not following speed limits. There are seven stoplights and six stop signs. In a police car, you can go right through them.

Justin and Hannah's chests are like iron bands. If they don't breathe all the way to the station, James will be back. If they don't move all the way to the station, if they don't cry all the way to the station—

"Where is he? Can we see him yet?" Justin can't get the words out quickly enough. Both parents have tears flowing down their cheeks, which they completely ignore. They're standing in a room with Detective Blair. The room has a lot of chairs, as if someone expects the Woodrows to sit and wait. Everything is rushed and blurred, all of the edges are fuzzy, the only thing that will bring the world into focus is their son, their James, James, James—

"He's in with the psychologist now," Detective Blair says. "We need to evaluate him first. We'll let you see him as soon as possible."

"No," Justin says. "We have to see him now. Please." He's squeezing Hannah's hand so tight her knuckles are white. She can't even

talk, her lips are smashed together, eyes pressed closed, tears run silently down her cheeks.

"I'll tell you what," says Detective Blair. "They're in a room with
a one-way window. You can look at him, all right?"

"Yes, yes, please. Please."

"We just can't disturb this," he explains apologetically, "or we
might lose our chance to figure out what happened to him. But you'll
have him by you very soon, I promise."

The scenery begins to change, the parents seem to be moving
through the blurry space. Hannah finds her eyes and mouth open. She
grabs Detective Blair's elbow.

"Wait," she says. "What does he say?" The words are out of her
mouth before she even knew she thought them.

"James?" he says.

"Yes." She grips him a little harder. Something is starting to form
in her brain, a little cloud of something. "Do we know what happened? Has he said anything?"

The detective shakes his head. "He says he doesn't remember anything. The last thing he remembers is being in the chair. We'll see
what the psych guy says after talking to him—"

"Was there anything in the auditorium? Any evidence?" The
cloud is growing bigger and bigger.

"No," he says. "Nothing."

"So, you don't know how he came back?" Hannah asks. Her voice
is quite squeaky now. What did she expect? That there would suddenly be an explanation?

"Not yet," he says, "but we're working on it."

Justin is watching her. "Come on, Hannah," he touches her shoulder. "Let's go. Let's go see James—"

And there he is, right there, in the next room. There's just a wall
of dark glass between them and their son. Everything is perfectly silent. But James is there, it is really James, all orange hair and dimples,

squeaky and new, wearing the blue sweater that looks so nice with his eyes. The parents gasp and grab onto each other. He is there, he is James, he is all right. Hannah slowly traces his outline with her fingers against the glass.

The parents press themselves as close to the one-way mirror as they can. James can't see them, but he must be able to sense them, he must. He's in a little room that's designed for children. There are schoolroom posters on the walls, stuffed animals and books on the shelves, and toys spewing out of the drawers. James has blocks in front of him, he's intently making piles. A balding man in a purple sweater is leaning into him, talking softly.

"He doesn't like strangers," Hannah says through her tears. "He might not like this. He should see us."

The detective says gently, "It's all right, Mrs. Woodrow. In a few minutes."

So the parents stand perfectly still against the glass, watching their son. It is a curious hell to have him so close suddenly and not be able to touch him. He is the sweetest little boy in the world. The psychologist says something and then James says something, and then the psychologist says something else and James smiles! He smiles!

"Please," Justin says whispering hoarsely. "Please let us see him now—"

Detective Blair sits them down in his office. They will strangle him if they have to. "I've talked to the doctors," he says. "James is just fine. There's no sign of anything physically wrong with him. The psychologist says he seems to be healthy, although he is concerned that James says he doesn't remember anything that happened. He wants James to start seeing someone regularly to work through whatever he's been through. I have a name—"

"Fine," Justin says.

"And the psychologist recommends that the whole family see a counselor for a few sessions to work through any issues that might arise—"

"Fine," Justin says.

"Meanwhile, we're going to keep investigating, and trying to put together what happened. If James tells you anything that might lead to the culprit—"

"Fine," Justin says.

"Okay," Detective Blair says. "I'll bring in James now—"

And James toddles in, holding Carlos's hand. Carlos is grinning. Hannah and Justin exhale in a gasp/wail, and the world exhales with them. Everything comes into focus now, everything is perfectly clear. James is clear, there, sharp and present—James is *James*, their boy, that is all. James sees his parents and his whole face breaks into a smile. Carlos lets go and James runs into their arms. The parents gather around him and squeeze him as close as they can. Carlos and Detective Blair stand back and watch, whispering quietly to each other. Outside of the office, the hum of the station goes on; phones ring, radios blare, people shout. But in here, wrapped up in each other's arms, all Hannah and Justin can hear is their son's heartbeat.

Where We Go from Here,

Take Two

Once upon a time, there was a

boy named James. James went to the circus one day with his family. There was a clown at the circus, and James liked him very much because he had funny pants and could do magic tricks. The clown asked for a volunteer and James raised his hand, because he wanted to meet the clown and help him. And the clown picked James! And James went up onstage! And all these people clapped for him like he was the one who could do magic tricks! And they laughed and James laughed too and he sat in a chair and went up in the air—

And then he disappeared.

Poof!

And his family was very, very sad. They loved James very much and missed him very dearly.

And then he came back.

Poof!

And the family was very, very happy. And they held on to him so very, very tightly.

And they asked James where he went and what happened to him there. And James didn't say anything. And they asked James how he disappeared. And James didn't say anything. And they told James that it was okay, that he didn't have to say anything. And at night they closed their eyes and said, "Please, please, don't ever take him away again."

Well, then. The Woodrows are

whole again. Four. Doctor Hannah, Stay-at-Home Justin, Hyper Greta, Quiet James. A family.

The news of James's return crackles and pops through the network of family and friends. The phone begins to ring constantly again, but now they have no Tom, no Carlos to answer it for them. Sometimes, Catherine takes a shift, but mostly they let it ring. Their answering machine is constantly chattering at them, *It's Rod and Lisa Wilson, we just heard, thank God, thank God.* People are always stopping by, delivering balloons and flowers and toys for Greta and James. Hannah or Catherine answers the door, and they can't help but cry, every time. People are good. They understand. The family wants some time together. Thank you. We'll call you later. We'll see you soon. My best to your family. Friend or neighbor shakes their hands or hugs them or pats their backs, and then turns to go—if it's Hannah, they just leave; if it's Catherine they stop, turn, and ask softly, reluctantly, *Don't they have any idea what happened?*

And Catherine must just shake her head and say, "No. No, they don't."

And a ghost of something passes through the expressions of friend and neighbor, their eyes close, their shoulders hunch, their bodies wither slightly—they hug themselves and purse their lips and walk slowly away.

Greta Woodrow has no ghosts; her brother is back, she's done her job, and that is all that matters. Greta lives in a state of perpetual motion, whizzing through time and space. She sits James down and goes over the book she made for him. "You like hot dogs!" she says, and James nods enthusiastically. "You don't like bananas," she instructs and James squishes up his face and shakes his head, no no no!

She quizzes him on where he was, and Hannah and Justin find themselves hovering in the background, listening. "Were there dwarves?"

James giggles and shakes his head dizzyingly.

"Wizards?"

Giggle. Shake enthusiastically.

"Fairies?"

The parents do ask. They can't help it. If only they could know more, it would be so much easier to keep away all those dark thoughts. They hold James close and whisper into his ear, "Where have you been, baby?"

He just looks confused when they ask; the question doesn't mean anything to him. Sometimes he grins and says, "Circus!"

"Yes, yes," they say encouragingly, "you raised your hand. Then what?"

He thinks. "I went onstage."

"Yes, yes, and you were so good. You made everyone laugh, do you remember?"

He blushes. "Yeah . . ."

"And then what?"

He thinks again. You can tell when he's thinking because he crinkles up his nose, he always does this, maybe he'll be forty years old and he'll still crinkle up his little nose because he thinks so hard. "I sat in the chair?"

"That's right, James. You did. That's right! And then what?"

And then he crinkles and crinkles, but nothing comes. He just shakes his head and looks worried, like he's gotten something wrong, and all they can do is hold him close.

What can they do? They have to know. The whispers won't stay away. They are up at night staring at the ceiling, wondering—now that James is back, the explanation for his disappearance and reappearance seems the most important thing in the world. Otherwise what's to keep him from going away again?

The deep red curtains are closed.

No one is in the plush seats in the small, dusty, yellowish auditorium, except Justin himself. The house lights come down. A pause. The curtains creak open; the sound echoes through the auditorium. The stage is dark for a moment, and then a single spotlight illuminates a chair in the middle of the dark floorboards. A tall, thin man in a top hat walks into the light. He bows. He clears his throat. He takes off his hat. He turns it over and shows it to the empty seats. He picks out a magic wand from his pocket and waves it over the hat. Nothing happens. He raises his eyebrows and waves it over the hat again. Nothing. He scratches his head and does it a third time. He peers inside the hat. He looks apologetically at the seats. He holds his hat up over his head and shakes it. He knocks on it. He sighs and puts the hat back on his head and sits in the chair, chin in his hands. And then, there is movement on top of his head. He perks up and looks over his shoulders. The hat falls on the floor and there is a white bunny sitting on top of his head. The man stands up, knocking the chair over. The bunny jumps off and runs offstage. The man bows. He waves the magic wand over his whole body, there is a puff of smoke, and then he is gone, poof.

The stage is bare except for an overturned chair and the top hat. The spotlight goes off, and then the whole stage is illuminated. The bunny hops on from stage left. He checks his pocket watch. "Oh dear!" he says. "Oh dear, I shall be late!" He begins to hop across the stage.

"Oh dear! Oh dear!" James runs in from stage left. He is following the rabbit, giggling. The rabbit runs over to the top hat and dives in. James runs right over to the hat and before Justin can shout, "No, James, don't. How will you get back?" James jumps in after the rabbit. He disappears into the hat. Justin runs onstage. He grabs the hat. He turns it over and looks inside. It is empty.

Hannah has been here before.

She knows there is something behind that innocuous-looking white panel door that she does not want to see, but she can't remember what it is. And she has to open the door, she knows that. There is no choice. Her hand reaches for the knob; it is a child's hand, but hers all the same. Is this Hannah as a child? She should remember. She hasn't had this dream in so long. She had it all the time when she was James's age; she would wake up screaming and screaming. What is it behind the door?

The hand reaches out and wraps around the knob—because this is what hands do in dreams—twists, and begins to pull. Darkness floods in from the room behind the white paneled door, and Hannah tries to slam the door shut, but it keeps opening on its own.

And then there is no door anymore at all. Hannah is alone in a great blackness. There is no shape here, no time, no nothing. This is an endless void.

Hannah cannot see herself, she can't see anything. It is as if the world has ended, everything has been extinguished and now there is only Hannah.

Hannah remembers now; there will be a chair, hanging there surrounded by all this blackness. She'll see it, stark and solitary against the darkness. There will be a figure in the chair, a person floating there in this perfect aloneness. The figure will grow clearer and clearer, and when she can see who it is, then she will wake up, shaking.

It used to be her father sitting there in that chair, her father alone in all that blackness. And now, the image of the chair appears right on schedule, there is a figure in the chair, Hannah takes a sharp intake of breath and she sees James—it's James all alone in the dark, still, expressionless. She reaches her hand out to him, she calls to him, but her voice won't come out. She screams but there's no sound. She can't get to him, he won't even look at her. And suddenly she can't move at all, she's floating in blackness, alone, forever separated from her son.

And that's how the dreams go.

The parents wake up, trembling and sweating. In her dreams, Hannah searches all over the house for James and can't find him—is that a memory? A premonition? She wakes up, climbs out of bed, careful not to disturb her twitching husband, and creeps down the hall. She peers into James's room through the crack in the slightly opened door, and he's still there, under mountains of covers, snuggling his gigantic soft purple bear. The nightlight in the room casts a soft glow. He breathes in with determination, force, insistence. It's the question; his exhale—long, loud, steady, relaxed—is the answer. Mountains of blankets rise and fall. His mouth is slightly open, his eyelashes flutter, and he might be drooling a bit on his bear.

Hannah stands and watches and tears begin to run down her cheeks. Everything she is exists for this moment. She doesn't even notice her husband come up behind her until his hand rests at the small of her back. He fits into the spaces around her and pulls her close. Together, they stand watching their adorable son sleep adorably, marveling at the terrible fragility of it all.

Visiting hours at the hospital are

from one to six. Justin called ahead to make sure. He and James arrive at two-thirty on Monday with a fern and a stuffed monkey that James picked out from the gift shop. Justin and James walk in slowly, James holding on to his father with one hand and the monkey with another. Hannah and Justin were a little worried about taking him—the hospital is a lot for him, with all the flurrying and beeping and rushing. But he wanted to go, and, for some reason that he can't quite identify, Justin wanted him to go, too. James is fine—alert and engaged—it is Justin who cannot handle all the noises and the bodies, the whooshing and the buzzing and the chattering and all the smells, and his grip on his son grows firmer and firmer.

There is penance to be paid, for a crime Justin only had wanted to commit, there is a son who was gone and now is back, and an ordinary man who was there when he disappeared and is now hurt, there are forces that Justin does not and cannot understand and a boy to be held on to at all costs, and there is the knowledge—ugly and bright—that it could happen again at any time.

This was a mistake, of course, a mistake to go outside at all, a mistake to take James out, a mistake for Justin to leave the house when the world is so full of whooshes and buzzes, and what if Justin is all wrong, what if Mike was the cause somehow, what if there's something about Mike that made this happen, what if there's something here that might make this happen again? But they can't turn around and leave, James wants to see the Magical Man.

Michael Simmons is in a private room on the fourth floor—he doesn't have any insurance, but Carlos said the city is paying all his expenses, and then some. There are already some scattered bouquets and cards in his room—it never occurred to Justin that Michael had friends.

Michael is on the bed, his leg propped up. The television is on—some talk show—but Michael is looking at a magazine. He doesn't notice them in the doorway, and Justin finds himself shifting a little. He clears his throat.

"Uhh ... Mr. Simmons?" Justin hears how strangely the words come out, but just because he's beaten Mike up, threatened his life, dreamed about his daughter, and seen him get shot, just because Mike was the primary witness to his son's disappearance, does not mean they are on a first-name basis.

Michael looks up. He sees Justin, and then he sees what Justin has by the hand. He breaks into a cheek-bending grin. "James!"

Justin looks at his son, who is always so reticent, but James just grins back and says, "Hi!" and runs up to the side of Mike's bed, and Justin's hand is cold and empty and he tries to suppress the urge to reach out and grab his son.

"You want to sit down, James?" Mike shifts a little and pats the bed.

"Yeah," James says matter-of-factly. He plops down on the bed, then stares at Mike. "You got hurted!"

Mike smiles. "A little."

"How?"

Mike leans in and whispers momentously, "I got shot!"

James's eyes grow wide. *"Really?"*

"Yes!" Mike grins. James has no idea what he's talking about, and Mike knows it.

James looks at the leg—he's about eye level with it now. "It's so high! Does it hurt?"

"Nah," Mike says. "Knock on the cast. Come on!"

James looks at him like he's nuts.

"Really! Take your fist and punch it, like this!" Mike balls up his fist and punches the air, "POW!"

"POW!" James squeals and punches the cast.

"You can do it harder than that! Come on, James, POW!"

"POW!" James says, and punches again.

"POW!" Mike punches the air again.

"POWWWWWWWW!" James starts his arm all the way back at his shoulder and propels his fist forward.

"OW!" Michael says. A flicker of concern crosses James's face. Then Mike smiles and James breaks out into wild giggles.

Justin just stands in the threshold and watches. It is strange—around this man, James has no shyness. He acts completely trusting; there are no boundaries to be broken. Justin has spent so much time thinking about this man—somewhere, deep down, does Justin still blame him for what happened to James? And does he believe, deep down, that that was what caused the shooting? And is he over-compensating, is that why he's here? Or is it a test of the world and the rules so that if maybe James does disappear again, at least Justin will know why, so when he comes back they know how to keep it from happening again? Or if he can hold on to him here, next to the man with the magical act, does that mean he'll never go away again? And why is Justin thinking this way, this is just a man in front of him, an ordinary man—Michael Simmons has been so much to Justin, he went from hero to villain to victim, and now here he is, just a man.

"Nice monkey!" Mike says to James, nodding at the stuffed crea-ture in his left hand.

"It's for YOU!" James says, thrusting it forward.

"Really?" Mike says.

"I picked it out," James puffs. "You can snuggle him if you want."

Mike takes the monkey and makes a show of squeezing him.

"He can keep you company," James says seriously. "His name is Moe."

Mike looks up. "It's the nicest present I ever got, James," he says softly. "Thank you very much."

Justin clears his throat and steps forward, lamely wielding the plant. "We got you a fern," he says.

Michael smiles awkwardly at him. "Thanks . . . um, how is everything?"

"Good. We're good . . . How are you feeling?"

Mike shrugs. "Okay. I'm just a bit sick of daytime TV." Michael laughs in a forced way. Justin understands suddenly; this man can talk to children all day—that's what he does with his life—but doesn't have a thing to say to grown-ups.

"POW!" James yells again.

"Do you know when they might let you out?"

Michael shrugs. "Another couple of days . . . They want to watch for blood clots. Apparently, the city really doesn't want me to die."

"Oh." Justin steps closer to the bed. James has found the buttons on the side of the bed and has started to press them. "James, careful— Oh, I think he just called the nurse."

"It's okay," Mike says. He turns to James. "These are magic buttons. See? I just press this, and"—the foot of the bed starts to drop, and James with it, "—Wheee!" Mike grins. James giggles wildly. "Now you try."

"Hmm," Justin says thoughtfully.

"What?"

"He's . . . different . . . with you."

"We understand each other, don't we, buddy?" Mike jolts forward as the head of the bed lurches up.

"WHEEEEEEEEEE!" James says, as a woman in pink scrubs pops her head in the room. "You rang?"

"Kim, could you bring my young friend here some apple juice? Make it a double."

She raises her eyebrows, shakes her head, grins, and disappears, calling, "You've got PT in fifteen minutes."

"Physical therapy." He laughs awkwardly. "I think my therapist is a former KGB operative."

"WHEEEEE!" James says.

"So," Justin shifts. "What are you going to do now? When you get out? Can you go back to the tour?"

"Oh, I don't think they want me to come calling. They're still not getting in audiences, and having me on the bill . . . Though I'm no longer a suspected kidnapper." A little bitterness creeps into his voice. A waft of blood flirts with Justin's senses, and he looks at the ground. "But I've got," he coughs, "a little more money now. There's a settlement . . ." The lower part of the bed begins to sink, and Mike's suspended leg is pulled a little higher.

"Ah," Justin says.

"I'm going to Chicago. I'm going to live there. It's a good town for this work, and, well, nothing like getting beat up and shot to make you want to be closer to your estranged daughter." He shrugs. "We'll see."

They both shift a little. The air hangs between them. There is nothing left to say. Mike smiles at James. "You be good, okay?"

"Okay!"

"And thanks for my monkey. Remember, if anyone gives you any trouble, POW!"

"POW!" James squeals and punches the air. Justin tries not to look too concerned. He picks James off the bed, but not before James reaches over to hug Michael Simmons and give him a wet kiss on the cheek.

A few days later, they send Greta

back to school, because she has to go back sometime. She's only missed two weeks—and since it's still the beginning of the year, her teacher feels she'll be able to make it up, no problem. Another child, she'd think they might have some socialization problems, but with Greta, well . . . (and here, Mrs. Olson paused a little), she should be running the class again in no time at all.

So, almost one week after James reappears, Justin finds himself seeing the family off again. He has not left the house since the hospital visit. He makes breakfast—waffles, because it is a special occasion, and possibly because if he can't keep his children from disapparating without warning, at least he can make them a good breakfast. James comes down, wearing a green sweater, jeans, and two socks, and Greta watches carefully while he eats, instructing him, "You like more syrup than THAT!"

Hannah helps Justin clean the waffle iron before she goes. She's driving Greta to school today; the idea of the bus is more than either parent can take right now.

"So, do you think you're going to take James to preschool today?" Hannah asks softly.

"I don't know," says Justin. "Maybe."

"I guess I agree with Miss Rose, we should probably try to make things as normal as possible for him. And the longer he's gone . . ."

"I'll take him," Justin says. He looks at his wife and shrugs. "I might duct tape myself to him, though."

Hannah smiles and puts her hand on the back of his neck. "Good, then I'll know where you both are." She moves to get her coat and collect Greta. "I'll call when I can, okay?"

"Okay," Justin says. He kisses his wife on the cheek, then turns to his daughter. "You ready for school, pumpkin?"

Greta considers the question. "Will there be snack time?"

Justin nods, "I bet there will be."

"Okay," Greta says solemnly. "Then I think I'm ready."

"Good." He kisses her on the forehead.

As the Woodrow women make their way toward the door, Justin cannot help but add: "And Hannah?"

"Yeah?" she turns.

Justin smiles sheepishly. "Um . . . drive safely . . ."

Hannah steps back through the doorway, takes her husband's hand and says with all the earnestness in the world, "I promise . . . You too, okay?"

"Okay."

He is the most pathetic man in the world, and he knows this, but accidents happen, everything changes so quickly. They leave and Justin watches them drive down the block, and Hannah does indeed seem to be driving perfectly safely, she does indeed, but what happens when they go out of his sight, and how to possibly bear life anymore?

Justin breathes and turns to his son and says, "Well, buddy, let's have some Man Time, huh?"

For the rest of the morning, Justin divides his attention between James and the clock. If he's going to take James to preschool, he has to start getting James ready to leave at twelve-fifteen. Sometimes you hit lunch traffic, you just never know. Justin knows he should probably send James back to preschool today, he and Hannah have been obsessing about this all week; Miss Rose feels strongly that James should be back as soon as possible, that in fact they should try sending him five days a week now, that perhaps, then, in the winter they could try some morning kindergarten and see how James does. *It's important that things be normal for James, now, I'll watch him carefully, you have my word on that.*

(Of course she'll watch him. Maybe she could make little notes on his progress too, and then talk to counselors and doctors about his son, and make recommendations, and draw up a whole profile, collect paper after paper, make a whole file, and then if James disappears again they can cuddle the file close to them at night.)

Justin could still get there if they leave at twelve-thirty, lunch traffic isn't that bad, now that summer's over. Even twelve forty-five— they would be a little late, but James would be there, Justin would have done it, he would have taken James to preschool. But as the clock ticks on, Justin's stomach balls up, his blood coagulates, his legs stiffen, while James keeps yelling, "POW!" and punching the air and giggling. He considers saying, "Come on, James, get your coat, let's go to school!" but the words do not come. And anyway, it's too late, really, Justin hasn't even mentioned preschool to James and he should prepare him. And besides, they would be late, and that would be weird for James. They can try again tomorrow. Or maybe next week . . .

Do the other kids know what happened to James? What has the school told them? They're so young, but maybe their parents have said something, and maybe the kids would treat him funny—differently. Maybe they should try a different school, maybe they should home-school James, maybe what he needs is the attention, and someone who really understands him and isn't going to evaluate him all the time. Justin could do it, he could do it until James is eighteen, and there are all sorts of wonderful programs for homeschooled kids so they can socialize and be with other homeschooled kids—he's read all about this, and maybe those kids would be good friends for James, and Justin would be a good teacher, and then he could make sure James is really getting the right kind of attention, and then . . .

"POW!" James yells suddenly, with a little giggle. Justin starts with a little yelp—and everything in James's body changes. His face wrinkles up, his eyes pop open, his mouth forms a perfect O. "Are you okay, Daddy?"

"Ohh," Justin gets on his knees next to his son, carefully avoiding a few stray blocks. "Yeah, buddy. I'm fine, you startled me that's all. What are you playing anyway?"

The O collapses. "Uh . . . blocks."

Justin is about to ask what on earth playing blocks has to do with the new "POW" game when the phone rings.

That will be Hannah. Ah. Well. He should get that. He will have to eventually explain to his wife why he did not take James to pre-school, how he's never taking James to preschool again, how he is absolutely incapable of letting his son out of his sight, how he is a complete and utter basket case, how he is this close to getting out the duct tape, how James just reappeared—Poof!—and there's nothing Justin can do to keep his kids safe, Superman can't keep them safe, tanks can't keep them safe, but at least he can keep them close, and there are so many wonderful things about homeschooling, and maybe it would be good for Greta as well, and is Hannah sure she got off safely, and who is watching the playground during recess and how old is the school building and has it passed all its current inspections—so he better start now. "Hello?"

"Mr. Woodrow?"

Well, it's not Hannah at all. "Yes?"

"Hi, this is Nancy Olson, Greta's teacher?"

And Justin freezes. "What is it? What's wrong?"

"Oh, nothing, nothing!" the voice trails off and Justin reattaches his heart to his body. "I just wanted to tell you that Greta's doing well today, that's all. She seems to be doing really well."

"Oh," Justin says. "Oh!" he gulps. "Thank you . . . thank you . . ."

Homeschooling might be a good idea, Justin thinks, breathing more easily now—Hannah works and Justin is home and the most important thing in the world is his family and he will keep them as close as possible.

This is Hannah's first full day back at work. She's gone in a little, here and there, for half days, seeing a couple patients, sorting through paperwork. Everyone has been so nice. Hannah has never been hugged so much in her life, and she's starting to get used it.

Her partners have been taking care of her cases while she's been gone—she's been reviewing the patient charts from her absence to find Betsy Pinzon's bronchitis has cleared up, Margaret Harris's abdominal pain has been referred to a GI for an endoscopy for a suspected ulcer, and Gertrude Pacheco sprained her ankle. The patients keep coming. Everyone knows of course; everyone's seen Hannah's name on the news, "I'm so glad you're back," they say with a big grin. "How are you doing?"

But the people are sick, and it's hard. Hannah frequently has to close her office door to cry during the day. All these wide-open spaces contain so many bodies, and the bodies can tear, break, wither, decay, mutate so easily. The world is full of infections. Nobody comes to her because they are happy and healthy. She can prescribe medications, she can advise, she can refer to a specialist, but there is so little she can really do. She can't lay on hands and heal.

All of these people come to her wanting explanations, reassurances, diagnoses of a long healthy life, assurances that if they eat right and exercise and ask her all the right questions and follow her advice to the letter, they will live forever—and what can she say?

Kenwood Medical Group may treat the whole body, but the whole body is too damned much for Hannah. Heart, lungs, glands—it's all too much, there's so much that can go wrong. And not just in the body; the pulse may sound normal, the blood pressure may be good, the temperature may be only slightly elevated—but do they know where their children are?

She has just seen Colin Peterson. She's been seeing Colin and Marie for ten years, and she's just started to see their lovely daughter Emily, who has outgrown her pediatrician. Colin is fifty-four. He exercises, his cholesterol is 184, his blood pressure is steady at 125 over 70. He doesn't smoke, he drinks a little red wine, but nothing else, and he has no family history of anything at all. He came to her today with lethargy and a strange pain in his side. His arms are covered with bruises. Colin has lymphoma; Hannah knows it in her bones, she knows it even before she sees the results of the CBC. She's referring him to an oncologist immediately, "just to rule things out," she says, but she lies. She could just tell him now, as of this moment, he is a marked man.

That is enough for one day.

She used to think the body was beautiful, poetic—now she knows it is malformed, hideous—there are too many breakable parts.

Hannah knows in a few weeks she'll be able to get through the day without crying, that she will be able to look at a sprained ankle as a sprained ankle, and not as a symbol of the greater terror of life, and that soon, she can harden her heart as she has to to keep doing this job. You want your doctors to have compassion, but not that much.

She has two people left, and she gets through them—ear pain (an inner ear infection) and a rash (eczema). She cries for Colin on the way home, for his family, for his wife—

At night, in bed, she lies next to her husband, still afraid to sleep and fall back into that other universe where James is still gone or has disappeared again, and still afraid to wake up and find he is gone.

Justin is sleeping. He's curled up fetally around a pillow. Hannah could mold herself around his back, she could easily do that. His mouth is slightly open, and he's snoring, just a tiny bit—he claims he does not snore, he "gently coos." Hannah reaches her hand out to his back.

What will I do when I lose you?

It has to happen. One day there will be both of them, and then there will be just one.

Our children, we made. They grow and change all the time. We are giving them water and sunlight, and we tend to them, and then we set them out in the world.

You, I discovered. You were out there, all my life—someone else cared for you and watched you grow, and you came, fully formed to me.

And, now, together, we are fully formed.

How will it end? Hannah's hand cups her husband's shoulder and she sees a future. They are eighty years old, she is cupping his shoulder with her hand, as she sits in vigil by his hospital bed while he breathes raspingly. They have not had nearly enough time yet, but bodies are malformed, hideous, so filled with breakable things. She is faced with saying good-bye and there are no words. Something is eating away inside of him—a cell mutates, then another, then another, and it is taking her husband's life bit by bit.

This is what happens. It's part of the deal. You never get enough time.

What I will do when I lose you?

Hannah lays herself down next to her gently cooing husband—both now and forty years from now—and holds his body to her to keep him close and safe and here.

On Saturday afternoon, two weeks

and one day after the reapparation of James, the family is at home. Greta and James are at each other's side constantly—do they feel the same need to hang on tight? Or is this just how it's always been? Now, the children are in the playroom, James is making a village with his blocks and Greta is assigning villager roles to various plastic figures, while the adults sit in the living room—Hannah talking on the phone to Angie Post, who is really rather nice once you get to know her, and Justin going through some bills—in spots perfectly suited for peeking through the playroom door.

The doorbell rings, as is its wont—though it has gotten a lot quieter this past week as friends and neighbors move on to other things. Hannah's on the phone, so Justin gets up from the table and heads to the front door, ready to accept whatever offering is presented to him.

He wasn't really expecting to find Tom there. He'd almost forgotten. Tom has slowly been disappearing from their minds—he was important, but he just isn't relevant anymore. (This isn't so for Greta, who still pairs the Tiny Town girl with the smiling plastic policeman, and they have adventures all over the playroom. He lingers in other ways too: at night, with Otter held close, she still dreams of loud pops and men having great falls. She cries a lot now, still, and appears in her parents' bed in the middle of the night more often than not, and

Hannah and Justin are getting names of someone for her to see and praying it passes.)

So Justin starts a bit when he sees Tom on his front step, carrying a bouquet of flowers in one hand and two giant stuffed animals—a seal and a dragon—under his arm. Justin's world shifts a little bit, and then settles back into place. Okay, this is Tom. He lived in your house. He answered your phone. He soothed your mother. He took care of Greta when you did not. He tried to keep you from attacking Michael Simmons. Then he shot Mike himself and traumatized your seven-year-old daughter.

A wave of something comes over Justin. Tom seems to want to come in. He lets so few people into the house these days. Catherine and, once, her blowhard boyfriend. Everyone else stays on the front stoop, deposits their offerings, gives sincere best wishes, and goes—leaving just a little doubt and uncertainty behind. People bring all kinds of things with them, wherever they go. What would happen if they came into the house—who knows what they'll leave behind?

Tom is wearing a blue shirt and khakis, like he always has. He's freshly shaven and nicely starched, but he looks ... puffier. He's gone from looking exactly like a short, stocky plainclothes cop to looking exactly like a short, stocky man who watches too much daytime television and is starting to take it to heart.

"Mr. Woodrow," he says, shifting. Justin has the distinct impression he is the last person Tom wanted to open the door—except perhaps for Michael himself.

"Officer Johnson," Justin says. His heart's going a bit again, and he's been down that road before—he has a distinct urge to run to his children and leap on top of them.

And then Hannah appears behind Justin, she touches his back, and says warmly, "Tom! Come in, please."

So Justin can only step back and make way, and wonder when his wife became the one who didn't consider the things people brought with them. Tom hands her the flowers and looks cautiously at Justin who looks cautiously back.

"Why don't you come sit down, Tom," Hannah says. "Do you want—"

"Oh!" Everyone stops at the sound of Greta's voice—she's appeared in the doorway of the playroom. She has James by the hand. She is staring at Tom uncertainly.

"Hi, Greta," he says. He looks at the boy next to her, a littler, male version of the girl herself, and he can't help it. He smiles. "James," he says gently. "It's so nice to see you."

James looks up at his sister for a cue on how to act in the face of this stranger, but she doesn't seem to know herself.

"I brought you guys presents. Um, the seal's for you, Greta. Her name is Seal, I thought she could play with Otter. And this," he holds up the dragon, "is for James."

And then something quite strange happens. James Woodrow lets go of his sister's hand and steps toward this stranger. He glances at his mother, who nods her approval. Tom crouches down and says softly, "Hi, little buddy."

"Hi," James says.

Tom offers up the stuffed animal.

"Dragon!" James says. He takes it with both hands and hugs it to his chest. Tom beams, and Hannah clears her throat and looks pointedly at her son. "Thank you," he says quickly.

"You're welcome, James," Tom says. Greta watches her brother and Tom very carefully. Tom glances over to her and straightens up a bit. "Hi, Greta," he says. "I've missed you."

"You have?" She looks doubtful.

"Yeah," he says. "I would have come by earlier, but— Do you want to look at Seal?"

She nods. She looks, in the moment, more childlike than James. Hannah and Justin only watch as Greta takes a step forward. Tom holds the plush white seal out to her, and she grabs it and holds it close. She begins to sniff a little, and buries her face in the fur of the seal and rocks back and forth.

"Thank you, Tom," she says softly, her voice shaking.

"You're welcome, Greta," he says.

Tears start pouring from Greta's eyes. No one knows quite what to do. Tom wants to reach out to her but doesn't know if he should. Hannah wants Tom to reach out to her but doesn't know if he will. Justin wants to forcibly remove Tom from the house for making his daughter cry but doesn't think he should. Greta buries her face deeper in her new seal, and all the adults step forward as one, notice the others moving toward her, and then step back as one. So it's James who comes up to his sister—he's started sniffling too—and he holds out his dragon for Greta, who takes it and starts crying all the harder. And then Tom sits down, on the floor, holds out his arms, and says, "Come here, Greta."

She shakes her head and cries, and he whispers, "I'm so sorry for scaring you. I'm so sorry. I didn't mean it, Greta. I'm so sorry." And his voice begins to waver a little, and his arms are still out, so James goes over to sit in his lap, at which point Tom begins to cry like he has not cried, ever. Hannah and Justin just look at each other, absolutely unable to take any action at all, while James cuddles into Tom and reaches his hand out to Greta, who runs and plops into her superhero's lap, next to her brother. Tom and Greta cry and cry while James, the stuffed seal, and the dragon do their best to comfort them all.

By the time the sun has begun to set on the fifteenth day after the reapparation of James, Tom is gone. That night, Carlos will take him to a movie and they will run into Catherine Bennett and her blowhard boyfriend. Tom will shake his head and tell Catherine, softly, "I don't even know how they go on, loving something that much." And Catherine will just nod.

Meanwhile, the Woodrows are alone and together again. After dinner—macaroni and cheese, Greta has pictorial evidence that James likes it—the children retire back to the playroom while the parents clean up. They talk in low voices about Tom, and whether he'll come back—he said he may move to another city, another force—or whether he'll disappear from Greta's life. And when she is thirty years old, will she remember the Tiny Town policeman whose heart grew three sizes when he met her, or will he fade in the rush of newness that growing up brings. She will never disappear for him, that much they know—his life will be forever marked into two periods, before and after Greta Woodrow.

After they are done in the kitchen, the parents take their posts quietly in the doorway to the playroom, and freeze in the threshold. Night terrors are thrust aside, fear is put to bay, for now they only live for this. They have never seen anything like their children, they are completely helpless in the face of them. They have nothing to do with it—Greta and James are what they are because they have each other.

The kids are together in James's corner of the playroom. James's village is getting massive now, and Greta's running out of plastic people. The new stuffed animals sit sentry next to Otter and James's two bears.

"Jaaaaaaaaaaaaaames," Greta pleads. "Can we play something else? I'm sick of blocks."

James scrunches his nose. "Something else? Like what?"

Greta looks around the room. "Wellll," she takes a deck of cards from her pocket. "I could show you some magic tricks."

James's eyes go wide. "*Magic* tricks?"

She nods importantly. "Uh-huh!"

"Okay!"

So Greta spreads the cards out on the floor. "Pick a card," she says. He considers carefully, carefully, carefully, until Greta squeals,

"Just pick!" and then he giggles and picks and she shuffles it back into the deck, dropping cards everywhere. This is a long process. "Now cut the cards." He looks at her. "Make two piles it means," she explains. So he does, and she puts them together and shuffles again. Then she stops, and leans in slowly, and then whooshes a card from the deck. "IS THIS YOUR CARD?" she proclaims.

"Yeah!" he says, eyes like small moons.

Greta grins and James grins back. He looks at his hand. He looks at Greta. He makes a connection. He leans in and asks breathlessly, "How'd you do that?"

Greta smiles and leans into her brother and whispers into his ear, but Hannah and Justin cannot hear.

Acknowledgments

Mike the Clown's act—minus the disapparation—has been lifted entirely from that of Michael Lane Trautman. Trautman (solotheater.com) is a terrific performer and a stand-up gentleman, and I thank him for allowing his wonderful act and his craft to be used and abused in such a way.

My adoration and firstborn to Lisa Bankoff, the Platonic Ideal of Agent Itself. My undying love to my editor, Peternelle van Arsdale, for her wisdom, humor, friendship, and great patience. My gratitude to the people of Hyperion: Natalie Kaire, Karin Maake, Katie Long, Caroline Skinner, Jane Comins, Robin Moses, Phil Rose, Will Schwalbe, Ellen Archer, and Bob Miller.

Thanks to Drs. Dziwe Ntaba and Chris and Jeff Hummel, to Michael Phillips, Jessica Hill, Brennan Laskas, and the e-denizens of Readerville (especially Mark Perez), for being so generous with their knowledge and their time.

To Caroline Leavitt, Susannah Melone, and David Fischer for their advice on the text. To Gretchen Moran Laskas and Lisa Tucker, fellow travelers. Jon Van Gieson, web designer extraordinaire, and his lovely assistant Brian Warshawsky. To Patrick Price. M. J. Rose. Brent Boyd. Suzanne Marx. And of course, John Erck.

To Mom and Dad, and all my family. And, most of all, to my husband, for apparating.